CW01024147

EXIT 202

J. B. ARNOLD

TWISTED TALES PRESS

For my Love, my Light, my Life.

CONTENTS

A Broken Man

The security door slammed against the house's siding seconds after he dropped the phone. The receiver clattered against the linoleum, bouncing in rhythm before coming to rest.

He cleared the stoop in a single stride, rushing to the red Datsun nestled in the driveway, fumbling to get his keys from his pocket. Within heartbeats, the truck door was open, and he slid inside, starting the engine with a flick of the ignition.

No, no, no! This can't be happening! Not now!

His weary eyes, catching the streetlight's dim glow across the road, darted to the rearview mirror while shifting the vehicle into reverse. The tires screeched against the pavement as the truck sped down the driveway and onto the road. He slammed on the brakes after leveling the truck. As his hand leapt for the gearshift, he paused, turning to look back at the house, his home. The home he bought for his new bride. The home he brought his sons into after they were born. Their home.

There, through the truck window, he could make out a figure by the doorway. His wife, sheltering herself from the chill of the night with her pink robe. The porch light accentuated her auburn hair, messy from the few hours of peaceful sleep. Her face hung low, staring into the street, staring at him. He promised this night would be different.

From the fogged window, he met her solemn eyes, returning the look. His mind was spinning, thinking about what was coming. Thinking about his life.

Agony brewed in his gut, recalling his mother's voice on the phone, hearing exasperation and dread spewing from her lips. The screams and sobs. It looped in his mind, tormenting each thought. You can't prepare for this. Nothing can prepare you for that call, even with the doctor's warnings. When it comes to those you love, death is never a thought.

He forced the pain away, burying it in his gut, and shifted into drive, speeding away into the night—leaving her again, alone with the boys.

The streets were empty and quiet, facilitating a speedy commute. It also provided a chance to think and reflect on the illness plaguing his life. Ever since his mother's diagnosis, he had slowly spiraled out of control, burrowing deeper into the rabbit hole with no hope in sight. His mind splintered and cracked under the pressure. He couldn't lose his mother. But he also thought of his wife; how their marriage was crumbling because he constantly let her down. The lies. The drinking.

I'm coming, Mom. I'm on my way. Hold on.

He wiped his eyes with his sleeve while turning onto Cedar Avenue. Panic bubbled in his core as he looked at the dash clock, and his fingers tightened around the steering wheel.

Six minutes, shit!

His mother lived three miles north in a two-bedroom condo near the college, and he prayed the EMTs would already be there. Prayed they would help her, and end the nightmare. He ignored the 35 mph speed limit, racing down the nearly empty road until he entered the apartment district. Parked cars lined both sides of the street, limiting access to two-way traffic.

His momentum ended with the first red light of the trek, forcing the truck to halt behind an aging Volkswagen van. His eyes fixated on the digital clock in the dash as he waited, watching it blink with each second. Panic percolated, not knowing his mother's condition mere blocks away. *Was she alive?* He sat there helplessly, knowing there was nothing he could do but wait.

Every second passed like a lazy caterpillar devouring a green leaf, and he felt an anxious sweat gather at his nape. As he sat there, obscenities flew from his mouth as he violently slapped the steering wheel. Yet the red light remained.

Seven minutes!

The traffic signal finally changed, shifting from the vibrant glow of red to a calming green, contrasting with the darkness surrounding the overcast sky, but the van didn't move. He paused his outburst, staring in disbelief at the green light and the stationary blockade in front of him.

Tick. Tick. Tick.

Unaware of his actions, he slammed his palm on the truck's horn, holding it. And then the scornful swears resumed.

Seconds passed before the van's brake lights disengaged, and the vehicle crept along, inching forward. His grip tightened around the wheel, watching this obstacle stroll without gaining momentum. Another wail of the horn, with no urgency registering from the van's driver.

"Move, you idiot! Get the fuck out of the way!" He gritted his teeth after the curse, navigating ever so slowly along, only blocks away from his destination. He was at this person's mercy. With all the parked cars on each side, he was boxed in, forced to wait.

Eight minutes!

Anger manifested, engulfing his thoughts and actions, and he felt he could wait no longer. With a swipe of the wheel, he veered to the left and sped up, nearly clipping the back of the van. During the maneuver, his side mirror collided with a parked car. Shattered plastic and glass exploded from the impact, going unnoticed. There was only one thing on his mind: her.

The little truck zoomed past the van, leaving it in the crisp night. Within seconds, he swerved right onto Barstow, heading for his mother's apartment. Turning the last corner, strobes of red and blue light overwhelmed his sight. The paramedics had arrived first. He slowed the truck and parked it in the middle of the road.

Reality seemed delayed as he opened the door, staring at the rotating lights of the orange and blue vehicle parked on the grass. Each movement was slow, and a pulsating buzz filled his ears as he took in the scene. He didn't bother closing the truck's door, nor did he acknowledge the broken mirror hanging from the fender as he walked forward. Numbness grew with each reticent step, and his vision blurred.

Exiting his mother's door, two men steered a gurney toward the ambulance. *She* was lying on it, propped up by pillows and covered in a gray wool blanket, an oxygen mask over her nose and mouth.

In an instant, his entire world collapsed. His cautious strides turned into a desperate sprint, running to his mother's side, right where he belonged.

He stood there, shocked and motionless. Staring in disbelief at her frail frame, pale complexion, and thinning hair. How did this happen? Where was his real mom?

Through the frantic breaths, she wept in horror. She lunged out toward the EMTs, grasping a hold of their uniforms and the itchy blanket. "I can't breathe, I can't breathe!" she chanted. The entire moment was hazy, filled with dubiety and deception as if it weren't real, but rather a terrible dream. He wouldn't wake from this nightmare, however.

"Ma'am, ma'am! Please calm down." The medic's deep voice knifed through the confusion, bringing him back, but he was in shock, legs paralyzed. His stare shifted to the medics and then back to his mother, watching her glide farther away and listening to her gasp and cry for help.

She clung to an EMT's forearm, eyes desperate as she was rolled down the walkway. Her vision suddenly diverted from the men and landed on her son, locking onto him.

The hysteria escalated, and she lurched back on the gurney, trying to whirl around. Trying to maintain eye contact with each foot that separated the two. She dropped her grip on the EMT's arm and reached out for him, thin arms extending beyond the headrest for her loving son. For hope.

"MOM!" The haunting image forced his hand, and he broke through his shock, running after them, running after the woman who was a shell of his loving mother. "Mom, it's okay. I'm here." His pace slowed, walking beside the gurney and grasping her outstretched hand. Seeing the hues of green and blue veins striping the length of her weak arm. "You're going to be okay, Mom."

The sobs continued to echo amongst the brisk night as she listened to her son's empty words. She knew she wouldn't be okay. That was clear as her thoughts drifted to darkness. This attack wasn't like the previous: subtle and defused with a few puffs of her inhaler. No, this attack broke her, and it fed the ill thoughts swirling inside: suffocation and death.

"Micah ... I can't breathe, I can't breathe, son! I'm dying!"

"Hold on, Mom. Hold on!" He bellowed through choked, tearful words.

The EMTs finally came to rest, opening the back of the ambulance. Each side door extended outward in a wide arc, revealing bright artificial light from within. They lifted the gurney with precision, rolling it into the back of the emergency vehicle, forcing Micah to lose his tight grip. Her hand remained outstretched, reaching for her son with fearful, dilated eyes even after the doors were closed by the paramedic climbing in to accompany her.

Micah stood there, jaw hanging open, staring through the left door's small window. His mom's cries could still be heard outside the van. His mind raced, thinking of everything that had led up to this fateful moment. How many mistakes he'd made, the choices he'd regretted. Thoughts of ending it.

The other EMT, the driver, spoke firmly in his direction: instructed him to follow them, provided the hospital's address, and assured him they would do everything possible to save her life.

The promise fell on deaf ears as his body turned numb. He didn't feel real. Nothing felt real. He couldn't hear, and that familiar haze blurred his vision. Life was void, and he was hollow, staring at the nothingness before him.

This can't be happening. This isn't real. My mom's a fighter, strong, stubborn. The doctor said she had the strength to live with it, to beat it.

The driver side door slammed moments later, and the siren's blare forced a trembling flinch. His senses returned, and he stared into the ambulance, seeing his mother in agony: gasping, clutching her throat, screaming at the man attempting to save her.

The red taillights flared before the engine sparked to life, and the ambulance rolled off the grass onto the dark street. He gaped as the vehicle floated away like a hazy dream, leaving him lost and useless.

As it vanished in the distance, he dropped to his knees, solemnity taking control. He knelt there, staring at nothing as his mind twisted in torment. A sickening feeling brewed deep within him as tears ran down his cheeks. He was going to lose his mother, his rock, his anchor. He knew that, and he was alone. He couldn't even stomach the idea of following the ambulance, knowing the end result. She will die tonight.

Slowly, the trauma and heartache of the inevitable sank to the bottom of his gut, replaced by something new, something dark and unforgiving.

Neither his wife, Lynn, nor his sons showed much concern for his dying mother. They rarely visited or called, merely asked how Grandma was doing over dinner. Nonchalant, petty inquiries. They weren't here now, either, suffering through the pain with him. No one seemed to care. The thought devoured him, leaving a bitter taste in his dry mouth. Anger bloomed deep within him. There was no support, no love, no empathy. Lynn wasn't here. He was utterly alone.

How could she be so selfish? Why doesn't she care? Why is she so heartless, so cold? Why isn't she here supporting me through this? Why?

He remained there for several minutes, kneeling in the cold, thinking about his mom, his wife, and his broken life and family, as the first drops of rain fell from the dark sky.

PART ONE

THE BREAKDOWN

1

"David, bring me those suitcases. Don't take your time either, boy." Revamping the trunk space, Micah didn't even look up to see if his son heard his demand. He knew his son, knew he would hear him, and knew he would obey. "What the hell is all this shit, anyway?" Micah mumbled to himself while stacking duffel bags and gathering loose pieces of clothing and pamphlets.

Gripping each suitcase by the handle, David promptly rolled the baggage off the inn's sidewalk toward their parked tan hatchback. "I'm coming, Dad. Here they are." The distressed boy approached the car and peered into the trunk, already jarring. "How are you going to get these in there?" David looked on as his father continued to move baggage around, hearing him softly mumble curses under his breath.

Micah ignored the question and grabbed the first suitcase, tossing it into the trunk with ease. After throwing the second in, his head emerged from the pile of baggage overflowing out of the back of the car. "Where's your mom and Will?"

David looked back toward the inn, uncertainty crossing his face. "I think Mom's getting a coffee in the lobby. I'm pretty sure Will's with her." He looked back at his father, delivering a weak smile.

Micah gave his oldest son a nod. "Okay, you guys get everything out of the room, like I said?"

David stood a little taller as he answered. "Triple-checked it, sir. Looked under the bed too." He smiled at his father, hoping for a smidgen of praise.

"That's good, David, very good. You're doing a lot better. Make sure you always listen to what I'm saying, understand?"

"Yes, sir, I understand," David said, never breaking eye contact.

After giving his son another nod, he slammed the hatchback's trunk, ensuring it was closed. He looked past David toward the inn's lobby, spotting his wife and other son exiting the automatic doors. A smirk pierced his lips as he thought about their holiday weekend.

Micah's wife, Lynn, planned the entire trip. She was good at things like that, organizing and mapping out itineraries.

It had been late February when she'd spotted the newspaper ad for an all-inclusive weekend package at Disneyland. A new attraction had opened inspired by the *Star Wars* films, sprinkling even more enticement over the colorful two-page advertisement. When she had first brought it to Micah's attention, he brushed off the idea, complaining about their financial problems.

The boys snatched the paper from their father's grasp in curiosity, and as they read, they lit up in excitement. Micah pursed his lips as they babbled, then had a surprising change of heart witnessing their eagerness. It had been ages since they'd done anything as a family, so it seemed only right to let them have this, regardless of their tight pocketbook.

The past few years had not been kind to Micah: shitty, tragic, full of death. His mother had finally caved to incurable emphysema. The consequence of smoking three packs a day for the past forty years. Her death lingered close, a gritty whisper tormenting his thoughts.

As her only son, he did his part. After the diagnosis, he visited her after work and on weekends, comforting her as best he could. Still, he wondered if he could've done more. Should've done more.

Then, there were the layoffs. Micah had a decade in at the local energy plant when he received the same dreaded phone call as so many of his colleagues. Ten years of service, and for what? Utter betrayal was how he and his work friends perceived the action, but the economy was in a downward spiral. Companies had to cut costs and shave salaries. They were just another American family sent to the chopping block.

The family moved to Bakersfield shortly after the new year—not their first choice, but it met their needs. Micah finally found employment after eight long months of searching, landing a low management position with a mid-box retailer,

Montgomery Ward. The pay was nowhere near his previous salary, but it was something. Considering how they had lost their house in Fresno, and the fact that banks don't take pity on those unfortunate enough to be without an income, paycheck to paycheck was their way of life now, and it wasn't getting any easier.

The move had been the easiest on the boys—even with being uprooted in the middle of the school year—but kids are more resilient than adults. David and Will had settled into their new school quickly, making new friends and getting involved in a local soccer organization. They barely spoke of their old school or friends anymore. They had moved on and started anew.

The hardest part of their lives now was repairing the damage left behind from all those months of uncertainty. Their meager savings had deteriorated trying to stay afloat, causing broken bottles and harsh words over heaps of bills. The verbal abuse didn't help matters, obviously. It's a miracle the family was still intact after all they had endured. But they were here, patching up the loose pieces of their lives, trying to move forward and not live in the past.

Lynn stepped off the curb and approached the car. "Got you some coffee. Thought you could use some to keep you awake on the drive home." She handed over the steaming Styrofoam cup, leaning in to mumble under her breath, "I heard you again last night."

He mirrored her forced smile. "Thank you, babe." He accepted the drink while locking eyes with her, regret and remorse in the back of his mind. "It was just another dream. Don't worry about it."

He turned to his sons, raising an eyebrow. "Are you guys all set? Ready to get back home?"

This weekend was their first trip anywhere in years, and the most exciting thing they had ever experienced. They never wanted to leave. But they knew better than to whine or tell their father no. He made the rules. Whatever he said, went. No ifs, ands, or buts. Considering that, the boys nodded silently.

"Well, let's get on the road then. Maybe we can beat some of the traffic and get back to the apartment in record time." He gestured toward the car, and his sons quickly sprang into action, ambling alongside the passenger side of the car and climbing into the back seat.

Lynn started to move with her sons but paused. She turned to Micah, an unreadable look on her face. "We had a great time this weekend, you know? I'm glad we did this, Micah. This was good for us, and especially them." She sipped from her coffee, never averting her eyes. Fierce green eyes.

His gaze was pure as he responded. "I did as well, babe. I know they had a good time and, if I'm not mistaken, you had a little fun as well. You look pretty sexy wearing mouse ears."

Lynn playfully waggled her brows at his banter.

Micah replied with a smile, shifting his eyes to his watch. "It's nearly eleven. I think we can get home by two as long as there are no hiccups, and you know there will be at least one on that damn freeway. There always is." A grimace crossed his face, thinking about the interstate.

"You just make sure you get us there in one piece, Dale Earnhardt. I don't care if it takes six hours, mister." Lynn smirked at her husband as she climbed into the passenger seat, buckling her seatbelt.

Micah thought to himself for a moment, reminiscing about his family's smiles over the weekend. He missed those delicate, precious smiles.

This had been a great weekend, one that, hopefully, they would remember for years to come. This might be their chance to put it all behind them. Maybe this would repair his mistakes. Maybe this would allow her to forgive him for all of those hateful nights. He lightly tapped the top of the car's roof with his fingers and then opened the door, sliding inside.

"Get those seat belts buckled, you two," he declared while looking at his sons through the rearview mirror. He also strapped himself in, checking his surroundings and side mirrors in the process. Safety first. After watching them complete the demand, he pulled out his keys, inserted one into the ignition, and started the car. The used hatchback was affordable, reliable, and new to them. Based on their lives currently, it met all their needs.

As they left the parking lot of the inn, merging onto the busy interstate, Micah felt at ease. He longed for this feeling, hoping it would stick around for a while. His only thought was getting home safe and sound, hopefully in record time.

2

Only minutes on the interstate and they were already gridlocked. Bumper-to-bumper, as the saying goes. Micah knew this would happen, especially on a busy holiday weekend. Everyone trying to get home after a blissful getaway. The stress rapidly escalated as he looked through the bug-splattered windshield, knuckles whitening from the tight grip on the steering wheel. Thoughts festered in his mind while scanning the stagnant cars around him.

I knew this shit would happen. Why weren't they ready when I told them? Ten o'clock, it's not that hard. He glanced at his two sons in the rearview mirror, clenching his jaw and shaking his head. *At this damn rate, we won't be home until after dark. Ten o'clock! Why won't they listen? If I say ten, that means ten. Not ten thirty, not ten forty-five. Ten!*

Lynn looked over at her husband, concern growing in her eyes as she observed his clenched jaw and twitching eyes. "It's just a little congestion, Micah. I'm sure it'll clear up soon," she stated in a low voice. Her hand reached for his atop the gearshift, gently brushing against it. "Are you okay?"

Micah ignored the question, anger swelling up inside him, filling his veins as he looked around at the stalled cars. *Look at all these assholes. Where did they come from, and where are they going? Isn't there another freeway out of this cesspool?*

"Micah, you okay?" Lynn said again, sterner, more of a warning than anything else. She squeezed his hand.

The quick pressure brought him back, recoiling from her touch. "Yeah, yeah, of course. I'm okay, babe. Just a little pissed about all this damn traffic." With a slight nod, he again turned his attention to the congestion blocking his passage home.

Lynn removed her hand and rolled down her window. "Well, at least it's not that hot yet. I guess we can enjoy the Los Angeles weather a bit longer." She kicked off her sandals and placed her feet on the dashboard, enjoying the slight breeze.

Micah's behavior ascended, and his attention flowed to David and Will from the rearview mirror. The boredom from the back seat had settled in, igniting some sibling roughhousing. The volume escalated before a knee jammed into his back through the driver's seat.

"Boys, stop kicking the damn seat."

Lynn turned and gave David and Will a look only a mother could, halting the rowdiness. It seemed Micah wasn't the only one that could redirect with a stare.

She settled back in her seat when she deemed the boys compliant, explaining gently, "They're kids, Micah. They're just having fun."

Micah released a long sigh. His temper was a problem, and he knew it. "I know, I know. I just need to focus. The left lane is moving, see?" He gestured toward the left side of the freeway. "And I need to get over, now."

Lynn's eyes met the cars creeping along next to them. "Well, take your time, and when you see an opening, take it. Just do it safely, Micah."

The stress of the moment forced him deeper into the pit he had nearly crawled out of months ago. He gave her the side-eye, clenching his jaw.

A few tense moments passed before another knee jolted his back, followed by a flash of red above his head, triggering a second aggressive outburst. "What did I say, boys? Stop the horseplay and quit swinging those fuckin' swords around!"

Instantly, the back seat fell silent and motionless. David's eyes darted between his father's scowl and mother's confusion as he lowered his souvenir from the weekend, expecting more torment and aggression. His brother's eyes welled with tears, hearing the hostility in his father's voice. Not one outburst like that had occurred over the weekend. There had been no anger, no yelling, no threats. In the back of their minds, they childishly thought maybe things would be different now.

David apologized while dropping his eyes to his lap, his voice shaky.

Lynn faced her husband, contempt sketched across every inch of her face. "Do not talk to them that way! They don't deserve that bullshit, Micah!"

He faced his wife, a mixture of disbelief and enmity forming, "I can't focus because of all that damn noise in the back seat, Lynn. I already told them to stop and they kicked my seat twice," he growled.

Lynn listened to his words, his aggression, and held back. Her leer slowly faded, replaced by empathy and sincerity. Her husband was no saint—that was for damn sure—but deep down, she still loved him. They had been through hell during the past year and a half, but she had to keep up the good fight. She knew she could talk him down, and the only way to do that was to control her emotions. If their marriage was to continue to mend, she had to be the bigger person here. She had to lead him, gently and patiently, to redemption.

So with a hesitant, faint smile, she responded, "I know, honey. I know, but it's okay. They're just kids. Try to remember that."

Micah could see the concern in her eyes as she spoke, every word bringing him an inch farther away from the ledge. He dropped her gaze, eyes closing as his face fell into his palms. With deep breaths, rationality crept back in. *She's right. Stop pulling this shit, Micah. You've come too far to fall off again. Control it! Control it!*

She looked at her husband, watching as the despair washed over his body. She leaned over, rubbing the back of his neck. "It's okay, Micah. Everything's okay. Just drive and get us home. We're in this together." Her attention redirected toward the back seat, brushing away a tear from Will's eye. "We're okay, guys, all of us." Her voice was confident and loving.

David's reluctant nod proved he understood. Being the older of the two, he had more opportunities to watch these moments climax. Until recently, though, his mother didn't have the upper hand when his father's aggression boiled over. This was new, but he was grateful for it. Too many haunting nights had ended very differently.

After consoling Will for a moment more, she leaned her weight against the door, staring out the open window.

Micah slowly lifted his head from his palms, blinking heavily. A myriad of emotions and memories meandered through his mind in a split second as he recalled the previous year. All the misery and despair that was his daily life came rushing back. All the blame, all the shouting, all the nothingness. *This is not me! This is not me anymore. You're better than this, Micah. Control it.*

He breathed calmly through his nose, channeling his emotions as he turned his attention back to the traffic lanes, his back straightening as he spotted an opening. From what he could see in the mirror, a yellow semi had stalled, allowing for an easy lane change on this sardine-packed highway that was barely moving. With a flick of the turn signal and a rude gesture out the window to those behind him, he merged and joined the snail's pace. At least they were moving again.

The next ten minutes carried utter silence from all parties. It was Lynn who broke the tension in the car, still nonchalantly staring out the window. "Well, guys, at this pace, I'd say we will get home in fifty years. Any takers on that bet?"

Neither boy responded. The reticence in the back seat continued as they stared at their laps, stoically still.

The car's pace increased now that they were in the left lane. Micah leaned his head out the window, staring down the interstate. Clear passage ahead, bringing a smirk to his lips. He leaned over to Lynn. "Hey, we're almost out of it. It's clear about a hundred yards ahead."

Lynn didn't look toward her husband immediately. She didn't respond to him right away either. Her thoughts were heavy, thinking about them, about what could have just escalated. She never wanted to go back down that haunting road again. She knew what he was capable of, regardless of the effort he had shown recently. There was a beast lurking deep within him, and she had to continue to help him suppress it. It was the only way. He needed someone there to anchor and support him in case the monster seeped through the cracks again.

"Lynn?" He reached over and lightly squeezed her thigh. "Hey, we're almost home free."

Finally, she turned and faced him. "Told you. I knew it wouldn't last too long," she said with a knowing smirk. "Now get us home safely."

Her smile was contagious as he gazed at her. "That's been the plan the whole time, babe." The car was in third gear by the time he turned and faced the road again. "Finally moving again, boys."

David could see his father's eyes through the rearview mirror, eyes of regret. Nerves were still racing through his body as he spoke, thinking about the violence in his father's voice moments ago. "When ... when do you think we'll be home, Dad?"

"Knowing this freeway, who knows, David? Let's hope the worst is behind us, kiddo."

It was smooth sailing as they finally broke away from the rest of the traffic. Everyone's nerves settled as Micah shifted into fifth gear, praying not to see another obstacle until Bakersfield.

Lynn leaned over after minutes of silence. "Hey, by the way, they're called lightsabers, Micah. Not swords, babe."

The playful jab brought a grin to his face as the car raced north on the freeway.

3

NINETY MINUTES ON THE road and not a single brake check. The interstate was wide open, not even an eighteen-wheeler to slow the progression toward their destination. Micah's irrationalism dissipated moments after leaving the cluster of once-happy vacationers behind him.

His aura of hope radiated throughout the vehicle, inviting the others in the car to relax and enjoy the journey back home. This is what it felt like all weekend. No tension, no stress, no uncontrollable blowups. This is how it was supposed to be. The model family returning home from a much-needed trip to paradise. If you were to look in the Sears catalog, this was the family you would see on vacation.

"Dad? Hey Dad, what's the name of that lake again?" Will was pointing out the window, looking back and forth from his father to the reservoir parallel to the interstate.

Micah casually looked over at the vista on his left and then back to his son through the mirror. "That's Pyramid Lake, son." His grip on the steering wheel was light, mirroring the curves of the road as he drove.

The abrupt break in silence caught Lynn's attention, taking her away from her memories and thoughts. "We're already here? How fast are you driving, Micah?"

He didn't face her as he answered. "I set cruise control to sixty, babe. Smooth sailing." The words purred out of his mouth.

"Well, you better not get pulled over. You know we can't afford to pay a speeding ticket."

The passive order brought a sneer to his stubbled face as his mind wandered once again. *How the hell am I going to get a ticket out here in the middle of nowhere? There's no cops anywhere.* His jaw clenched, trying to ignore the feelings that were festering on the surface.

Will leaned forward, head poking between the two seats in the front, redirecting the negative energy slowly manifesting in Micah's mind. "So, when we left on Saturday, Dad, you said that we had been on the road for an hour when we passed the lake. That means we are about an hour away from home, right?"

Micah's attention turned to the back seat of the car, to his son, pride in his smile and voice. "Yeah, that's right, Will. Very good. You have been paying attention."

Will's eyes widened at the sound of the genuine praise flowing his way, feeling his heart skip a beat. Given that he was the baby of the family, the positiveness traditionally directed at him regarded manners and behavior, nothing more. A nine-year-old should know the proper way to act, right? His big brother David's academic and inquisitive nature prompted regular commendation and acclaim, creating a sense of resentment, if not envy.

But this was *his* moment, and he felt ecstatic about it. For the first time, based on recent memory, he had earned this praise. His father actually complimented him, and he deserved it. A smile leaked from each corner of his mouth as he looked at his father.

"Move out of the way, Will." David leaned forward, pulling his brother by the T-shirt, forcing him back into the seat. "Hey, Dad? I remember you saying that the lake isn't natural. What did you mean by that?"

Will abruptly grabbed a handful of David's hair, yanking him backward. David had monopolized their father's time from the moment they left on Saturday morning, and enough was enough. Even through the scream coming from the back of David's throat, Will held on, gripping the back of his brother's head with his right hand. He was tired of always being number two, always second fiddle. This was his time.

"Will, what has gotten into you?" The screech echoed through the car as Lynn attempted to break up the scuffle. "Let go, let go now, young man!" Her hands were entangled in the mess of knuckles and matted hair.

With the addition of a few threats, Will finally broke his grip, releasing his brother to sob in the back seat's corner.

The soothing, carefree drive vanished in mere seconds. Will sat there, arms crossing his chest, a scowl draping his face as he listened to his mother's scolding. It didn't last long, though. Lynn had a unique way of turning every difficult situation into a teaching moment. The harshness in her voice abruptly ended, replaced by concern and encouragement, as she probed for a motive. The rationality of her words, directed at both boys, soothed the tension that peaked during the confrontation and also calmed Micah's nerves.

His temper was malicious. Everyone in the car knew that, but during this brief hostile exchange, he had kept his cool. Or at least it seemed like that. On the inside, his dark thoughts were festering to a boil once again.

Control it! Damn, Micah, control it. These little ungrateful shits, pulling this crap after all I did for them this weekend. Long exhales came from his lungs as he attempted to suppress the darkness lingering. *Breathe! Just control it!*

Lynn halted the crooning of her voice, eyes flicking to the way Micah's chest heaved, his hands on the steering wheel, back too tight. Angry, brutal Micah was scary, but silent Micah was scarier. Instinct took over as she watched him spiral downward, the closest to the edge that he'd been the entire car ride.

She had already talked him down once on this car ride, and she could do it again. After enduring his blowups, she knew what to say. Lynn's throat clicked as she swallowed, softly whispering, "Micah, are you—"

Without notice, a thunderous bang sounded outside the hatchback, bringing screams from Lynn and both children. The vehicle's right side instantly sagged, and Micah fought to control the car's path, resisting the internal urge to slam on the brakes. *What was that? What the hell? Hold on, just hold on. Don't panic. It's a flat. It's just a flat tire.*

As maddening chaos ensued within the car, Micah's wits and comprehension took control. "Settle down back there. We just blew a tire, guys. It's okay. Everything is okay." His eyes were focused, scanning the road in front and behind him, slowly easing off the gas, and drifting the car to the right shoulder. Given his emotional volatility, he uncharacteristically held it together when it really mattered: when the lives of his family depended on it.

Both boys sat still, watching as their father cleared the final lane of the interstate, merging onto the shoulder and coming to rest.

4

Two nights, that was it. Not a week, two damn nights. Why did they have to bring all this shit with them? Micah pondered as he yanked bag after bag out of the loaded hatchback to get to the spare.

As he cleared the last piece of luggage, he hunched headfirst into the vacant space and sought the thick piece of gray carpet securely Velcroed to the floor of the trunk. Lifting it, he peered into the empty cavity, shaking his head with disgust.

That lying son of a bitch! I knew something was wrong with the deal for this piece of shit the second I signed the papers. When it's too good to be true, it's too good to be fuckin' true!

From the passenger side, Lynn approached, worry strangling her like a noose. "Can you change it? I can help if you need—"

"There's no spare!" Micah whipped his head in her direction, spittle flinging from his lips. "That piece of shit, Larry, sold us the car without one. What are we supposed to do now?"

Lynn halted, watching her husband's nostrils flare. "He ... he said there was a spare, right under the mat." She approached the back of the car, staring at the nothingness below the piece of carpet. "It was there when he gave us the keys, Micah. He showed us the spare. What happened to it?"

Micah dropped his glare, shaking his head in disgust. "That cheap bastard took it out at the last minute, trying to save twenty bucks, I bet."

"Well, what are we going to do now, Micah?" Lynn asked, eyes pleading for guidance. "Will's scared in the back seat, worried about being stranded here all night."

Violently, he slammed the trunk closed and released a yell, mumbling curses under his breath. He whirled, pacing the area. *Why me? Why does this shit keep happening to me?*

After a few moments, he looked at his wife again, trying to be the husband and father he was in the early years of their marriage. "Tell Will everything will be all right, okay? And make sure David's not planting shit in his ear like he always does."

He broke his gaze, averting his eyes to the lonely highway. "I'm going to get help. I'll try to flag someone down, get a ride to the nearest town, and buy a new tire."

Lynn's eyes wandered to the freeway. "How far is the nearest town? An hour?"

He shook his head, dropping his eyes to the ground. "No, no, not that far. I think there is a small rest stop a mile or two north of us. If no one will pull over and give me a ride, I'll walk. Either way, I'll be back soon." Knowing he had a job to do, his eyes were full of pride as he spoke those words. This was not a moment to be the new Micah, the angry and resentful man he had become. He had to protect and lead his family. He had to do what was necessary to keep them safe and get them back home. The new Micah, the parasitical asshole, had to be suppressed.

She gave him a curt nod, respecting his efforts to keep everyone, including himself, calm in a situation as stressful as this. Usually, these moments yielded a fist in the wall, or a door slammed after a violent outburst. She knew deep down the effort was there. The effort to be a better man.

"I'll be back, babe. You and the boys stay out of sight the best you can." He paused, looking at the interstate again, shielding his eyes from the fury of the sun overhead. "If anyone stops and something doesn't seem right, remember what my mom always said."

Lynn responded, simpering lazily. "Yeah, I remember, Micah. Kick him in the nuts, scream, and *run*."

The suddenness of her response brought a smile to his lips. "She always had a way with words, didn't she?"

The playfulness in her voice ended as she said, "Be safe. And hurry back, Micah."

"An hour or two at the most, babe. I'll be back. Hang in there."

"We will." She paused, staring at the man she had fallen in love with so many years ago. Her eyes said everything, but she mouthed the words anyway. "I love you."

"Love you too, babe."

The interstate was quiet as he turned north and started his trek. *Too quiet*, he thought. *Where is everyone? Is everyone still stuck behind that wreck?*

With a flip of the thumb toward the few cars and trucks passing by, he walked, praying someone had the generosity to lend another human being a hand. Maybe, after all the shit he'd endured during the past year and a half, he had a little luck on his side?

5

AFTER CLEARING A HILL a half mile up the interstate, he turned around, trying to get a last glimpse of his family and their car. They were still there, leaning against the railing on the shoulder. Lynn had her arms draped around both boys, keeping them from their worries and thoughts. *They're safe,* he told himself as he again headed north, thumb pointed out toward the minimal traffic.

He had taken less than twenty paces before the clamor of an approaching vehicle startled him. Whipping his head around at the sudden commotion and jumping back a few feet from the freeway, he watched with weary eyes as a beat-up,old Chevy plodded along in the lane next to him. Black exhaust spewed from its tailpipe, creating a trail in its wake as it inched closer, slowing considerably. He could see there was only a lone driver. One man that could help them all.

The truck passed by, skidding off the asphalt onto the dirt shoulder a few feet in front of him before stopping completely. Micah watched as a thick left arm hung out the driver side window, gesturing for him to come closer. *Thank God someone stopped*, he thought, observing the man flick a cigarette butt onto the interstate.

As he trotted to the truck, he noticed it had some writing on the door. The oxidized paint, worn and weathered but still legible, read: G. C. Motors Inc. Est. 1938.

After a second look at the door, his attention focused on the driver, who was now exiting the less-than-cared-for truck. The man was portly, and that's being kind. Concern struck Micah as he took in the extent of this man's physique. Well over six and a half feet tall and easily weighed four Benjamins, he was a monster of a man.

After slamming the door of the truck, the man stared in Micah's direction, not breaking eye contact. Eventually, he cocked his head to the side and spat before calling out, "Need a lift?" His voice was deep, demanding.

Relief hit Micah like a ton of bricks. Help had arrived, and he didn't care where it came from. His family was alone, waiting alongside the freeway, praying for his safe return. "Thanks for stopping, friend. I didn't think anyone would. You see, my car—"

He cut Micah off before he could finish the weak response, holding his eyes with a glare. "That piece of shit down the road, right? Tan one?"

Micah nodded slowly in response, a little offended, gaping at the towering man. He wondered how he knew the hatchback was his. Dumb luck? To Micah, the man looked like he was stuffed with raw dimness. "Yeah, that's my car. It has a flat, and I don't have a spare. Think you can give me a ride to get one? I have little to offer, but I could use some help, sir."

"Yeah, yeah, I can help. Got a shop up the road in Gorman." The man paused, removed a handkerchief from the back pocket of his Dickies overalls, and wiped his brow. "Got a few used tires in the yard. I reckon one of 'em will fit."

Micah couldn't believe what he was hearing. This was exactly what he needed, what his family needed. With a little hope, they could be back on the road in no time. Maybe his luck was changing after all.

"That's great," he said, nodding his head in surprise. "Thank you so much, sir. Not just for stopping, but for—"

The man held up both hands, waving them back and forth. "I ain't done nothin' yet, friend. Save your thanks for later. Let's just see if we can get you up and running." He gestured to the truck's cab, not waiting for Micah to respond.

Without concern, Micah approached the passenger side of the truck, noticing significant damage. The entire right side of the vehicle had heavy Bondo work, not done by a professional, from what he could tell. *What the hell happened here? Are those fucking bullet holes?*

The sight caused him to halt, wondering what this old truck—and, more importantly, the hulking man in it—had been through recently. In seconds, the sound of the truck's horn interrupted his stillness, bringing him back from his thoughts.

"You comin' or what, friend?" The man yelled, hanging his head out the window.

With reluctance, Micah lifted the handle and opened the door. Peering into the cab, he found the interior even less desirable. If the sight alone wouldn't make a man think twice about entering, the scent would. Oil and grime and stale beer. This was definitely the vehicle of a man who did not give a shit what others thought. Micah didn't have a choice, though. If he retreated now, who knows if anyone else would stop or offer help? He had to do this. He had to do this for them, the ones he owed so much. *If he backed out now, wasn't he still the deadbeat husband and father he knew he had become?* Regardless of his reservations, he hopped into the cab.

6

Minutes passed with neither saying a word. No small talk, no shooting the breeze. Absolute silence, except for the radio. An old Waylon Jennings song played in the background as Micah looked around, without making it obvious he was looking around. He knew this would be a short trip. He had traveled this interstate many times and knew where the Gorman exit was. He just prayed the shop this mysterious man was taking him to was right off the interstate and not up in the hills somewhere.

"The name's Clyde," the man said, eyes fixed on the road, finally breaking the tension that had built up in the silence.

The sudden sound of the man's voice caused a knee-jerk reaction; Micah's foot struck an empty beer bottle rolling around on the floorboard. "Nice ... nice to meet you, Clyde. My name's Micah. Micah Carter." He nonchalantly responded, attempting to conceal his nervousness.

There was no response from the man known as Clyde. He didn't even look over to acknowledge that Micah had responded to him. His eyes remained in front of him, pinned on the curves of the road as if he had memorized every turn. Micah wondered if he had. *Has he lived here his whole life?* The car turned awkwardly silent again until a sudden sound came from within the car. Clyde tapped the turn signal, initializing their exit from the interstate.

The constant ticking echoed in Micah's head as he eyed the asphalt, spotting the exit sign less than a hundred yards in front of them.

Yup, there it is. The Gorman exit. As the vehicle slowed, merging onto the off-ramp, he noticed some bright yellow graffiti on the green sign. *Dumb punks,* he thought. Below the Gorman sign was a smaller green sign with white lettering for Exit 202.

"Shop's not too far off," Clyde mumbled as they glided down the off-ramp blanketed on each side by gnarled oaks and pines.

Micah had taken this exit during his many journeys home from Los Angeles in the past. Quarterly retreats from his days in the energy field. It wasn't a regular rest stop for him, but he had stopped several times to fuel up or grab a quick snack. He knew of a few gas stations and a McDonald's at the end of the off-ramp, but he had never traveled past these initial businesses. Again, his thoughts revolved around the shop's location and how long it would take to find a tire that would fit. Worries of Lynn and the boys stranded on the side of the road compounded that.

The off-ramp ended at a T-intersection, west or east being the only options, except for the Beacon Station directly across. As the truck slowed near the stop sign, Clyde signaled right. Eastbound it was. Micah inadvertently looked over his left shoulder as the truck turned, narrowly catching a glimpse of the Shell Station he had been inside a few times, except it was no longer a Shell. There was no sign marking the establishment that he could see from his point of view. *Hmm, that's new.*

The silence was deafening, and it went on for miles down the road. Looking out his window, Micah observed the nothingness of this part of the state. The landscape was void—nothing of interest or value—just trees and hills with the occasional trailer and a few cabins sprinkled here and there.

Eventually, the sound of the turn signal brought Micah around once again, steering his attention to the road. With the lingering tick, Clyde slowed the vehicle. The twisting road, thickly lined on both sides with forest, had no visible signs or clearings indicating a residence or business was nearby, but the truck came to a stop in the middle of the road anyway. Micah's nervousness heightened as he looked around, wondering what this man was doing, until he saw it. A razor-thin clearing of the trees on the left side of the road, barely wide enough for the truck. Anyone traveling at a decent speed would never notice it.

"This is it," Clyde mumbled as he guided the truck across the oncoming lane into the tight opening. Micah watched wide-eyed as the forest surrounding them seemed to enclose and swallow them whole.

7

THE SUNLIGHT FADING AWAY as the truck continued down the enclosed natural tunnel escalated Micah's anxiety; he fidgeted in his seat, looking side to side and behind the vehicle. Even the radio seemed to stop as they rolled forward into the darkness. Only static coming out of the speakers. Micah's eyes scanned the scenery, not knowing what to expect. *Where are we going? Where's he taking me?*

After a hundred feet or so, the uncertainty racing through Micah subsided at the wonderful sight of light again. There was an opening in the forest, bright and vibrant with sunshine. A deep, relaxing sigh came from Micah's lips, knowing this must be the shop Clyde had mentioned minutes earlier. *What the hell's wrong with you, Micah? This guy's just trying to help. He picked you up, remember? He's one of the good ones.*

Once the vehicle cleared the tunnel of trees, the sight wasn't unexpected. A large single-story workshop adorned with a familiar logo: G. C. Motors Inc. The building wasn't anything to write home about, four shabby walls and a roof, but it still filled Micah with hope as Clyde steered the old truck into a parking space to the left of the structure. Parked beside them was an old Chevy Malibu from the late '60s, and from the looks of it, it was slowly being restored. Still primed and missing most of the chrome.

"Here we are. The yard is in the back," Clyde mumbled as he opened his door and climbed out of the cab.

Micah followed suit, climbing out of the truck and taking a final look at the Chevy and the sights of the surrounding forest. He inhaled deeply, breathing in the rich, clean air. The mountains were beautiful this time of year, but the remoteness of the location still had Micah scratching his head. *Was this place actually open?* It was a wonder how this could be a thriving business. No signs directing customers, no advertising, no way of knowing that this establishment was even here. *What is this place?*

The crunching of footsteps on gravel sounded behind him, startling him back into place. Flinging his head around, relief flooded his veins. There in front of him was the behemoth known as Clyde. "Shit. You snuck up on me. Pretty light-footed for a big guy, you know."

Clyde didn't respond to the statement. He just stood there glaring at Micah, head slightly cocked to the side. A light breeze cut through, waving the man's long, unkempt beard. Their stare-off filled the calmness of the serene environment with tension and anxiety. After a few more moments, Clyde dropped his eyes and started sauntering toward the side of the building. He gestured for Micah to follow with a wave of his arm, followed by a question, "You comin'?"

What the fuck was that? Micah thought, watching this monster stroll away. He stood there puzzled, perplexed by the strange encounter.

Why the uncomfortable stare? This man was a stranger, not a friend, a colleague, or an acquaintance. Not that Micah had any of these anymore after all his shit this past year and a half. He didn't have a choice. He followed, monitoring the man and his whereabouts, ears perked.

The gravel at the front of the shop ended where they turned the corner, and the ground transitioned to dirt and sprinkled vegetation. Beyond the bothersome weeds, someone had cut a firebreak thirty feet or so into the surrounding forest. *That was smart*, Micah thought, given the wildfires that occur in this region every summer and fall. As they walked the perimeter, "the yard" came to fruition.

It was a junkyard. Old beaters ruined and picked apart, forever parked amidst scrap metal and rusty sheds. There was a little bit of everything, it seemed—a fender here, a bumper there, forgotten in the dirt like lost souls. It was eerie. Micah quickened his pace among the omnipresent milkweed that sighed with the breeze. This area did not look like an active work yard. It was long forgotten and disused.

Clyde continued to wade through the yard, passing an oxidized blue Volkswagen Beetle set on wooden blocks. Micah followed reluctantly, being cautious with each step. Behind the car was the treasure they had come for: a pile of used tires, worn and cracked by the intense sunlight of the summer months. Clyde began sifting through them, tossing unwanted tires to the side.

The broadness of Clyde's shoulders obstructed Micah's view until the man turned around, holding a tire in each hand. A sly grin crossed his face as he held them up to be viewed. "Choices, choices. Either will work, but let's take 'em both, just in case. You'll need a new one soon, though. Not much tread left."

He was a man of his word, and he had come through. The sight of one tire that could fit would have brought relief, let alone two. They were saved, and it had only taken roughly an hour. Micah's appreciation poured out of him like a leak in a ship's hull. "This is great, Clyde, I can't thank you enough. I know I have a jack and some tools in the car, so—"

Clyde cut him off, "Hey man, it's nuthin'. I already told you, let's get you up and runnin' before all the damn thank you's." There wasn't any aggression in his voice, just matter of fact. With a wink, he lightly tossed one tire in Micah's direction, which struck him in the chest and issued a groan, then turned back toward the front of the building. As he began his departure, he mumbled under his breath, "Let's get you back to your sons and that pretty *wife* of yours."

The unexpected strike caught Micah off guard, and he staggered back a step, gripping the center of the tire with both hands. *What the hell was that for?*

He watched as the monstrous man ambled away, not waiting for him to follow. The verbal blow distracted him for a few moments before he regained his bearings. His mind chewed over the words that Clyde had spoken. *Did he just say something about Lynn? I didn't bring them up in the truck, did I?*

He chose to ignore the comment, not sure whether he heard the man correctly or not. Knowing he had to get back to them and be the man of the family, he followed, carrying the tire in sweaty palms.

As Micah turned the corner, Clyde was already climbing into the old truck. He hurried his pace and tossed the tire into the truck bed beside the one Clyde had already placed. As he reached for the door handle, something beyond the firebreak caught his eye, hundreds of yards down the slope into the surrounding forest. He would have never noticed if he weren't at this perfect angle. It was the same color as this supposed shop, sun-bleached yellow with blue trim. The thick forest made its visibility difficult, but it seemed to be another structure. *It's too far away to be a part of this establishment. Another abandoned business from the early days,* he thought. He pondered this thought for a few moments before the familiar horn sounded, catching him by surprise.

"Hurry up and get in. We're burnin' daylight!"

Not waiting another second, Micah pulled down on the door handle and climbed into the truck. He would be back with his family in no time, thanks to this man, this complete stranger. This was far easier than he ever expected.

8

THEY WERE NEARING THE interstate minutes later, racing down the two-lane backwoods road. Again, the truck had fallen into uncomfortable utter silence, with the exception of the radio. Hank Jr. and all his rowdy friends were in the background. Passing the Beacon Station, Clyde slowed the vehicle and pulled into what used to be the Shell near the southbound junction. Micah looked on in anticipation, wondering what they were stopping for. The truck had plenty of fuel, based on the gauge. He needed to get back to Lynn and the boys. He didn't have time to make a pit stop.

The truck stopped in front of the establishment. There was no visible sign labeling the place, no logo either. Just a dusty brown building with a flashing red OPEN sign in the front window.

"Hey, what is this place? Why are we stopping?" Micah asked, apprehension gripping each syllable.

Clyde looked over, grinned, and arched his brow. "Gotta get some suds and smokes, friend. Be right back," he stated as he climbed out of the cab.

There was no response from Micah. He sat there, mouth agape, watching Clyde stroll away. He thought about his family, wondering if they were still okay. Wondering why this man would stop knowing they were alone on the side of a busy interstate. The questions piled up in his mind as he stared at the blinking OPEN sign. His appreciation for the help dissipated in seconds, replaced by hostility.

Suds and smokes? Are you fuckin' kidding me? I don't have time for this shit. What the hell's wrong with this guy? Doesn't he know my situation, my family's situation? We should be on the freeway, heading in their direction right now, not screwing around in some shitty convenience store getting a pack of cigarettes and beer! He sat there, emotions festering to a boil as he leered out the windshield, eyes narrowed.

Minutes passed without Clyde returning, minutes that escalated Micah's irrationalism. Eventually, the anxiety of the wait gave in, and he exited the truck, slamming the door and storming toward the shop's entrance.

As he approached, he saw Clyde inside, leaning over the cashier's counter, engaged in what looked like a playful conversation. The sight stopped him in his tracks as he thought about what he was about to do. Not acting impulsively was something new he had been working on the past few months, and this was a great opportunity to stop and think. *What was he supposed to do anyway, barge in and demand to get back on the road? Piss and moan at the man? He didn't have any pull in this situation, let alone the natural ability to influence others. He was no leader. And Clyde had come to his rescue on the highway. He didn't have to stop and offer help. He did anyways, though, so Micah should give him at least an ounce of respect for that.*

He slowly dropped his stare, unclenched his fists, and breathed in deeply, attempting to gather himself. After a few moments, his stare redirected through the glass door. He was ready to try a different approach.

The jingle of the bell above the front door sounded through the small store, garnering Clyde's attention. He turned his head around and found Micah standing just inside the doorframe. He delivered a weak nod Micah's way and returned to his conversation, not saying a word. The rude dismissal usually would have caused an angry outburst, but Micah's thoughts were clear. He had a job to do and he needed to get back on the road to do it.

"Um, Clyde? Everything okay? We should ... um, probably get going."

Clyde turned around again, an expression of pique across his face. When the man shifted, Micah's view behind the counter was unobstructed. The person on the other end of the conversation sat on a stool, cold beer in his hand as he, too, stared in Micah's direction. *Maybe this was a bad idea*, he thought, leaning backward in anticipation.

Instantly, the man behind the counter stood up and called out, "What ya doin' here, boy? Lookin' for somethin'?"

Confused and nervous, Micah's eyes met the man's, but he couldn't answer him. If there was such a thing as the polar opposite of another human being, this man was Clyde's. Not a hair over five feet and skinny as a rail. The blue sleeveless coveralls he wore appeared soiled and caked with grime. *Was this place a convenience store or an auto shop?*

"Well, what is it?" The man questioned, louder this time, firmer, spreading his frail arms out to the side, gesturing for an answer. As he spoke, his eyes widened, revealing hints of yellow.

Micah's wits returned, and acknowledging there was a necessity to say something, not just stand there like a dipshit with his mouth sewn shut, he spoke. "Just … just waiting on Clyde. He's helping me with—"

Clyde turned back to his counterpart, cutting Micah off mid-sentence. "Piece of shit import broke down on the freeway. Needs a spare, probably more than that, though."

Stunned, Micah stared as the two resumed their small talk. *Probably more? What is this guy talking about? It's just a flat!*

He could see there were two empty beer bottles on the counter where the two laughed and joshed with one another. *Is this really what we are doing? Happy hour while my family is out there waiting for my return?*

As he glared at the two, watching them clink their beers together and hearing the *slish-slosh* of the liquid inside, memories from long ago flooded his thoughts. He hadn't had a drink in months. One more thing he had forced himself to change after he hit rock bottom. One more thing from his past he knew he couldn't return to, but …

Memories from years ago sifted through his mind, when he still had friends and acquaintances. Having a beer or two with his coworkers from the energy plant on Fridays, sipping a scotch with his dad at a BBQ, and drinking margaritas in the backyard with Lynn during the summer while the boys ran through the sprinklers. Those were wonderful memories, but like all good things, they came to an end.

His father passed a year after Will was born, in the fall of '79. Tragic and sudden. It affected him, but not like the death of his mother. She was his everything. Her decline started the downward spiral that almost ended his marriage and his life. As her health slowly deteriorated, the drinking became more frequent. The weekend six-packs turned into nightly six-packs, while the social drinking became isolated binge drinking.

How could anyone just sit back and watch their mother die without something to take the edge off? Lynn expressed her concerns countless times, questioning if he was self-medicating to cope with the pain. Every time the concerns and questions piled up, his denial and irrationalism bloomed. The thought of losing his mother was too much.

He had found a way to numb the misery.

Coinciding with the heavy drinking, Micah's dishonesty with his wife began. It started with staggering into the house late at night, claiming he had a single Coors while sitting with his mom. It continued with disappearances into the garage in the middle of the day, only to return with beer or scotch on his breath. These behaviors slowly fractured Lynn's trust. She knew he was lying about this, knew he needed help, but he wasn't willing to listen or do anything about it. He wasn't only lying to her; he was lying to himself.

Along with the dishonesty came the heightened aggression and anger when confrontation came his way. Common deflection behavior with addicts of any kind. It wasn't until after his mother's first ER trip that the anger turned physical.

After the initial diagnosis, Micah's mother's physical health was better than her mental health. She could function as long as the oxygen tank was nearby, but she hated being tied down and dependent. She was a strong woman, proud but humble. This disease had stolen that. After a few daunting months of using the tank, she broke down and had a panic attack.

At eleven p.m. on a Tuesday, the phone rang in the Carter household, awakening Micah from his deep slumber. He had been sober that night, going to bed conscious and focused for a change. Groggily, Micah picked up the phone from the nightstand, spine straightening as the mortified voice of Grace, his mother, rang through his ears. She cried and claimed suffocation, ignoring Micah's alarmed pleas for answers.

Within seconds, he was out the front door and racing down the somber streets toward his mom, his rock. She lived minutes away, but every second seemed like an eternity as he frantically swerved in and out of the traffic separating him from the one woman in his life that he would do anything for.

The ambulance arrived first, but he had a split second to see her. Wearing her light pink robe and white cotton bath slippers, he found her on a gurney outside the medical transport vehicle. The hysteria from the phone call continued as he ambled forward, not believing this could really be happening. His eyes swayed from the flashing blue and red to his mother, taking each step reluctantly, not wanting this to be the last moment he spent with her.

"Mom?" His voice was frantic, approaching manic. "Mom, I'm here! What's wrong? What the hell happened?"

Her eyes were full, dreadfully full, as she leered at him. Not with hate or indignation, but with desperation and fear. The timorous look halted any response as the EMTs moved the gurney and loaded it into the back of the ambulance, saying little but trying to be supportive.

He followed them to the hospital but couldn't see her despite his pissing and moaning. He spent the night in the ER waiting room—antsy, with a sick feeling brewing in his stomach— as the hours dragged on with no news of her status. Eventually, in the wee hours of the early morning, a doctor named Jacobs approached and shared his findings. She was indeed dying.

This event broke him. Micah always claimed to be a vigorous man, but all men think that, right? He understood the sickness that was spreading through her lungs, but her mind? It was too much for him.

After leaving the hospital, he found comfort in an old bourbon bottle stashed in the garage behind some half-used gallons of paint. After draining the contents and some much-needed sobs, he staggered into the house around six a.m. to find his loving wife waiting and worried. Initially, her concerns involved Grace, but her demeanor changed as she embraced him and smelled the whiskey on his breath. The confrontation didn't last long, but a few pieces of drywall had to be replaced. He also had to drive himself, unaccompanied, to the ER for a fractured wrist.

The nostalgic clanking of two beer bottles brought Micah back from his thoughts. As his eyes focused, he watched as Clyde and his counterpart joked and bullshitted with one another. It looked natural. It looked fun. He missed moments like this. He had been so wound up these days, trying to steer straight as an arrow, to be different from what he once was. *Why couldn't he join them? Just one beer wouldn't hurt, right?*

He took one step forward, intrigued and a little confused, when Clyde rose from the counter and slammed the remnants of his third beer, leaning back far enough to stare at the heavens, suds sliding down his thick throat. He placed the empty bottle on the counter and turned around, latching onto Micah before releasing a heavy belch.

"Let's go get that piece of shit you call a car. See ya around, Sid." He waved at his friend and slid past Micah, exiting the quaint little station, not waiting for a response or acknowledgment. Nada.

Micah just stood there inside the doorframe, staring at the man behind the counter, not understanding what this was all about or why all of these memories came pouring into his mind. He slowly turned around and followed Clyde to the beat-up old truck, hopping in without a sound. *Hopefully, this would be the only pit stop.* That was all he could think about as Clyde threw the truck into reverse and started toward the southbound junction.

9

After flipping around to return northbound, the ride down the freeway was much like the ride up. Silent. Through the dusty truck's windshield, Micah could make out Lynn sitting on the interstate shoulder railing. The boys were behind her throwing something back and forth, passing the time. The sight filled him with joy, knowing they were only moments from being reunited and could put this total fiasco behind them. But deep in his psyche, he knew he had nearly made a stupid choice and almost relapsed. This wasn't the year for that, '87 was the year of *change*. The year to fix things and revert to the decent husband and father he once was.

The turn signal sounded, marking their exit from the now busy lanes. Lynn stood, caution painting her demeanor, as the truck slowed to a stop in front of her and the boys. The exterior was ghastly, and the look on her face as she eyed the damage and shoddy body work confirmed that. The boys halted their game, jaws slackening as they watched the dust settle around the truck's chassis.

Micah hopped out of the cab, smiling as he headed toward his awaiting family. He glanced down at the gold watch strapped to his wrist, then gestured toward his sons. "Eighty-two minutes, guys. Told you I'd be back before you knew it." He met Lynn near the railing and joined her in a slight embrace. He met her eyes. "Everything okay? Did anyone stop to check on you?"

"No, we're fine. Not a single car stopped." She looked past him to the truck. "I see you found a ride. Did you find a spare tire?"

Micah glanced back as well. "Yeah, yeah. This guy stopped and helped me out. He has a mechanic shop up the road." He faced his wife once again, joy in his voice. "We have a spare in the truck bed. If it works, I think we can be home before nightfall."

Suddenly, Lynn's eyes widened as she looked beyond her husband, her complexion fading.

Micah whipped his head around, wondering what had caused the trepidation in her eyes. There, standing next to the beat-up vehicle was the man known as Clyde, glaring at the couple, arms crossed over his barrel chest. Micah realized the reason for his wife's concerned expression. His size was intimidating. "Oh, this is the man that stopped and picked me up." He stepped forward, grabbing his wife's hand, pulling her toward the hulking man and his truck. "Lynn, this is Clyde. He helped me. He saved the day. Saved all of us, that is."

Lynn sized him up, observing the scuffed brown work boots, denim overalls, frayed white T-shirt, and grizzled, unkempt beard. She thanked the man reluctantly, a cautious look in her eyes.

Clyde simply nodded in her direction, never breaking eye contact. His stoic nature was unsettling, and the staring was awkward, as if neither party knew what to do next in this situation.

Micah observed both. *Why's he looking at her like that?* He knew what Lynn must be thinking. He had just traveled with this monster for the last hour, anxiety coursing through him every second of the ride. Regardless of the fact that he helped him out of this jam, the last thing he wanted was to spend more time with this stranger leering at his wife.

In an instant, he broke the tension by strolling toward the truck bed. "See, Lynn, here are the spares." He reached in and grabbed one, holding it high in the air like a trophy. "This little piece of rubber is going to get us home, babe," he stated with a toothy grin, trying to conceal his nervousness.

Lynn's attention shifted from Clyde to her husband. There wasn't a response to his optimistic claim. She simply delivered a weak smile and nod, then dropped her eyes to the dirt. She turned around and walked toward her sons, still watching from the other side of the shoulder railing.

What the hell was that about, Lynn? He thought as he watched her stroll away.

Micah had sparingly worked on cars as a youth, so he could handle a tire change. And he knew Clyde's presence was affecting his wife and kids based on their mannerisms. He was grateful for the help but he, too, felt a tad uneasy around Clyde. Maybe it was because it seemed prudent, maybe it was because the awkwardness in the air had turned suffocating; either way, now was the appropriate time to dismiss this monster of a man. The sooner he climbed into his truck and drove out of sight, the better.

"Well, Clyde, thanks for everything. If you hadn't stopped, I'd probably still be walking along the freeway. I have a jack in the trunk and should have this changed in no time. Thanks again." He paused and held out his hand, expecting a friendly shake.

Clyde looked down at the outstretched hand, then back to Micah's eyes.

A smirk tugged at his lips as he responded, "Well, hold on there. We're not out of this just yet, *partner*." He emphasized each syllable of the last word. "I want to make sure you folks are up and runnin' before leavin' you out here all alone. It can be *dangerous*. Get what I mean?" His eyes were full as he looked from Micah to Lynn, now standing on the other side of the railing with her sons. He delivered a wink in her direction, then started toward the tan hatchback. "Let's get that jack you mentioned."

This was not the response Micah expected or wanted. His mind wandered, spinning in circles, searching for this man's MO. *What the hell's this guy's problem? I said I had it. He's freaking out Lynn and the boys. I can see it in their eyes. What the hell does he want? Is he really just some good Samaritan trying to help? Son of a bitch better stop looking at her like that too.* He spiraled.

Shaking his head with eyes pinned to the ground, Micah followed the lumbering man toward the family car, glancing back twice to ensure his family was okay. He walked to the hatchback's trunk, still open from before. "You see? The damn salesman sold it to us without a spare. Can you believe that?" He eyed Clyde, disbelief painted across his face.

Clyde delivered a grunt as he reached into the cavity where the spare should have been and removed the jack. "Dealt with a few of them in my day. They're all shitty. Crooked as my daddy's back before he died." He held out the jack toward Micah. "Get started on the tire. I'll be under the hood. Want to make sure there's no other problem with this piece. Fuckin' imports, right?"

Micah's brow furrowed as he accepted the jack. "The engine's fine. We've never had a single problem with this car the whole time we've owned it until the tire. It's been really reliable. You don't need to do that."

Clyde looked to the side and spat, bloody phlegm hitting the ground. "You a mechanic?" The man lingered, letting the words sink in. "No, I'm the mechanic, remember? Trust me, you can never be ..." He paused again, making sure he had Micah's attention, "... too careful, friend." He tipped his head forward as he talked.

Then he walked toward the front of the car, leaving Micah standing there anxious and confused.

There's nothing wrong with the engine. But I guess he has a point. It's better to be safe than sorry. Maybe he is just trying to help, but why is he so persistent? Let's just get to work then we can all go our separate ways. I have to get us out of this mess.

With the jack in his hand, Micah approached the flat and got to it, lifting the rear passenger side of the car and prying off lug nuts. They would be back on the road in no time, and the memories of Clyde would vanish before he and his family made it down the Grapevine.

10

THE TIRE CHANGE WAS quick and efficient. Micah barely broke a sweat, and the spare fit just like Clyde said it would. He didn't even have to try the second one still sitting in the truck bed.

Wiping the grease off his hands with a rag, he approached the front of the car, expecting to hear that the inspection was over and that everything was fine. He knew it would be.

He stood there observing Clyde's thick frame under the hood. "It's in great shape, yeah? It's Japanese, but no problem, right?" Micah asked.

Clyde glanced up, pity crossing his face. "Well, it's a good thing I checked. Fuel pump's 'bout to blow, friend." He shook his head in disappointment. "You got lucky that it didn't fail while drivin'. That could have been *really* bad."

Micah couldn't believe what he was hearing. Since they bought the hatchback from that weasel, Larry, there hadn't been a single mechanical problem. Not one. *How could this happen?*

Struggling to grasp the situation, he spoke slowly, tasting his words. "What's our options here, Clyde? Can she make it down the hill to the valley, to Bakersfield, so we can at least get home?"

Clyde lifted his head from within the hood, uncertainty in his eyes. "You seem like a man with some integrity. You want to take care of your family, don't you?"

Micah didn't respond with words. A simple nod delivered the message while his thoughts meandered.

"If that pump gives out as you're goin' sixty downhill, that's gonna be bad news for everyone involved, man." He paused and shook his head, oozing empathy with every mannerism. "I reckon you need to get it changed out and fast. I can do the work. Not sure if I have a new one or the parts to rebuild yours, though."

Micah cupped his mouth with his hand and could feel his breath grow frantic. This trip was supposed to be the chance for change, for redemption, for forgiveness. Now he wasn't even sure if they could get home. How was he supposed to pay for the fuel pump, let alone the service to install it? He had twelve dollars in his wallet. Certainly, Clyde wouldn't do the work for free.

He had held it together for so long, but standing there looking at this man, thinking about his only option, he couldn't control it.

What are we supposed to do now, Micah? This could take days if he doesn't have the parts, maybe longer. Where are we going to stay if it is days? Oh God, this can't be happening!

He turned around, shaking his head with aggression as he walked away from Clyde, hands on top of his head, mumbling.

Lynn noticed his behavior, knowing her husband and what it meant. She didn't know what was wrong, but she knew something had triggered it. Her only thought was to talk him off the ledge he was teetering on.

Carefully, she stepped over the railing, approaching with caution. Walking up beside him, she reached out to gently touch his shoulder. "Micah? Micah, babe, what's wrong? What happened?"

As her hand gently brushed his body, he whipped around, eyes full of fury.

"What's wrong? What do you think is wrong, *Lynn?*" He was seething. "The damn car is about to die! This piece of shit that *you* had to have. The fuel pump's gotta be changed, and we have no way to pay for it!" He paused and released a growl as he scratched the back of his head. "We spent everything we had on this trip of yours buying cheap souvenirs and shit. There's no way to get home now. We're broke!" His glare was menacing, eyeing her like a predator before the inevitable pounce.

This sudden rage wasn't new; Lynn had seen it before. She knew it wasn't personal, but his aggression still affected her when he had these episodes. The worry that it might turn physical always lingered in the back of her mind, so she had learned to narrow her senses and straighten her back in alarm.

As she stood there, contemplating how to bring him back, observing how he was looking at her, the memory of the now faint scar forever on Will's cheek came to mind.

It happened the night of Christmas Eve, '86: the climax of their squabbles. Micah was absent most of the day, claiming to be last-minute shopping for the boys. When he returned empty-handed and reeking of booze and desperation, the agitation and lies began. As Lynn questioned him, violence erupted throughout the house in a drunken frenzy of broken glass and the kitchen table thrown over.

The boys were upstairs but inquisitively came down to check on their mother once they heard the screams and destruction echoing through the home. In the madness's wake, Will slipped and fell, landing face-first on a pile of glass shards. The cut wasn't deep enough to require stitches, but the blood ...

The sight of crimson flowing down his son's face stopped Micah's aggression, replaced by agony and despair. He fell to his knees, cradling his son in his arms while he sobbed on the kitchen floor. This was his rock bottom, and he hated himself for everything. He needed help, wanted help, but didn't know how to break this endless crippling cycle.

Lynn was at a breaking point after the incident. She packed some of their things, and she and the boys went to her mother's house for three nights, threatening to leave permanently if Micah didn't sober up and get help with his grief. Eventually, they reunited after he pleaded and begged for her to come home. The ultimatum seemed to work because he had been sober since. The aggression, though ...

The misery of the past haunted her to this day, a deathly grip wringing out her essence. She always wondered if she should just give up and leave, start over somewhere with the boys. The idea almost came to fruition many times, but her heart just couldn't take it. They needed each other, and the love she had for her husband survived, always. Deep in her psyche, she knew she could save him and bring him back from the pit he had fallen into.

The past year and a half had created this monster, and she kept telling herself that it wasn't his fault; it was his mother's death, losing his job, and the alcoholism that drove him to this point. She *could* bring him down, just like she had in the car earlier today.

A weak smile crossed her lips, and the anxiousness flowing throughout her aura subsided. Warmth surrounded her as she stepped forward, expressing her love and compassion with her eyes. She could do this. She could help him.

Micah's mind spun, trying to encompass the situation and his actions. He knew during these especially trying moments that he couldn't control it. But he also knew she was there for him, cared for him, and loved him more than anyone.

With resolve, his eyes tightened, and he lowered his head, inhaling deeply. The rage would pass. It always did.

Seeing his vulnerability at that moment broke her in two. *How had it gotten this far, and why? What was happening in his mind during these intense moments?* She didn't know, but she had to embrace him and drive these dark feelings away. She stepped forward, threw her arms around his neck, and held on, whispering in his ear.

After a moment, he felt a lot lighter on his feet. He pulled back from her hug, fixating on her loving eyes. With sorrow and devotion, he mouthed, "Thank you."

She held his stare, responding without making a sound. From behind them, David called out. "Mom? Dad? What's wrong? What's going on?"

They both looked over at their sons waiting on the other side of the railing. Micah was winded, trying to gather himself, so Lynn responded. "It looks like there's more wrong with the car than we thought. We might not get home until later now, that's all. Nothing to worry about, hon. Daddy and I are just talking about it."

With her smooth, confident delivery, David turned back to his brother and resumed playing catch, oblivious to the heightened emotions just displayed.

Lynn faced her husband, grasping his hands in hers. "Micah, we're going to figure this out. We always do."

As she spoke, he slowly lifted his head, eyes full of shame. "I'm so sorry, Lynn. For everything, and now this shit. I just, I just don't know how to control it when it comes on. The stress, I mean." He exhaled deeply.

"It's too much sometimes ... with my mom and everything else. I feel like I'm losing my mind, like I'm not in control anymore."

She chewed her bottom lip and listened, taking in everything he was saying. It had been so long since he had been honest and genuinely open with her. This was her husband, the man she had fallen in love with so long ago. This was her heart, her past, present, and future.

There was a reason she had stayed and never gave up. For the first time in what seemed like forever, she felt like she was actually bonding with the man that she vowed to spend the rest of her days and nights with. The man that she could trust.

Suddenly, behind them came the heavy sound of leaves crunching under boots. The two turned instinctively, alert, eyeing the intrusion upon their intimacy. There he was, the man known only as Clyde, eyes beaming at his targets.

"Well, if we're done pissin' and moanin', we need to get hooked up and towed out of here. I can fix y'all folks' pump, that's for sure. Hope I got everything I need, though. At least you won't be out here on the side of the freeway, right?" His eyes shifted back and forth between the two as he spoke.

They faced each other, uncertainty lingering within. *What were their other options, though? Stay and dwell on the unknown, or pray that they would be home later in the night, or worst-case scenario, tomorrow sometime?*

There was nothing else to think of. With reluctance, Micah turned to Clyde and nodded, signaling him to hook up the car and tow it back to the shop.

After Clyde walked away, Micah stated in a low voice, "He said he doesn't know if he has a new one or the parts to fix it." He paused, dropping his head and shaking it side to side. "We may be here overnight if he can't."

The news wasn't what Lynn needed at the moment. The thought of staying somewhere overnight where she wasn't comfortable made her nervous. She could feel her palms begin to sweat.

She didn't know this man, but something deep inside told her not to trust him. Something about this situation wasn't right, but she understood their dilemma. Getting towed was their only option, so she went along with it, showing her support and trust in her husband.

The car's front end was in the air minutes later. Clyde attached signal cables to the roof and offered the truck's cab to the family for the journey, which they declined after a whispered conversation. Instead, they climbed into the truck's bed, taking a seat below the back window. After Clyde started the truck, Micah scanned the dense forest, praying to get back home and for this vacation to come to an end.

PART TWO

THE SHOP

11

THE SOUND WAS FAMILIAR, yet unfamiliar all the same, as the brothers looked from a distance at an old tire lying on the dirt. Weeds had sprouted from within and around it.

David playfully punched his brother on the arm. "I told you it was in there, Will. Did you hear that? I saw its tail in the grass before it went inside. Bet you it's ten feet long. Thick as a Jolt can too."

Will looked at his brother in alarm. He squeezed his eyes shut as he shook his head, murmuring, "Ms. Jenson said that rattlesnakes are poisonous. I'm not going near that thing! We need to go get Dad, or maybe Mr. Clyde. They'll know what to do with it." He looked back to the front of the property, hoping to see anyone nearby.

David rolled his eyes at his brother's crying. "Dude, quit being such a sissy. It's not gonna bite us. I just want to see how big it is, that's all. Come on, let's get closer and see if we can find it." He gestured forward with his hand, encouraging his brother to follow his lead.

Will's bottom lip trembled as he took small, deliberate steps forward once, twice, before stopping altogether.

David continued, inching ever so closer, challenging his nerves with each step, not realizing that his brother had stopped feet behind him. The inner ring of the tire was in view now, but the vegetation growing around it didn't allow for a clear view of the creature. As he leaned forward, finally peering into the tire, that familiar sound emitted from inside, causing him to jump back a few feet.

"Shit! It's in there. Look, Will, look!" Pointing at the tire insistently, he looked back at his brother, noticing the alarm on his face. The excitement of the moment stopped as he observed his brother from head to toe. "Dude, it's just a *snake*. We're just going to look at it, not play it with. I'm not that stupid."

There was no response from Will. He stood there, frozen in place.

"Will?" He looked back at the tire and then toward his brother once again. "It's not that big of a deal, man. I didn't mean to scare you. I just thought it would be fun to—"

"*Shh*," Will hissed quietly, snapping out of his stupor. His eyes dilated as they seemed to look right through David at something behind him.

Confusion crossed David's face. "Will, what the hell? What's wrong?" His voice was cautious as he stepped in his brother's direction, hands on his hips.

Will finally diverted his eyes and locked on his brother's. He slowly raised a finger, pointing out into the forest beyond the yard. "There's ... there's someone out there, in the woods," he whispered.

David instantly turned to watch the trees beyond the firebreak. Eyes scanning left to right, looking for the slightest movement. "Where?" he asked in a low voice. "I don't see anything, just a bunch of trees."

Will stiffened, extending his finger while whispering, "Straight ahead, maybe fifty feet. There's someone there, hiding in the trees. I think he's watching us."

David looked again, carefully piercing the thick blanket of pines and oaks surrounding the shop's yard.. "Are you sure? I can't see anything, Will." He squinted his eyes, searching for a clue.

Then the murmur of voices heightened from the front of the property, gripping their attention.

"That sounded like Dad. We better go see what's wrong. Come on." Whipping around, David left the tire and the mystery in the woods to investigate the commotion.

Will didn't initially follow his brother; his eyes still focused on the forest and what he thought he saw. After a few seconds and a holler from his brother, he started pacing backward, watching the trees. His guard up.

He was convinced that something was out there. Or *someone*.

As they rounded the corner of the shop, the scene was revealed. There, near the garage, was their father, hands clasped behind his neck, pacing back and forth. They could see that he was mumbling to himself while their mother looked on, trying to bring him down from whatever had upset him. She truly deserved a break.

Micah shook his head in disappointment, eyes erratic as he thought about the news he just received. *I knew this would happen. No parts or new pump, what the hell! The last thing I want is to be stranded here in this shithole.* Clyde had shrugged when he voiced that he wouldn't get the parts for a few days, tops, causing Micah's stomach to curl.

Lynn approached her husband, getting within earshot. "Where'd he go, anyway? I heard the truck start then it left the yard. Please, please tell me he's going to get the parts for the car."

Micah stopped pacing and turned toward her, spittle flying from his clenched teeth as he spoke. "I don't know where he went, Lynn! The phone in the shop rang, he talked to someone, and then he just left. He didn't say where. Probably to get some more booze or some other stupid shit!"

Lynn took a step back. She had to be careful here.

"Micah," she hissed, voice cracking with concern, "Do you think we can use his phone? I can call my mom in Fresno. She'll come pick us up, and we can come back when the car's ready in a few days. I just want to go home. There's no way I'm staying *here* overnight."

Micah faced his wife, fury burning in his eyes. "Does it look like I've been worried about a damn phone, Lynn?" He buried his face in his hands, releasing a growl. "We are stuck here, and something's not right!"

"What do you mean, 'not right'? What's going on, Micah?"

Micah's jawbone clenched. "That son of a bitch just told me that he doesn't have the parts and won't for a few days! Wouldn't explain why either. Then he just left without explanation.

Lynn felt her throat tighten as if in a python's deathly grip. With panic in her voice, she lobbed a barrage of rapid-fire questions, not giving her husband a chance to respond. "A few days, what do you mean? What are we supposed to do? Stay here at the shop? That's not happening, Micah. We have to go. We have to get home. What are we ..."

Her tired voice trailed off.

"What? What are we going to do, Micah?"

Micah's jawbone clicked as he maneuvered it, thinking: the car, the boys, Clyde, Lynn.

With a deep exhale, he answered her. "I don't know, Lynn. I really don't. What I do know is that this whole situation is shit and feels wrong. Something is not right about him, or about any of this."

Lynn looked at her husband with dread, all traces of previous peace vanished. "What's going on, Micah? What aren't you telling me?"

Micah's eyes went straight to the open garage door, eyeing the hatchback inside. "I don't know for sure, but I'm going to find out. I need you to get the boys and stay here. Keep your ears open for the truck. If you hear it coming through that creepy ass tunnel, yell. I'm going inside to find a phone or any other way to get us out of here."

Lynn looked at her husband, praying that he was going to fix this, praying that he was going to protect them. She didn't understand all of Micah's reservations, but alongside the uncertainty and fear a sliver of hope emerged. Her eyes told the story as she watched him turn and walk into the dark garage.

12

LYNN TURNED TO WHERE she saw her sons minutes before, huddled near the corner of the shop. They were watching and listening to her conversation with Micah, but they were nowhere to be found now. Her motherly instincts kicked in; she needed to find them and make sure they were safe. *But what about the truck?* Micah had told her to watch and listen for Clyde's return. She was lost, not knowing what to do at that moment.

Panic-stricken, frantically scanning the area and listening for any hint of the boys' whereabouts.

With a shaky voice, she cried out, "David! William! Boys, where are you?" She ran to the corner where she had seen them earlier, only to find the side of the shop vacant and silent. "Boys!"

She looked back toward the canopy of trees, making sure there was no sign of the truck's return before venturing down the side of the shop, yelling for her sons. As she neared the back of the building, her fears and worries ended with the comforting sound of her sons' voices. They were in the back of the shop's yard. However, they were not alone.

David and Will stood shoulder-to-shoulder near the firebreak with their backs turned, staring at the ground with little movement. Someone was behind them, shorter than most adults, based on Lynn's view. The fear of her sons missing slowly subsided, now replaced with concern that they were talking to a stranger. She had told them so many times about creepy men in white vans, which they seemed to understand, yet here they were.

"Boys! Did you not hear me calling you?!" She approached at a swift pace as David and Will turned around, confusion in their eyes. "Well?"

Neither boy said a word, only glanced back and forth between the ground in front of them and their mother as she continued in their direction. Hesitation strangled every movement.

Lynn held out her arms, gesturing for an explanation as she walked up to them. The person who was behind them was in full view now, but it wasn't some creepy old man. It was a child. A young boy, a little older than Will but not as old as David, from his looks. Maybe ten or eleven.

He was a scrawny skeleton of a kid, dirt smeared across his cheek and under his nails. Flies buzzed happily around him.

To go along with his holey camouflage tank top, each knee of his soiled jeans bore large holes. A mop of platinum blonde hair fell to his shoulders, obscuring his vision as he looked up at her. In his right hand, Lynn noticed a bow. Not some makeshift one made of a twig and a piece of string either. This was a top-of-the-line hunting bow. And then she saw it. The thing on the ground that had dominated her sons' attention and focus.

In front of her, near an old worn tire, was a snake. A rattlesnake, to be specific. It wasn't shaking its tail or moving whatsoever. It appeared to be dead. Dead as stone, a frozen photograph of agony and demise. An arrow had pierced it just below the head, and someone had stretched out its lifeless body.

David and Will stared at the creature while the other boy stared at Lynn, squinting his eyes in the sunlight.

Lynn grabbed both boys by their shoulders and forced them to take a step back, not knowing whether the snake was still a threat or not. She quickly pivoted in front of her sons, back turned to the newcomer. With a stern voice, she demanded answers. "Why didn't you answer me when I was yelling? And what is this? Did you touch that thing?" She gestured behind her to the dead reptile laying in the dirt.

David attempted to respond, but he tripped over each word, babbling and stuttering. His little brother just looked up at Lynn with trying eyes, sheepish and unsure of how to answer. He simply shrugged his shoulders, praying that maneuver would quell his mother's inquiries.

"You both know that thing could have killed you, yet you're out here playing with it! What the hell is wrong with you two, and who's this kid?" She turned around, thumb pointed out, and faced the young boy, leering in his direction.

Finally, David's wits returned, and he was able to articulate the situation, even though he stammered through each sentence. "No ... no, Mom, we just got here and saw this boy. He shot it before we came back to look for it again. We didn't touch it or anything. I swear!"

"What do you mean, 'again,' David? You knew there was a rattlesnake here, and you came back to find it? What were you thinking?" She was exasperated. Unbelievable, these two. She glared between her sons, frowning hard in disappointment. Both boys dropped their eyes, shame settling in, not sure what to say or do.

Being a mother, she had a fierce streak whenever someone or something threatened her children. Mama bear complex, some would say. Too many times in the past, her sons were victims, preyed upon and traumatized. Too many times, she had felt helpless to protect them.

Those days were over, though. She had made that very clear one night, days after Grace's death. Before Micah could enter the home, after mourning at the pub down the street, she deadbolted all the doors, not allowing him access. He pounded repeatedly on the front door, cursing belligerent threats, but eventually gave up, opting to spend the frosted night on a wrought iron bench, curled up with his old jacket.

The next morning, when he walked inside red-eyed and staggering, she delivered her ultimatum. Get his life under control, or the marriage is over.

"Get your asses back to the front of the shop! Now!" A slight growl wrapped the last word. Her gaze was menacing, piercing through each boy.

Without objection, they both turned and ambled toward the building, leaving her and the mysterious boy near the firebreak.

Once they were paces away, she slowly turned to face the little marksman, caution and judgment in her eyes. "Who are you?" She firmly demanded.

The boy brushed a lock of blonde hair away from his eyes. They were blue, bright blue. Blinding blue. "Name's Tobias." He looked her up and down as he answered, voice low and mumbled.

"Why are you here? Where are your parents?"

The boy didn't answer. He leered at her with reciprocal judgment for several seconds. Eventually, he dropped his glare and stepped toward the dead snake, grabbing it by the body. He continued on to the line of trees, silent and slow.

Once he entered the woods, he looked back one last time, locking eyes with Lynn. He gave her a devious smile, winked, then slowly turned away. In no time, she had lost him in the trees, as if he had dissolved into the maze of vegetation.

Who was that creepy little hillbilly? She thought, still trying to catch a last glimpse. With her hand, she shielded the sun from her eyes and peered into the surrounding forest, gave up after a moment, and turned around. There were more pressing things to deal with: her boys, husband, and that damn car. With a strange feeling in her gut, she walked away to join her sons, glancing back at the woods every few steps.

As she rounded the corner, she found her sons just outside the garage. Will had a long stick and was drawing a circle in the dirt. The sight comforted her, and seeing the area empty filled her with relief. There was no sign of Clyde's truck. Micah had not come out of the building either. *Nothing to worry about, Lynn. Nothing at all.*

She strolled up to her sons, shaking her head with a smirk. "You know that was stupid, right? That thing could have bitten you, and if you haven't noticed, we don't exactly have a car right now to get you to the hospital."

Will stopped his doodling and looked up at her, guilt flowing through his eyes. David's mannerisms didn't match his brothers, though. Self-pride and defiance told his story as he eyed his mother. He folded his arms across his chest and held her stare. "We didn't even get close to it. What's the big deal?"

Any playfulness of the situation left in a heartbeat. Mama doesn't stand for back talk.

She held her eldest son's stare fiercely. "Maybe you don't understand the gravity of what *could* have happened. You're twelve now, I get that, but don't think for a moment that you know everything, boy. Something bad could have happened."

"Will and I were just messing around, okay? It's your stupid car that broke down. We just wanted to have a little fun while we're stranded here in BFE."

Lynn opened her mouth, but no words flew. Oh, her baby boy. She realized he was getting older, but he had never blatantly spoken to her with such disrespect. They were in enough trouble without a rebellious adolescent acting out.

"David Jacob Carter! I don't know who the hell you think you're talking to, but—"

She couldn't finish the tongue-lashing. A subtle noise and movement from within the garage demanded her attention. It was Micah, exiting the darkness and entering the light of the sun. And he did not look happy.

13

WHAT GOOD IS HAVING a damn phone if it doesn't work? Busy signal, busy signal! That ogre just used it twenty minutes ago. Why can't I even get a hold of the operator? He thought as he stepped out of the darkness of the garage. *What the hell's going on?* He rubbed the stubble on his chin, eyes glued to the ground as he approached his wife and sons.

Lynn watched as he neared, looking for clues of his distress. This look was just confusion, though, not a hint of anger. It almost appeared normal. He just couldn't figure something out.

"Did you find anything? Anything that might help us?" Her voice was soft as she spoke, not wanting to heighten any agitation possibly loitering on the surface.

He continued rubbing his chin but looked in her direction. In a low voice, he replied, "No, no, I didn't find anything that could help us." He gave his head a slight shake, cocking his chin. "I found that phone of his, though, but I can't get an outside line, just a busy signal. No operator, 411, or 911 either. I don't understand it."

"What do you mean?" Lynn worked her jaw, nervous, brow furrowed. "That's not possible. Didn't you say you heard it ring right before he barged out of here without an explanation? I mean, did you try hanging it up and—"

Micah cut her off, "Lynn, I swear I tried it five different times. Even unplugged it from the wall and plugged it back in," he sucked in a whistling breath, holding up two of his fingers, "*twice*. I don't know what the hell is wrong with it, but the shitty thing doesn't work."

She dropped her eyes to the ground, "I ... I don't understand how it can work one minute and then not work at all the next. Did you break it accidentally or something?" She took a step forward, moving toward the garage. "Maybe I can get it to work. Where did you see it?"

Micah shifted in front of her, blocking her advancement. "That's not a good idea, babe." He held out his hands, forcing her to halt. "It scared me shitless walking in there, and there's not a chance in hell you're going in that place. The thought of that Neanderthal returning while I was alone scared the piss out of me." He eyed her, hoping for understanding.

Lynn locked eyes with him, gazing deep into the blue gems, searching for answers. She had looked into those eyes for over fifteen years now. As she stood there, thinking about this shit show, she recalled the first time she met those beautiful baby blues.

After graduating from high school in '71, she started waiting tables at a diner near her family home. It wasn't anything special, but it put a few dollars in her pocket. Angelo's was the hotspot for high school kids on Friday nights, and Lynn loved the atmosphere. And the tips. Occasionally, an older crowd would pass through the dive, and one humid spring night, she met him.

The group Micah was with, rowdy and obnoxious, gathered in two booths in the back, smoking cigarettes after ordering burgers and milkshakes.

Once the order was up, Lynn had strapped on her apron, carried the tray of their food in one hand, and approached with caution—maybe it was immature of her, but she always felt her stomach do small flips, and her palms became clammy whenever an exceptionally cool group of kids came around here.

As she passed the first booth, a hefty twenty-something wearing a black leather jacket slapped her right on the ass. Stunned, she nearly dropped the tray but luckily stabilized it, avoiding disaster and the humiliation that would have followed.

All the young men in both booths laughed and cheered their buddy for his actions, except for one. He was the youngest of the group, but he carried a firm presence. With cheeks flushed from embarrassment, she watched as the young man strolled over to her and asked if she was okay. All she wanted to do was run and hide, but something about his eyes calmed her. He gently took the tray from her hand, set it down on a nearby table, and hissed to his friend that he was a dick.

Micah's eyes always had a story to them, and over the years, she learned to watch for clues. When the drinking escalated and the lying started, she knew. His eyes always gave it away. They told her everything she needed to know.

At this moment, as she gazed into his blue eyes, she couldn't find any clues. *What aren't you telling me, Micah?* She thought, nodding to appease him.

The fact scared her. Deeply.

"We need to come up with another plan to get the hell out of here." Micah paused and looked off into the woods, a slight nervousness in his motions before continuing. "When he gets back, I'm going to ask him to drive us to the convenience store down the road. At least we won't be here, and they'll have a phone. We'll get a hold of your mom or someone."

She knew something had to happen. The thought of staying there any longer kept her mind spinning in circles. "Do you think he'll take us?"

His eyes remained on the surrounding forest. "I hope so. He's trying to help us." He delivered a weak smile, knowing how uneasy she was about all of this.

Lynn's face slackened with exhaustion. "Just do something, Micah. I want to go home."

He turned toward her, focused on the anxiety in her voice. "Babe ... I'm going to get us out of this. I promise. We're going home as soon as possible."

"I know, I know. I just hate being here. And I didn't tell you about what the boys were doing in the back. Lucky we're not in the ER right now."

This news grabbed his attention. "What the hell happened? Did one of them get hurt, or ..." He trailed off, turning to find his sons. "Boys! Boys! What the hell happened back there?" He bolted in their direction, eyes distressed, as he approached his sons standing near the corner of the building. "What happened?"

David and Will's eyes ballooned as their father strode forward with clenched fists. Will was tongue-tied, but David mustered the courage to speak, standing straighter, knowing he had to come up with something quick. "It was nothing, Dad, honest! We ... we just saw a snake slithering through the grass. That's all." He paused, looking toward the back of the property. "Some boy killed it, though. Shot it dead with a bow and arrow. Nothing happened, we promise." He looked over at his brother, pleading with his eyes at Will to give his input.

Micah's eye twitched, an awful, hostile feeling swirling in his gut.

He looked back and forth between them, knowing there was more to the story. "Snake? What were you doing playing with a snake? What boy? Where's he at?"

Stuttering, Will attempted to answer. "Dad ... Dad, it was nothing." He looked over at David and then back to his father. "We didn't even get near it. I ... I told David we shouldn't even look at it. My teacher said that rattlesnakes are poisonous and—"

"You two were playing with a fuckin' rattlesnake?" Micah boomed, cutting his son off. "Are you kidding me? Are you two a couple of idiots or something? Why? Why?" he demanded, looking erratically between them.

Lynn rushed over, placing herself between her husband and sons. "Micah, they already told me they didn't get very close to it. They just wanted to see it, that's all. I already scolded both of them for it, and they know it was a dumb choice."

"It was a *mindless* move, Lynn!" He turned his attention away from his wife and back to the boys. "Does it look like we have a car to get you two to the hospital? Does it?" He was furious, eyes dilated and large.

"They know they made a mistake. They really do." Lynn pleaded softly, turning around to see her sons rapidly nodding in agreement. "They already told me they didn't even get close to it. They were just boys being boys, Micah, that's it."

He cocked his head to the side as he eyed his sons, his mind brewing on the situation. He stood there for a few moments listening to his loving wife's pleas and watching his sons tremble before him. The temperature of his eyes slowly descended as he thought about his actions and the trauma he was stirring up. This was the man he no longer wanted to be. This was the Micah who had caused all of their problems and the despair that had crippled their existence as a family.

Control it. Just control it! They're just a couple of dumb kids being kids. No one got hurt. He dropped his leer to the ground, shaking his head from side to side. "At least no one got hurt. If you two see another one, *stay* away from it. Do you hear me?" He looked up, making sure each boy heard his command.

Neither said a word. They just nodded in his direction, fear still striking their faces. A single tear slipped down Will's right cheek.

He let out a deep sigh and then turned and faced Lynn. "All right then, who the hell is this little boy you were talking...."

He trailed off as his attention moved toward the front of the property, turning and facing the woods. In the distance, he could hear a vehicle approaching. It was coming from the forested tunnel, and it sounded a lot like a truck.

14

THE OLD TRUCK RUMBLED through the thick canopy that was hiding the property from the two-lane road. It came to an abrupt stop in front of Micah and his family, dust floating in the air as the tires finally came to rest. Micah wrapped his arms around his sons, with Lynn behind him near the entrance of the garage. They stared at the vehicle, noticing that Clyde was not alone.

Simultaneously, both doors to the truck opened, two occupants exited through the settling dust. Clyde stepped out of the driver side, wiping his brow and peering at the overhead sun. The passenger stepped out as well, looking around the property, ignoring the four visitors and their inquisitive looks.

Clyde delivered a nod in Micah's direction and then stepped to the back of the truck, lowering the tailgate. Even behind the vehicle, the man's height was noticeable as he sifted through the space.

His counterpart finally stopped looking around the land and stared at the family, crossing his arms over his thick chest. The man wasn't as large as Clyde, but his size was impressive, if not daunting. His frame was more muscular, looking more like a lumberjack than a heavy-drinking automobile mechanic.

After a few tense moments, Clyde emerged from behind the truck, holding something and smiling.

He took a few steps toward the family before speaking. "I found one, friend. At least, *most of one*." He approached the family holding a used fuel pump, heavily greased up. "I pulled it out of an old shitty import like yours at my buddy's place." He looked over at his colleague. "Tank here lives up the road. Has an auto body shop in Castaic." He paused, allowing the news to register.

Micah looked back at his wife, still standing a few paces behind him and the boys, and gave her a pleased smirk, knowing this was the news she needed to hear.

"That's exactly what we needed to hear." He turned back to Clyde and asked, "How did you know he had one?"

This monstrous man let out a deep chuckle. "I made a couple of calls while I was inside." He cocked his head to the side and spat, bloody spittle stringing from his lips. "Sid didn't have shit, but Tank here," he paused and glanced at his counterpart, "he called me back pronto." He held the pump for all to see and grinned like it was the most precious prize. And frankly, to Micah and his family, it was.

Micah turned his sons around, gripping their shoulders, "Do you see that, boys? That's our ticket home." He leaned down to their eye level, passing an encouraging look to both of them.

Lynn approached from behind, peering over Micah's shoulder. She had heard the great news but was still hesitant with her steps. Cautious as she eyed the greasy instrument the man was holding.

Micah whipped his head around, greeting her with a look of relief. He noticed her reluctance as she moved and knew how she felt about all of this. "Everything is going to be okay, babe." His voice was calm, assuring. "We're going home." He nodded in her direction, hoping to receive the same in return.

After a few moments, she dipped her chin, acknowledging his statement, lacking confidence.

Micah returned his attention to Clyde and his counterpart, trying not to think about Lynn's unsettled expression. "Thank you, Clyde. This is fantastic news."

He paused, moving past his sons and taking a few steps toward this new man before halting his progression. "And ... Tank is it? I really want to thank you, as well. We all want to thank you for this. For finding the part, I mean."

There was no response from Tank, just a mindless gaze as he sized up Micah and his family. His eyes were twitchy and anxious as he glared at them with what seemed like aversion, pupils heavily dilated.

Maybe feeling confused, embarrassed, or nervous from the man's hostile stare, Micah shut his trap quickly. He laughed dryly, anxiously. "If there's anything I can do to help get it installed and—"

Clyde cut him off. "You a mechanic, *amigo?*" His voice was condescending, matching his derisive look. "How many hours you got under the hood, boy?"

Micah looked at his wife, insecurity escalating with each blink before responding. "Oh, not much. I just ... I thought maybe I could help."

Clyde laughed, a greasy, booming sound that made Micah's stomach curl, and the hairs at the base of his nape stand erect. "Leave this to us, yeah? We know what we're doin'."

With his ego bruised, Micah was taken aback. He smiled a plastic and forced grin, jawbone clenched in suppressed anger. "Yeah, man, okay. I just wanted to show my appreciation, that's all."

Clyde clapped a hand on Micah's shoulder, smiling crookedly. "I'll get that piece of shit runnin' very soon, amigo."

Micah nodded, looking over at Lynn and the boys. "How soon, if you don't mind me asking?"

The grin covering Clyde's face went flat. He took a stride toward his hulking counterpart before saying a word. "Well, here's the thing, friend. You need help, and Tank here needs some help too." He paused and looked up at the sun, now hovering in the west.

"Tank has run into a problem that I need to help him with. Shouldn't take too long, but we need to head up the road and handle a little situation." He raised an eyebrow, hoping Micah would understand the dilemma.

The news was disturbing. This was not what he wanted to hear. Micah dropped his eyes to the ground, thinking about the comments. "So, what does this mean? Are we stuck here until morning?" Micah's face dropped a few shades of color as he looked at the man.

"Not necessarily, friend." Clyde held out his hands, shaking them back and forth. "If I can get back here at a decent time, the pump shouldn't take but an hour."

Micah looked over at his wife, noticing the unsettled look on her face as she, too, heard the news. She had already expressed her concerns about staying any longer. A slight shake came from his head as he focused his attention back on the bearer of bad news. "Where are we supposed to stay? Here? At the shop?"

"Let's worry about that later. All we can do now is pray that I'm done with Tank before we have to make those plans." He looked back at the garage and delivered a shrug. "I have a futon in the back if it comes to that."

Micah turned and looked at Lynn again; God knows what was going through her mind. There was no way that it could come to them staying there overnight. She wouldn't go for it, and he sure as hell was not going to force his boys to put up with this.

"Well, we really need to get home. Do you think, maybe, you could take us to the convenience store or a motel off the highway?" He locked eyes with the massive man, searching for an ounce of empathy.

Clyde returned the look, knowing this man was at the end of his rope. He eyed the boys and then fixated on Lynn, starting at her feet, then ogling all the way up her body before returning to Micah.

After a brief pause, he answered. "Yes. I can do that."

Micah couldn't believe it. The nervousness of the situation subsided, hearing they would be away from this place soon. A smile crawled across his lips as he eyed his wife. Maybe with some luck, Lynn's mother could be there before nightfall to get them down the mountain and into the valley. Absolute relief.

"But not right at this moment," Clyde murmured while looking at the sun.

"Daylight's burnin'." He paused, hoping that the family would consider the situation. "You understand, right?" His look seemed sincere as he scanned all four members of the family.

So they were alone. Accompanied only by the worries that swam freely in their minds.

Clyde lowered his eyes and passed the family, making his way into the darkness of the garage, exiting minutes later with a small black case he carried by a handle.

What the hell is that? Micah thought, knitting his brow.

The four huddled together as they eyed Clyde and Tank clamber back into the truck, watching the dark exhaust pour out of the tailpipe once the engine started. Clyde delivered a lasting wave as he steered the vehicle through the canopy of trees. The last thing the family saw was the vibrant red of the taillights before they disappeared into the surrounding forest.

15

AN HOUR HAD PASSED without a single vehicle being heard on the road. The eerie silence drowning the place brought out the worst in Micah.

He sat on the ground, back against the shop's wall, looking into the never-ending forest beyond. *What the hell are we supposed to do, Micah? Sit here on our ass and just wait for something to happen. We are so screwed!*

Micah shook his head shamefully, thinking about everything that had gone wrong since they piled into the hatchback that morning.

Lynn was resting inside the car, reading People, feet hanging out of the passenger side window. She hated this place, wanting nothing more than to just walk down the road and flag down the first car she saw, but Micah forbade it.

He kept telling her he would figure something out; they would get to a motel, or gas station, or someplace soon. She didn't share his confidence in the matter but decided not to press any further. She turned away from him and went and sat in the car, her worries festering.

The boys were rummaging through some old cars to his right, clearly in sight. He had allowed them to go and explore as long as they didn't get close to anything alive or potentially poisonous.

After a period of self-torment, Micah raised himself off the ground and started toward the garage. While in mid-stride, he heard a muffled series of pops to the south that stopped him in his tracks. He turned and looked in that direction, only slightly alarmed, though he felt a chill run down his spine. *Gunshots*, he wondered?

After a long moment, Micah shook his head to clear it and walked up to the hatchback. He cleared his throat as he got close enough to Lynn.

She looked over, contempt on her face, expecting a verbal slaying of some sort, but that's not what she received. He looked calm.

Micah cocked his head to the side. "Comfy, are we?" he paused but didn't receive an answer to his snark. "Hey, I'm going to try the phone again. Who knows when that ogre's coming back." He looked toward his sons, making sure he could still see them. "Clyde said he used it earlier to call that Tank guy. It *has* to work."

Lynn dropped the magazine into her lap. "Do you want me to come with you? I know you said you didn't want me anywhere near the inside of this place, but I'm sort of already inside. If you count the garage, that is."

"No. No, just get the boys. I'll try the phone and if it still doesn't work, I'll be right out. If it does, and I'm in there for a few, listen up for Clyde." He held her look, making sure she understood what he wanted.

She reluctantly nodded before exiting and strolling into the fading light of day. When she got within paces of her sons, she looked back into the dark garage, hoping and praying for this to end, before calling out.

"You boys haven't been messing with another snake, have you?" she joked.

They both turned and faced her, a little shocked by her presence. They had been so wrapped up in taking parts off the old Ford they were tinkering with that they didn't hear, let alone see, her approaching.

A little startled, Will immediately shook his head, affirming he had not disobeyed his mother. If there was one thing about Will, it was that he knew when to never do something again.

His brother, however, played a different hand. "We've just been messing around with this old truck, that's all. We didn't even play with the first snake!" His sneer spoke volumes.

The playfulness exited her voice as she replied, "David, you better watch your mouth, young man. There's enough stress going on around here without your attitude."

She shifted her stare to her younger son, shaking her head in disappointment. "Thank you, Will. Thank you for answering my question politely. Maybe your brother here," her eyes went back to David, "can learn a thing or two from you." Lynn held her eldest son's eyes the way only a mother could, scolding without making a sound.

David's behavior and attitude had been escalating as of late. Adolescence, puberty, maybe a combination of the two. Very likely, the verbal bashing he received from his father also factored in. Lynn tried to take it all into consideration, but she was so fed up with his nasty temperament. Tired of the back talk and the negativity when Micah wasn't around.

While the two had their stare-off, Micah stepped over the entry point separating the garage from the shop. The smell of gasoline and grease lingered heavily as he reached for the light switch on the wall. A layer of dust covering the bulb deterred the illumination of the room, but enough shone through for visibility.

The phone was in a separate office in the back of the shop, but he felt the need to look around first. A need to search.

Clyde had made some pretty empty promises about getting them out of here, but there was no trust in the man's word. He had to find a way to save his family and get them out of this hellhole, with or without Clyde's help.

Lining the wall adjacent to the garage was a series of steel shelves riddled with cluttered auto parts, some loose and some still in their original packaging. All domestic, however. He couldn't fix the car. He knew that, and none of this would help him or his family. He passed the shelves shaking his head and entered the center of the shop, stopping at a table.

Invoices and debris littered the top, all dating back to the late '70s from what he could see as he scanned through them. Nothing dated later than '79. *What the hell's going on around here? When was the last time the bastard had a customer?*

Dropping the stack of papers back to the tabletop, Micah's eyes focused on a filing cabinet pressed against the opposite wall of the shelves. It had a different feel than anything else in this dingy room. It was spotless, as if freshly polished or painted. Not a dent or scratch anywhere to be found. The surface shone with brilliance, reflecting the minimal light from above. Micah approached, rubbing his chin, wondering what could be behind its drawers.

As he moved forward, he had to step over a spill on the concrete floor. It had a dark tint to it, like oil, but lacked the consistency. From the looks of it, it had been left there for many days.

He ignored the strange puddle and strolled to the cabinet, noticing a padlock hanging from the clasp, and it was unlocked. *What the hell is that son of a bitch hiding in here?*

Reaching forward and removing the lock, he pressed a button and pulled on the top drawer. It slid out effortlessly, revealing that it was empty. Not a scrap of paper to be seen. *There has to be something in here, something that will help us get out of here,* he thought.

The second drawer opened just as easily, and it was full of old documents: receipts, invoices similar to those on the table, and more. All dated before 1980. No order to them, just thrown into the drawer, long forgotten.

He felt as though this was a waste of time until the bottom drawer opened with a hesitant pull. His eyes swelled at the sight within. Inside was a case, much like the one that Clyde was holding when he left with Tank. Black, rugged, compact. As he knelt and lifted it out, he noted its weighty bulk. This wasn't something Micah was used to handling, but he had an inkling of what was inside.

He set the case on the floor, brushing away an old beer can in the process. Two hasps secured the contents inside and with a simple flip, both disengaged. As he lifted the lid, his presumption was confirmed.

It was a gun case.

His eyes hovered over the handgun for many moments while his mind trudged along, worrying about what could happen and what was going to happen. *Why would Clyde need a gun to help his friend, Tank? Why was this one left here? Why wasn't it locked up? I have children nearby, for Christ's sake! Were those actually bullet holes in the side of that bastard's truck?* It all became too much to handle and he fearfully slammed the case shut. Without care, he tossed it back into the drawer, shutting it with a slam.

As he stood, his eyes never left the drawer. Anxiety took hold as he ruminated on their dilemma and the discovery that this man was armed. *Were those two going to kill someone? Is that what he meant by taking care of something? Are we next on the list? Maybe he is screwing with us after all. Maybe we are next. Maybe I should—*

A sudden sound from the opposite end of the room brought him whirling back. He whipped his head around to locate the threat, only to find a rat scurrying through the old parts on the shelves. With his heart hammering in his chest, he turned back to face the bottom drawer once again. Thinking. Planning.

He shook his head, attempting to rid his mind of irrational thoughts. He had come in here to find something, anything that would help Lynn and the boys. A gun wasn't the answer. All that would do is provoke the giant and likely get himself killed. Or get all of them killed. He didn't want that. No one wanted that. He had to keep looking, searching for another way out of here in case all else failed.

In a corner outside the office door stood a seven-foot-tall bookcase. It held numerous mechanic books and old Chevy and Ford owner manuals, dating mostly from the '50s and '60s. On the third shelf, underneath a rusty oil can, was an unassuming, unlabeled cardboard box. It had a lid that could be removed.

Micah gripped a small opening on the side and slowly slid the box toward him, never removing it from the shelf, a trail of disturbed dust left in its wake. He lifted the lid and peered inside. *Another anomaly,* he thought as he removed the box from the shelf, cradling it in his arms.

He placed the lid on the shelf and reached inside, furrowing his brow as he pulled out a woman's purse, not one of the modern-day trendy designs. This was a relic from the past: red in color, bronze clasp, gently used.

He set the box on the ground, ignoring its other contents for the time being, and placed the purse on the shelf next to the lid. The bronze clasp opened easily, allowing him to spread the two bindings apart and view the internal contents. It was empty, except for a handful of loose coins and a driver's license. He pulled out the license, inspecting it thoroughly in the dim light.

Marsha Johnston, expired in September of '59.

He dropped the license back into the purse and left it on the shelf. Kneeling, he reached back into the box and removed a smaller object. A man's billfold: well-worn leather, black, stitching loose around the edges. Rummaging through the wallet, he found a similar driver's license, that of a man named Elijah Mooney. He pulled the license from its clear, plastic covering and studied it, learning that it was even older than Marsha's. Its expiration was '52. *Who the hell are these people and why does he have their stuff?*

He held the license in his hand while his mind wandered for a few moments. As he snapped back into reality, he realized that none of this new information was of any help to him or his family. He had to keep looking. He had to try the phone once more.

After returning all the items to the box, he slid it back into place beneath the oil can, but the damage had already been done. The dust surrounding everything on the shelf had been heavily disturbed, revealing recent activity and there was no way of correcting it. Panic struck him instantly, realizing the mistake he had made.

Oh shit! What did I do, what did I do? This is bad, this is so bad. He began quickly pacing the area, hands wrapped around the back of his head. *If he sees this, I'm dead. I know it. He's going to get that damn gun and blow my head off. I've got to warn Lynn, warn the boys. We have to get out of here, now!*

Suddenly, he paused his pacing, eyes focused on the open door of the office. *The phone,* he thought. *It will work this time, I know it will. I'll call the police, the operator, somebody. Anyone that will listen. It's going to work.*

He stepped to the right, leaving the shelving unit and its belongings, and approached the door frame, peering inside. The desk was littered with empty beer bottles, an overflowing ashtray, and pin-up girl magazines. On the edge, atop an old newspaper, was the telephone. Praying it would work this time, he stepped through the door and lifted the receiver, placing it near his ear.

Busy signal?

He reached for the base, fiddling with the switch, attempting to get an outside line, but the line was dead.

"Shit! How the hell did he use it earlier?" He mumbled under his breath, frustration brewing to a boil. He laid the handset back down on the base and dropped his eyes to the floor. *What am I going to do now? Think Micah, think!*

Why was this man toying with them at every turn? Why was he doing this to him and his family, anyway? Why? What motive?

He was so foolish for even following this man here, let alone taking his goddamned family with him. How could he have done this? Been so stupid? He needed a miracle, a way to get down this mountain. Fast.

As he turned to face the door, he found that miracle.

Next to the light switch was a hook. Hanging from it was a key chain adorned with a single key. The chain had a two-sided piece of rubber with logos attached to it. On one side was a blue shape with the brand Chevrolet in the middle. On the opposite side was the word Malibu in flaming red.

Without thinking or rationalizing his actions, he lifted the key ring off the hook, studying it before putting it back. His stare returned to the exit and he started back toward Lynn and the boys. *I'm getting us home. One way or another.*

16

Orange hues painted the western sky as Micah stepped from the void of the garage, finding his wife and son involved in a heated debate. This was becoming a more common occurrence. David always held his tongue when addressing his father, knowing the repercussions could be harsh, but this had not been the case with Lynn. Micah had blown it off each time Lynn approached him with her concerns, chalking it up to adolescence and puberty.

Deep down, though, Micah knew it was his fault for the disobedience. It was a direct reflection of his shitty parenting, one way or another. David was slowly, surely, turning into him.

Even so, there were bigger things to worry about as he approached his family. Lynn broke her condescending glare away from her son and redirected it toward Micah.

"Good, there you are. You need to straighten your son out, Micah!" She griped, pointing at her son. "He just doesn't know when to shut it. Back talk, back talk, back talk."

Micah attempted to put all his emotions and worries regarding the gun, the key, the purse and wallet to rest. He needed to warn Lynn of the dangers surrounding them. He needed to focus and come up with a plan, not deal with petty drama that felt like a thespian's wet dream.

But first, he had to end this. It was time for him to step up and be a father. His eyes wandered from Lynn to his son, fury burning within them. Preparing to unleash the blaze, he took a step forward but halted after the stride, mind teetering back and forth, thinking instead of doing. The wrath never came. He didn't even speak a word to his son, just glared at him in disappointment.

David dropped his eyes to the ground once his mother started speaking, knowing the fire that roared within his father, knowing that he had messed up again. He could feel his father's eyes hovering over him like a stalking beast, ready to attack.

Lynn looked on, observing her son's drastic change of behavior. Her eyes moved back and forth between David and Micah, wondering how this was going to play out. It was like the flip of a switch watching how different his mannerisms were when Micah was around. She hated it but appreciated the help. All she had ever wanted was support, someone to come to her aid in situations like these. The thought that they were a team, knowing they were in this together, left her warm and comfortable.

She hadn't felt that way in years.

Micah knew he wasn't a monster, not in a literal way, but he was also aware how much damage his actions had caused his family. The look on his son's face spoke volumes about that destruction. The self-loathing deepened as he stood there, fixated on his firstborn, knowing this was all his fault. He hated himself for his past and present, but maybe he could fix this. If he could get them out of this jam, out of this situation, he could be a real father again. Maybe his mistakes could be forgiven, forgotten.

David lifted his eyes, glanced over at his mother and then, for a moment, his father before returning them to the ground. He uttered a simple word, so quietly they almost didn't catch it. "Sorry."

"Sorry for what, young man?" Lynn pressed, expecting more.

There was no response. David just stood there, stubborn, fidgeting with the dirt under his sneakers.

"Well?" she asked again.

Micah looked over at her and then back at his son, feeling the pain and torment that must live within him. *How could I have done this to these people? How? How can any man create such anger, such hate, such despair in those that he loved? Maybe I am the monster they all think I am, after all.*

Micah dropped his head. "I think he knows he made a mistake, Lynn. I can see it and you can too. He's going to change. Think before he acts from here on out. Right, boy?" He asked after clearing his throat.

David stopped pushing the dirt around with his shoe and looked at his father. There was shame in his eyes. He didn't understand the feelings flowing through him. He couldn't explain them, but too many nights had ended with an earful from his father and the threat of more. He had felt a greasy, deep hatred toward his father for all those nights, but more than anything, he feared what could happen if his father lost control. With a slight nod of hesitance, he acknowledged his father. "Yes, sir."

Micah turned to his wife, proud of the way the situation turned out, frowning when her demeanor had not changed. Her jawbone stayed gripped. Her shoulders tense. She stood there, still, with that indignant look plastered across her face. She asked for his help and he delivered, but nothing had changed. Perhaps, deep down, she wished David feared her the way he feared Micah. Maybe she expected that power and influence. *Would that help anything, though? Would that fix these circumstances and bring control to David's hostility toward her?*

"That's good to hear, boy." Micah paused and started toward his son. "One day, you are going to be a man. A man who will have a house, a job, a wife. You need to start acting like one, David. No more of this shit, all right?" As he stepped in front of David, he placed a hand on the boy's shoulder.

David looked up with big, round eyes and gave him a nod.

"Okay, okay." He breathed, letting his grip fall from David's shoulder. His stomach clenched at the way the boy took a shallow step back from him, as if cautious. Micah ignored it. "I need to talk to your mother alone now, okay?" He looked over toward the tree line, listening, searching for anything. "Can you and your brother give us a few minutes?"

"Yeah, Dad. Sure," David started toward Will, pausing, turning back to face his towering father.

After clearing his throat, he said one last thing before joining his little brother by the junked Ford. "I'll do better, Dad. I think we can all do better, right?"

Micah blinked, but David had already gotten back into the beat-up Ford. *Was something implied?*

But he needed to talk to Lynn. Warn her about the guns and Clyde. His concerns about his son would have to wait. There was a threat out there and he had to save them all from it.

He turned back toward his wife, observing how her stance had not altered. She still looked pissed off, stiff as a board, wearing a sneer as she locked eyes with him. She was on the cusp of breaking. That was clear. And here he was, ready to deliver the news that would do it. It didn't matter, though. He had to get her out of here, get them all out of this cesspool and away from the unseen dangers he knew were out there. He had to. It was his duty as a man, a husband, and a father.

Micah tried to persuade her. "Lynn, the boy knows he messed up. He told both of us he was going to change. You heard him, right?" He cocked his head, looking for understanding.

Lynn reluctantly uncrossed her arms and listened to his words, never breaking eye contact. After a subtle sigh, she dropped her look, refocusing toward the forest. "How many times has he said that before, Micah? Do you really think he learned his lesson?"

A smirk crossed his lips, thinking about his childhood and how much trouble he used to get into with his mother, remembering a certain incident that involved a neighbor's mailbox and a baseball bat. *God, I pissed her off that day. I still can't believe I survived that ass-kicking. I don't think I've ever heard the type of cussing and trash that came from that poor woman's lips before or after that day in my entire life. Mom....*

"Micah? Earth to Micah. Hello."

The nostalgia of the moment ended as he snapped back from the past, noticing Lynn impatiently waiting for a response.

"Sorry, babe. Got lost in thought for a second. Anyway, I have something I have to tell you, Lynn—"

Suddenly, both whipped their heads around in the direction of the trees, watching headlights shine through the canopy. He was back.

17

THE OLD BULLET-RIDDEN TRUCK came to rest next to the Malibu, allowing Clyde to step out into the open yard. He was alone but still had the black case with him, carrying it by the handle as he trudged from the vehicle. His demeanor was chipper. One might even say that he seemed satisfied or content.

While approaching, he barely acknowledged the couple, eyes dancing over Lynn's chest for a split second before straying to the garage. Not a word or gesture issued. He just walked between the two, separating them, and continued into the darkness of the shop.

After watching him disappear, Micah and Lynn turned and locked eyes.

"What the hell was that?" Lynn whispered.

Micah shrugged, not having the words to respond. His eyes ballooned and panic pulsated through him, knowing Clyde would notice that someone had been in his office. Knowing he would return hostile, maybe carrying the weapon locked in the black case.

"Is he going to help us with the fuel pump?"

Micah glanced back toward the garage before responding. A bead of sweat trickled down his brow as his eyes shifted back and forth. "He ... he said he would. Looks like he's done helping that Tank guy out," his voice shook with apprehension.

Lynn dropped the addled look, straightening her posture. "I'm not staying here any longer, Micah."

Micah attempted to focus on his wife, but the anxiety was building. He looked back to the garage, waiting for the looming threat he was sure was on its way. He had to protect them, get them to safety, but how to do it without scaring Lynn or the boys? He needed his wits right now. The truth needed to be told, but that would only cause hysteria and panic, which is not a good recipe for survival. There had to be a way.

"What's wrong? Why do you look so anxious, Micah?" Lynn stiffened, observing his body language. "What aren't you telling me?" She began to get nervous.

Micah snapped back to her, trying to recover from the stress. He had to think, had to do something. There was no time to waste. They had to get the hell away from this place, and fast.

A rapid gesture came from his hands, waving her forward. She cocked her head to the side, wary of the urgency behind the motions, before stepping forward. "What is it, Micah? You're scaring me."

"*Shh*, just get over here." He stepped forward, standing right in front of her, keeping his eyes glued to the garage. "I found something while I was inside. This guy isn't—"

A clatter came from the yard where David and Will were playing, using rusty pipes and hubcaps in place of swords and warrior shields.

Lynn dropped her jaw, watching the two swing at each other without care or caution. "What are you two doing now?" She left Micah standing there, a scowl forming across her face as she approached her sons.

"Lynn? Lynn, wait!" His voice elevated. "I have to tell you—"

Lynn looked back for a split second. "Someone's going to lose a finger, Micah," she snarled before storming toward the two.

Micah's nerves were still firing, forcing his glance back to the garage, where his nightmare had come true. Clyde was there, standing just outside the opened garage door. His stoic nature was menacing as he glared at his guests, hands on his hips. The gleeful persona from his return was gone, distant. *Oh Shit! He knows!*

Micah stood there, jaw open, paralyzed by the thought of what was about to happen. *This is it. This is how it all ends. I know I failed my mom in the end. Hell, I've failed everyone in my life.* He looked over at his wife and sons, eyes glossing over. *I can't protect them, lead them, or be a father. Not against a monster like that. This is it. It will just be me. He'll let them go, right?*

Waiting for the inevitable and thinking he was about to soil himself, something changed. Clyde's hands dropped from his waist and a smirk slowly appeared on his face. His gaze hadn't been at Micah, but rather beyond, where David and Will were reenacting scenes from the Roman Coliseum.

Clyde shook his head in amusement before chuckling. "Boys will be boys. Am I right, friend?"

Micah let out an exasperated sigh, not believing the situation. Clyde hadn't noticed anything out of place or disturbed. They were in the clear. Everything was going to be okay, and they would be on their way soon. Clyde would fix the car like he said, and this blasted day would be behind them. "You said it, but try raising two of them less than two years apart."

Clyde snickered at the rhetoric. "Hell, I've got five of 'em. Each one the twinkle of my eye."

Astounded by the news and still calming his nerves, Micah responded. "Really? That's impressive." He glanced over at his wife, scolding the boys and taking their makeshift weapons. "Five?" He asked, redirecting the property's owner.

"Oh, for sure. And that's not counting the daughters." His grin widened as he spoke, decaying teeth contrasting with his sun-reddened face. He paused, observing how low the sun was in the west. "Well, we better get that piece of shit of yours runnin'. I'm sure the missus is ready to get home where it's more ..." He cocked his head and spat. "Comfortable."

Why does he keep doing shit like that, and what's his deal with Lynn? In case you haven't noticed, she's spoken for, asshole! Micah hesitated for a moment before responding. "Yes, well, we would all like to get home, Clyde. Let me know what I can do to help." He gave the man a small and sideways smile.

"Oh, why don't you take your family to the pit over there?" Clyde paused, gesturing behind the old truck the boys had tinkered with earlier in the day. "There's a cord of wood over by the tree line, nice and dry for burning. Gets chilly fast out here once the sun sets." He looked back to the west and rubbed his calloused hands together, a wicked smirk attached to his lips. "Keep your family nice and snug while I get that pump in for ya. Unless, of course, you need a hand with that, too, friend."

The jab didn't sit well in Micah's mind. He wasn't some dumb kid unaware of the world and its surroundings. He could build a damn fire. He wasn't much of a husband or father, but he was still a man with basic skills. A little pride poured back into him while looking at the sly smirk on Clyde's face, thinking about what he would do if he had the power in this situation. Thinking about how he would belittle this towering buffoon if the roles were reversed. "I got it, Clyde. Good idea. We'll be over there."

With that, he strolled away, mumbling under his breath. He went to his family, gathering them to escort to the firepit, as Clyde suggested.

18

THE SCRAPS OF LUMBER littering the property and a few handfuls of dried pine needles and cones provided excellent kindling for the split logs of oak. Within minutes, Micah had a roaring blaze warming those surrounding the fire. He wasn't useless, regardless of Clyde's inapt and belittling opinion. But Micah still seethed inside, feeling emasculated by the man's words and actions. Left wondering what the giant's endgame was.

Look at this thing burn, you son of a bitch. Yeah, I'm not a mechanic, so why would I know how to fix a Japanese import? Bet you couldn't even spell Japanese, dumb Sasquatch. His thoughts bettered him as he stared into the flames, festering like a ruptured boil.

The boys sat on discarded paint cans, burning twisted branches while the flames danced around in the pit. Their shadows against the surrounding forest bouncing with every movement. This was bliss for them. Micah had taken them camping years ago before the shit hit the fan. Before his world collapsed at the news of his mother's rapid decline in health and imminent death. Oblivious to the worries lingering in their father's head, they were having fun.

Lynn remained standing, back to the flames, watching her sons wave the red embers of their sticks through the air. Her mind spun, thinking about Micah. She knew he had something to tell her, but his demeanor at the moment halted her inquiries. She had learned when to dig and when to leave it be. He'd reach out when he was ready, when he was done strewing. She knew it could wait.

What the hell does he know, anyway? He's probably never even been off this shitty mountain before. Man, If I see his beady eyes hover over Lynn again, I'm going to say something. Maybe he's the one who should be worried about what I may do when agitated. He released a heavy sigh, cradling his face in his hands. *Just get the damn car fixed already!*

Lynn looked over at Micah with his hunched posture, thinking she heard an agitated grumble. With the fire illuminating his face, she observed his lips trembling slightly while he fixated on the flames.

She approached by taking small strides, prepared for a reaction, either sudden or erratic. There was no telling with Micah these days, and she had figured out how to prepare for the worst when expecting the best. "Hey, babe. Are you doing okay?" Her words were confident and comforting.

Micah broke his gaze from the illumination, staring through her with vengeful eyes. His mind was distant, stuck in a spiraling cycle of what-ifs and whys, trying to deal with their situation. *Am I okay? Well, let's examine our sweet little situation, Lynn! There's a psychopath nearby that controls the outcome of everything we do, and I'm helpless to intervene or stop it. I can't do anything but wait for him to release us or slit our throats when we fall asleep. Am I okay? Yeah, doing just dandy, Lynn.*

Looking beyond the angry eyes, she probed again, hoping to bring him back. "Micah, help me understand what's going on. I can help you help *us.*"

After a few tense moments, his eyes dropped to the earth, releasing a much-needed sigh. He felt useless, unworthy of having the title of father or husband. There was nothing he could do to correct this problem, to get them all back home without the help of Clyde. Time and dependency were his enemies in this scenario. He had to inform her about the threats surrounding them.

His face seemed to morph as he looked up at her, the agitation and hostility peeling away. He hated showing this side of himself, the vulnerability exposing his faults. He had learned to bottle it all up, keep it hidden deep down in his core, but not at this moment. This was a chance to be honest and help repair the trust issues that had plagued them for the past few years. But being someone else was so hard. *Would scaring her with the truth help this situation?* He wasn't sure.

She could see the misery on his face, the pain, the anguish. She took another stride forward, getting to within a pace, studying him. She so wished she could crack open his skull and read all his thoughts if doing so helped her understand.

"Let me in, Micah. Tell me what's going on, what's causing all the grief I can see."

For the first time, he responded, blinking away glassy eyes. "I just want to go home and get you three the hell out of here. And I can't do anything about it. I feel like this is my fault."

"No, Micah, this isn't your fault. It's the damn car's fault. That weasel sold us a lemon, but it just took a while to discover it, that's all." She shook her head and placed a reassuring hand on his shoulder, squeezing lightly. "You've done everything that you could."

Micah shook his head in disgust, disregarding her warmth and compassion. "I don't feel like I have, Lynn. I feel I've let you and the boys down at every turn. I can't even protect you guys."

Lynn's heart squeezed. "But we are safe, babe. We're safe because you found this man, this place. If you hadn't walked to find help, we would probably still be sitting on the side of the road waiting for the car to get fixed, not next to this scorching fire." She cocked an eyebrow, hoping he understood the appreciation in her words.

Micah released a small chuckle. "*If* he gets the car fixed, you mean. I'm still not completely sold on his ... mechanic skills."

"He's going to fix it. I know he will, and you are the reason we will be on our way within the next hour. You!"

There was no response. His eyes glassed over as he stared at her, thinking maybe she was right. *Maybe none of this was his fault. Maybe this wasn't his fault because he was the victim here. Could he have done more, and if that were possible, what and how?*

Micah stepped in and wrapped his arms around her waist, pulling her close. He held her green eyes, telling her all she needed to hear without saying a word. He wasn't the perfect husband or father, but he wasn't a monster like Clyde. There was no deception or con coming from his lips when he spoke. He just wanted to keep working on his mental health and patching up his mistakes. There was still a chance to become the man he knew he could be.

"You're going to get us out of here and off this mountain, Micah. I've always believed in you and I believe in you now."

As the two lovingly stared at each other, the sound of footsteps approaching broke their focus. Clyde was standing there, cleaning his oiled hands with a handkerchief. The light from the fire flickered across his face, exposing a grimace and disdain. This was not the look of a man prepared to deliver good news.

Micah called out, breaking the tension of the moment, praying the man's look had nothing to do with the office being disturbed. "Everything okay, Clyde? Pumps all right, isn't it? You look like something is bothering you."

Clyde continued wiping his hands with the cloth, muttering under his breath. He looked up at the stars overhead while shaking his head back and forth before redirecting his attention to his guests. "Well … How do I put this, friend? The pump I got from Tank is bad. Rear gasket is cracked and won't hold the fuel. It doesn't look like I can get you guys on the road tonight."

19

"Micah, what the hell are we supposed to do now? Just stay out here, in the dark? Overnight?" Lynn demanded in a shaky voice, arms crossing her stiff torso.

Micah was seething, thinking about what Clyde had told them earlier. He couldn't figure out why, but something told him this man had a personal vendetta against him, sabotaging every hope of progress: the car, the phone, and now the fuel pump. *Why was he torturing them and stringing them along?* The thoughts burrowed deep, taking him into the darkness.

Lynn cleared her throat. "Hello? Micah? Where are you?"

The agitation in her voice snapped him back to reality. "What? What is it, Lynn?"

She cocked her head, annoyance pricking at her features. "Have you not heard a word of what I said, Micah? What's the plan now that we can't get home? What are we going to do?"

Micah couldn't give her the answer she wanted. He didn't have a plan. He was still trying to navigate the whole scenario and figure out what Clyde actually knew, versus what he assumed he knew. Deep down, paranoia was eating at him, wondering how Clyde would act, and *when*.

"We don't have a choice here, Lynn. We're stuck until we can fix that piece of shit car." He turned away from her and looked into the garage, now illuminated with a hanging drop light, glaring at the hatchback. "Always buy American. It's the only way. That's what my daddy always said," he mumbled under his breath.

"What?"

"Nothing, Lynn," he snapped, whirling around. "There's no alternative here, okay? We're stuck until the morning and that's how it is."

She returned the stare, considering him. "Why, Micah? Why can't we find a motel off the highway? It's littered with them at every exit."

"If you haven't noticed, *dear*, we are flat broke!" His posture stiffened and his arms became animated, waving around. "You and the boys splurged pretty heavily at Disneyland, remember? Your little *getaway* has put us even deeper in the hole, and there's no way to dig out now." He paused, dropping his stare to the dirt, trying to collect himself, trying to find a way out of this mess. "There's nothing I can do, that *we* can do."

"Micah, we can't just wait for something to happen, because it may never happen. You're being paranoid! Get us out of here, with or without the damn car," she implored. She waited for a response, staring a hole through him.

There wasn't one to give. Even up here on a rural mountain road, he couldn't be completely truthful with her. He couldn't be the man he once was, and it was slowly drowning him. He had no answers.

Lynn sighed, looking off into the tall reeds surrounding them.

"I'm going to talk to Clyde, Micah." She looked to the garage, seeing movement from under the hood. "He has to be reasonable and understanding of this situation. We have young children, for Christ's sake." Moving around her motionless husband, she stepped away from the vibrant glow of the fire.

Without a word, Micah reached out and grabbed her wrist as she passed him, halting her from advancing.

She turned and faced him. "Somebody has to do something. Let go and I'll take care of this."

His stare left the ground, locking on Lynn as his grip tightened around her frail wrist. For a brief moment, before it disappeared, he saw alarm flash in her eyes, a perceived challenge: *What will you do?* He couldn't let this happen. What if Clyde threatened her, or revealed that he knew someone had been snooping in his office? What if this was the moment he acted out the final scene of his plan? There was zero chance that she was going by herself to engage with that man.

Micah didn't let her go, instead pulling her body closer to him. He had to alter her thoughts, get her to stop digging. "Lynn ... you need to listen to me," he muttered. "I know you're trying to help with this situation, but nothing good can come from these actions. The twelve dollars I have in my wallet will not get us off this mountain." He looked over at the garage, acknowledging the activity under the hood. Clyde had disclosed the bad news about the pump, but he was still working, tinkering with the engine. "I know it's not what you want to hear, and it's not ideal, but this is our situation."

It wasn't what she wanted to hear at all. His willingness to accept their fates in this situation pissed her off. She knew he wasn't disclosing all he knew, and that made things worse between them. But pressing and probing would only push him off the ledge. This was another moment when she was helpless, and any action would be disastrous and confrontational. Togetherness was the only way to keep them all safe, so she swallowed her emotions and instincts and nodded, as wrong as it felt.

He pulled her even closer, embracing her warmth and understanding. He knew they weren't going anywhere soon, but he also knew there was a looming threat. *What was Clyde's MO? It's for her own good, for everyone's. I'll get us out of this shithole safe and away from that son of a bitch. I might not sleep tonight, but I just have to wait until first light, and then I'll make my move. He's not getting his chance.*

She could feel his heart beating under the brown sweatshirt he wore. It was calm, normal. *Maybe he's right? This sucks, but I can make it one night. I think we all can. He'll get us out of this and I'll support him. I just wish he would open up and tell me what he's thinking, what's wrong.* She pulled back, staring into his eyes. *What aren't you telling me, Micah?*

A smirk crossed his lips as he returned the stare, stroking her hair lightly. "It's just one night, and we'll stay in the car, babe. I'll even stay awake to make sure you three are safe. It wouldn't surprise me if there were bears out there to go along with the snakes."

She let out a giggle and playfully slapped his chest. "Okay, but you know I don't like this. It is what it is, though, right?"

He nodded, eyes full of pride and confidence, shrouding the guilt deep within. "We'll be home in the morning, with or without the car. I'll even call your mom if I have to. We're going to get through this, together."

20

Rubbing his eyes with his palms, his surroundings revealed after a series of heavy blinks, Micah searched the setting for any clues to his whereabouts. A white room lined with miscellaneous shelves and countless doors. Trinkets, tools, old books, and loose papers, all stacked unevenly along these shelves lining the room's perimeter. The place was foreign, yet familiar.

I've been here, right? Where the hell is here, though? he thought while circling and taking in all the strange scenes of the elongated room. Turning to face his original direction, a door to his left crept open, echoing throughout the space. Oddly, the event didn't startle or shock him. Intrigue set in, engulfing his focus as he watched the door come to an abrupt stop. Inside the doorframe hid absolute darkness, void of any hint of color. His curiosity was piqued, forcing him to stroll toward the door and the unknown beyond.

Inching closer with curious steps and never averting his eyes from the blackness within, a sudden whisper sounded near his right ear, causing a jolt in that direction. There was no one there. "Who's here? Who said that?" He shouted while spinning like a top, investigating the room from ceiling to floor. *It's just nerves, that's all. It wasn't real, I'm just hearing things.*

Mustering courage again, he continued forward, eyes flickering above and to his sides with each stride. The comfort and fascination that flowed moments earlier waned with each step. Something wasn't right about this place. Once he was within feet of the door, gazing into the dark, it slammed shut, causing him to jump in surprise. He slipped and fell on his ass, pushing himself backward along the concrete floor with his hands, never blinking or taking his eyes off the door.

The whisper snuck into his left ear, causing another flail, then searching for the voice's owner. Finding nothing, he leapt to his feet, whipping his head back and forth, scanning for movement or threats. *This isn't real, it's not real. This isn't happening!*

He turned to run, but stopped in his tracks when his eyes caught a figure. It was tall, thin as a rail, and hovering in a doorframe that appeared to be the exit. A haze shrouded its face, cloudy and gray, seemingly staring at him. There was no movement by either party for a few tense moments, only utter stillness.

His nerves were boiling with anxiety. *Was this figure a threat or the answer to the mystery?* Either way, some action needed to take place. With his heart hammering, he called out, the nervousness flowing through his veins resonating in each word.

"H ... Hello? Who are you?"

The figure did not respond, merely swaying its head from side to side as it lurked in the doorframe.

"Where am I?" His voice was more insistent. "What is this place?"

Suddenly, the figure flipped around and vanished through the door it was blocking. Like the previous door he approached, absolute darkness filled the room beyond. However, unlike the previous door, there was no longer intrigue in finding out what lay on the other side. He wasn't following this thing into the void.

Lacking comprehension of what had just happened or what to do next, dread swept through his body. One door slamming shut and another hiding something mysterious, yet terrifying. Getting away from this haunting place meandered through his mind repeatedly. He no longer cared about any of the other doors or what was beyond them. The only thought looping now was safety.

He turned his body away from the door the figure disappeared into, knowing there must be a second exit on the opposite side of the building. With darting, dilated eyes, he found it, but the long room seemed to lengthen as he searched. The door at the end of the growing hall slipping farther away with each passing second.

What the hell is happening? What is this place? Why am I here?

Without knowledge of doing so, he broke into a sprint. His eyes focused on the inverted rectangle of the exit in the distance, praying it was his way out of this nightmare. Faster and faster, he raced down the corridor, never averting his eyes from the door. Winded and panting, he slowed as the door neared, but as he approached, he noticed it was open. Something wasn't right. Something was in front of the door, towering and menacing.

The mass of another figure engulfed the doorframe, a sliver of darkness visible beyond it. There was no mystery here. This was a man, larger than physically possible, however. Working class from the looks, and rural based on his attire of grimy coveralls, a red checkered flannel shirt, and work boots. A sneer crossed the man's unkempt face as he gazed forward, staring a hole through his prey.

Trepidation growing heavier with each passing moment, uncertainty thick in the air. Fight or flight being the only option. Adrenaline flowed freely as he looked at the monster in front of the doorway, barring his escape from this madness. As he observed the agitation in the behemoth's face, a memory clicked in his mind. He knew who this was. This was the man, the obstacle in his way. The lingering threat that plagued his thoughts and feelings. It was Clyde. But he wasn't alone. There beside him was someone else, petite and beautiful. Lynn.

"Lynn! What are you doing?" Micah stepped forward, his voice full of alarm. "Get away from him!"

She didn't acknowledge him. She didn't even look at him as he approached the two hovering in the exit, shouting demands and threats at them. Her attention was on the man beside her, eyes looking up toward the mountain of a man. She looked at peace, enjoying the embrace and strength of the power that existed within him. She reached up and gripped his anvil of a hand, smiling with the naiveness of an adolescent's first crush. Her expression was love, and Micah could tell where that love projected. Clyde returned the sentiment, dropping the sneer and replacing the look on his face with a gentle, intimate smirk. They looked like a happy couple, passion oozing out of their pores as they gazed at one another like lovestruck teenagers.

"Lynn! Lynn! What is this?" He stared at the two, not believing the reality that was transpiring before him. "What did I do, Lynn? Why are you doing this?"

With his last plea for answers, Lynn turned away from her love and stared at Micah. Her look had changed when she completed the movement, however. It was now one of indignation as if she despised the man in front of her. The disgust strapped across her face spoke volumes about what she must be thinking. This was an unmistakable look of hate.

Micah dropped to his knees, watching as his wife, his love, the mother of his children spat his existence from her teeth. The type of pain he endured at the moment couldn't be described. Agony set in as he wept, continuously calling out the single word, "Why?"

As his world crashed down around him, something unexplainable occurred. Lynn's face morphed before his eyes, altering her appearance. The youthfulness of her skin aged in seconds, deep lines developing in the corners of her mouth. Wrinkles appeared under her eyes and forehead, making it seem as if she were in her sixties, not a young mother on the downhill side of thirty. She was no longer the woman that he had fallen in love with so many years ago. Micah was staring at another significant female figure in his life. One that had left him heartbroken and crippled within. It was his mother.

Micah gasped for air, nearly hitting his head on the driver side window of the hatchback. He looked to his right, acknowledging Lynn curled up in the seat next to him, a gentle snore exiting her mouth. His brown sweatshirt draped her torso as she slept. Turning around, he found Will and David asleep in the back seat.

What the hell was that about? Just a dream, just a dream. His attention turned toward the open garage door, where the morning sun was rising behind them.

Already morning? When did I doze off?

Lynn mumbled something next to him, diverting his attention from the morning's brilliance. He watched her for a few moments, inhaling, exhaling, thinking about their life together and how he had fucked things up. He wanted his old life back, but there was no returning after his history. After the torment and fights. He was a broken man and questioned whether he still deserved her by his side.

A few minutes passed while he contemplated the dream, trying to remember every detail. Most moments were hazy, full of uncertainty, but others were vivid, clear, and focused. His mother's face on Lynn's body seemed to be suppressed, but not the emotion Lynn expressed while looking at Clyde. The love radiating from her eyes, her actions. It sickened him to think about it and plunged him farther down the spiraling rabbit hole.

Why was she with him, straddling his side and looking at him that way? That's stupid, Micah. What's wrong with you? He shook his head, trying to rid the picture from his warped mind.

There's no way she would be interested in a creature like him, let alone love him. I know there's resentment deep inside her about me, but she's still here, still by my side. She still loves me, right? But why would I dream about that shit? She would never leave me, would she? Especially not for someone like him.

"Hmmm, would she?" he mumbled.

21

Shuffling from behind him tore Micah away from his worries about Lynn. He turned around, once more noting his sons in the back seat. Will had shimmied away from his seat and was using David's shoulder as a pillow. The sounds and mumbles came from David, who didn't care much for the idea. He had always been a little grumpy when his sleep was disturbed, and was mumbling his displeasure with the new sleeping arrangement.

Micah didn't intervene between the two, knowing both would reposition shortly and not have any recollection of the dispute once they were awake. Instead, he turned back around and slipped out of the car, being careful not to make too much noise or awaken Lynn.

As he closed the door, he knelt down, taking in her features. She was amazing. Truly amazing. And beautiful. *How did I let this get so bad?* He thought. *Why can't things just be normal again? Why can't we just go back in time and start over? I know I can be a better husband, a better father, a better man.* A smile crossed his lips while he watched her sleep, thinking about the life they should have. The life they were projecting toward before the shit hit the fan with his mother. *There's still time. I know there is, even if I don't deserve it.* He stood and walked away from the car, exiting into the morning light surrounding the yard.

Micah brought a hand to his eyes, shielding them from the beauty of the morning. As he scanned the yard, jays and finches fluttered through the canopy of trees, squawking and chirping with eagerness. A squirrel scurried up the trunk of a pine, carrying an acorn in its mouth. The area was alive with activity, but he hadn't come out to watch nature. He had to find Clyde.

Knowing that the monster had a plan, a goal, keeping a watchful eye on Clyde and his whereabouts was critical. A bit of self-loathing snuck into his core, wondering how he had dozed off last night, leaving his family vulnerable. Wits were the only way to stay focused and alert. He had to be prepared at all times, just in case.

Ignoring the wildlife and the majesty of the early morning sun, he turned to his right and saw the Malibu still parked in its original spot. *Did the thing even run?* He wondered while noting that the truck was absent again.

"Where the hell are you now?" He mumbled under his breath while turning and searching the rest of the barren yard. Neither Clyde nor the truck was anywhere in sight. He and his family were alone for the time being, not safe, but alone.

As he turned back toward the primed Malibu, a flashback hit his mind from the previous day. An action he had somehow suppressed deep within his consciousness, forgotten and lost. *Oh shit! What did I do? Oh Shit! This is bad.* He reached down, patting his front left pocket, feeling the key ring. The Malibu key ring. *What the hell am I doing with this? I put the fuckin' thing back. I know I did. Why is it in my ...*

He dropped his face into his palms, pacing the area, panic striking like a caged animal. His mind warped, bent, trying to remember how this could have happened. *Why did I take the key and why didn't Clyde notice?* This was just added fuel to ignite the toxic flame that was coming his way. He knew it.

But ... what if Clyde already knew about the missing key? What if this was just another ploy to terrorize me? Another mind game aimed at tormenting his thoughts, like a mad scientist carrying out a lethal experiment with rats. He had to regain control, focus on getting his family to safety before it was too late. He had to get the key ring returned, whether or not Clyde knew about it.

He knew he had to worry about Clyde's overall intentions, but maybe the man hadn't noticed anything out of place. Maybe he didn't realize someone had rummaged through the office, found the decades-old belongings of the old couple, and took the keys to the old classic parked out front. Maybe all this was just Micah's anxiety creating scenarios that didn't actually exist. Scenarios that heightened the stress of his family's situation. Just maybe.

Either way, that key ring had to be returned, and fast. It wasn't like he planned to steal the car. There's no way he could be that bold.

He couldn't risk being seen reentering the building by Lynn or the boys, either, so it was now or never. Clyde was gone, and everyone else was still asleep. He had to act now.

Swift strides led him back inside, where he silently shifted past the car and his family.

Two minutes, in and out. Then I'll head back out front and wait for that bastard to return. You're not getting her, asshole! She's my wife, and we are leaving here together.

22

Thirty minutes had passed without Micah exiting the building. The bright sun's rays had awoken Lynn and the boys from their slumber, and they stretched their legs outside in the yard, wondering where he was.

Lynn's initial emotion was panic at waking up to Micah being nowhere in sight, but she couldn't reveal that to the boys. She had to be strong and acknowledge that Micah was surely searching for a way out of here. Maybe he was with Clyde right this moment, picking up a new pump that would end all this. He would return any minute now with the news they had all been waiting for. He had to come through. There was no alternative.

Movement caught her eyes from within the darkness of the garage. She grabbed Will by the hand, hair a matted mess, and pulled him closer to her. With her free hand, she shielded her eyes from the sun, squinting into the darkness. The three watched as a figure exited, revealing themself.

Micah stepped out of the darkness and approached his family, brow furrowed and carrying a black object in his right hand. The veins in his neck were noticeable as he rubbed the stubble on his chin with his free hand, eyes locked on his wife. This was not a man that had just solved a problem.

David and Will looked on, unable to move. Lynn stiffened as he got closer, anxious and perturbed. "Micah, did you find anything? What happened?" she asked, lacking confidence.

He ignored her questions. He just stood there, feet away from his family, eyes shallow and dead. Slowly, he raised his right hand, showing them the object that he had carried out of the building. It was the handset to the telephone, and the cord had been severed.

Lynn stepped forward, unable to grasp what he was showing her. "Is that … is that his phone? Didn't you say it rang right before he left yesterday? Who did that? Who cut the cord, Micah?" She was a few feet away now and could see him, truly see her husband. The bloodshot eyes, the lifelessness to them. She knew this look, knew this man. This was how he looked after his mother died, the way he looked when he had given up on life.

Micah dropped his eyes to the ground, but Lynn could see a hint of life returning as they teared up. He shook his head from side to side, mumbling under his breath. He had tried so hard to keep it together, to control it during this trip. And now, another obstacle was in his way. Another hiccup preventing him from being the man he longed to be.

Lynn dropped her eyes before moving any closer, attempting to hide her nerves about what could happen if she zigged when she should have zagged.

Micah didn't lift his head until she was a foot away, desperation swimming in his eyes. A repetitive chant came from his lips, but she couldn't make out what he was saying. She slowly reached out to touch his arm, to show him she was there.

His eyes immediately shifted to the outstretched hand, and he jerked back a step. The hopelessness that was expressed seconds before ended, replaced with agitation. Fury blazed in his eyes as he glared at her, his loving wife.

"Do you see what the son of a bitch did, Lynn?" He screamed, holding up the phone. "He's screwing with us at every turn! First the fuel pump, and now this?" He turned toward the woods and released a growl, throwing the severed handset into the towering trees.

Lynn stepped back. Her mind spun in circles listening to his rant, thinking about Clyde and his actions. How could anyone deliberately do this? The dread in her mind about this man's intentions haunted her every thought. What was he planning? Was he going to hurt them, hurt David and Will?

The thought of her sons in any capacity of danger brought her reeling back, regaining focus. Fearing for their safety, she looked at Micah, searching for hope.

"Why's he doing this, Micah? Why? What does he want from us?" She cried.

He faced her, breathing heavily, fingers interlocked behind his neck. He shook his head before responding. "I don't know what he wants or why he's doing any of this! He's a psychopath and a monster!" His rant paused while he collected himself, taking deep breaths. "I don't know what he's planning, but I'm not waiting around to find out. We're leaving without that shitty car."

The rashness of his declaration surprised her, but she agreed. The sooner they left, the better. From the moment she first saw that man, a feeling of uneasiness surrounded her. Was it his massive size or his mannerisms? Now, Micah's claims about these sabotaging actions. She wasn't sure, but she knew they needed to get away before finding out. With confidence, she nodded.

"Boys!" he called out after nodding in return. "We're leaving! Now!"

They both looked at their father, perplexed at the demand.

"Why? But what about the car? Where are we going?" David asked, still blinking away the sleep in his eyes.

Will looked into the garage, tilting his head in confusion. "Yeah, Dad, what about the car? What about all of our stuff?"

"We can't worry about that crap right now, guys. Right now, we need to get away from this place. It's not safe here any longer, and we need to get away, fast." As he spoke, a sound was heard in the distance, garnering all their attention. It was a vehicle coming up the two-lane road, and it sounded a lot like Clyde's truck.

PART THREE

THE WOODS

23

THE THICK LAYER OF vegetation partially obstructed Micah's view as he watched the old truck come to a stop near the shop's garage, leaving a wake of dust stirring in the air. Peering over the rotting remnants of an old stump, he watched Clyde exit the vehicle. No one exited the passenger side. It appeared he was alone and searching the area, looking for them, looking for anyone. On the hunt.

The boys and Lynn were thirty paces downhill from him, hidden amongst the saplings and brush growing in an opening of the forest floor. He instructed them to take cover while he watched, trying to discover the level of threat that was present. There was no telling what Clyde's intentions were. The man was steering them to stay here as long as possible for a reason. And the looks he kept giving Lynn....

He watched, scarcely breathing, observing the monster that was toying with him and his family. Clyde looked confused, looking to the north and then the south, searching for his four captives, circling the area. Instantly, he dropped his search and marched into the darkness of the garage, evading Micah's watchful eyes.

Micah leaned forward over the stump, trying to glimpse anything or hear the man's exit from the shop. The tension of the moment warped his mind as he waited, expecting the worst. *Where the hell did you go?*

After a few tense minutes, Clyde emerged from the darkness and released a deafening scream which echoed through the forest. The volume caused Micah to drop to the ground, ensuring he was out of sight. He crouched and began his trek toward his waiting family, avoiding pine cones and splintered branches underfoot. Moving as fast as he could without making much noise, he found them huddled together, confusion and fear streaking their faces.

Lynn had her arms wrapped around both boys' shoulders, facing the direction of the scream as Micah approached. Fear pulsated through each mannerism as she locked eyes with her husband, trembling.

"Move, move, we have to move now," he demanded in a hushed voice, gesturing at them with his arms. "We have to go. There's no time to wait."

But Lynn couldn't move. Her body was paralyzed as she held onto her sons, watching Micah inch closer with each careful stride. Her eyes told only an iota of the emotions swirling through her. Facing him, she forced herself to respond. "What the hell's going on, Micah? Was that ... was that him?" She shifted her eyes behind Micah in the scream's direction. "Clyde?"

He didn't answer. There was enough worry and alarm pulsing through his family already. "We have to move, Lynn." He looked back toward the property. "I don't know what he wants, and I'm not finding out." After grabbing Will by the hand, he locked eyes with her. "Now, Lynn. Now."

The confidence in his voice brought her back. She didn't understand what was happening, but she knew that voice. She remembered that voice. That was Micah, the man she had married, delivering for her, for all of them. She removed her arm from around Will's shoulders and followed as Micah led them away, keeping a tight grip on David's hand. The four slinked their way through the trees, looking back every few steps, cautious of their footing.

Micah came to a halt as they approached a sudden descent on the forest floor, stopping the caravan of Will, Lynn, and finally David. The decline wasn't significant, that's not what stopped his progress. His eyes caught something that signaled alarm. A towering oak stood before them, hovering above all the other trees in the area. Its broad, arching limbs reaching far into the morning sky. Protruding from the thick, coarse bark of its trunk was an object. The shaft of an arrow with red fletching. From the looks of it, the tree was recently penetrated.

But the deadly arrow wasn't all that concerned Micah. The shaft pierced the remains of a gray squirrel sans thick, fluffy tail, its front paws still twitching. A trail of blood streaked the bottom of the animal, dripping down onto the trunk and the forest floor below, creating a purple puddle of coagulation.

Micah flinched at the scene, turning back to shield the sight from David and the others behind him. As he looked at his sons, he held up his hands, palms showing, signaling all to stop. Neither the boys nor Lynn needed to see this brutality.

"Hey, hey, hold on for a second. We need to go in a different direction." He stood a little more erect, shuffling the line to the right of the oak, attempting to block the view with his shoulders and arms. "Keep going, guys. We have to keep moving." He paused and looked over his shoulder, making sure no one could see past his torso. "Faster. Eyes in front. Watch your steps."

David and Lynn passed without a glance at the massive tree, avoiding the grotesqueness pinned to it like some twisted ornament on a Christmas tree. Will, bringing up the rear of the group, looked past his father's unsubtle attempts and took in the sight. His jaw dropped, and he froze for a split second before being ushered along. Micah held a finger to his lips, silently instructing the boy to keep the scene to himself, which Will agreed to, also nonverbally, with a continuous nod.

As the group cleared the tree, Micah glanced back and prayed no one was following them. Scanning and searching for movement and not finding any, he turned and caught up with his family, again leading the way. The forest continued its natural descent westward away from the shop and its dangers.

There has to be another road out here! Where is it? He slowed, brushing away a condensed group of saplings with his left hand, scanning all around, cautious with each step. Another road had to be near. He could feel it. *But would they be safe walking along its perimeter, out in the open, once they reached it?* He hadn't thought about that until now. *Maybe that would put them right where Clyde wanted them, sitting ducks waiting for the predator to strike from any direction.*

Finding himself in a conundrum that could be lethal if he made the wrong choice, he stopped his advance. Lynn and the boys also halted their progression, staring at their patriarch, awaiting the plan's next steps. Utter silence followed. Micah had neither a plan, nor any idea how to get them off this mountain. He simply crouched there, gazing to his left and right, eyes darting, hoping the answer was in front of him, or that it would soon reveal itself. But it never came. *What was next? Keep marching and hope for a way out of this, getting farther and farther away from the beast that lurked behind them somewhere? Or solidify a plan that will save their asses?*

Micah released a deep breath, dropping his chin to his chest, his eyes shut tightly. The boys and Lynn looked on, not knowing what to do or how to react to the behavior. They were confused, scared, and worried about what was happening. About what could happen if they stopped and didn't advance their escape. There wasn't time to sit and wait without confirmation or dialogue. Something had to be done with efficiency and swiftness. It was the only way.

Lynn slinked forward, keeping low to the ground, gesturing for David to take a step backward. She needed to see Micah, see his eyes, and make sure he was still with them, not lost due to the stress. As she approached, he opened his eyes, acknowledging her presence and allowing her to see him. She observed the lifelessness swimming throughout his blue eyes. The lack of cognition and feeling in his features. He was lost.

She inched forward, "Micah, I'm here. We need you, babe." She stiffened with each minute stride, trying to get as close as possible without forcing the expected aggression to futility. As she reached out to touch his slouched shoulder, he flinched, avoiding the gentleness of her attempt. He whipped his head around, staring into the forest as a thunderous echo exploded through the trees, sending birds and animals scurrying away.

Micah flipped a 180, staring into the denseness of the forest they had traversed, eyes shifting left and right. He saw the movement of someone in the distance—shrouded by the ancient oaks and pines—approaching swiftly in their direction.

24

OH SHIT! THERE HE IS! The statement spiraled in Micah's mind. This threat was real, and it was right behind them. Micah instinctively whipped around, facing his family, terror flushed across his face. Lynn and the boys couldn't understand what was happening, not noticing the looming figure ambling down the slope, but Micah's appearance infused them with a similar dread.

And then a twig snapped to their left, followed by the crunching of pine needles under someone's feet. A dark shadow flashed in Micah's peripheral vision before vanishing into the trees. It was time to panic and run.

Without saying a word, Micah bolted down the descent, grabbing both boys by the hand and pulling them along.

Lynn was matching each stride, keeping pace with all three of them, chaos and horror flowing through her like ice water. Her mouth hung open as she ran, trying to release a shrill scream, but it wouldn't come.

"Why are we running?" David cried, full of alarm. "I didn't see anything!"

Neither parent acknowledged the question, merely increased their speed in the opposite direction.

Clusters of fallen branches and forest debris made for treacherous footing. The thick layer of fallen leaves hid twisted roots that jutted out from the base of trunks. In the run's chaos, David's toe snagged a root, causing him to fall and land face-first on the forest floor, yanking his hand away from his father. Micah slid to help him up, but Lynn was already there. With a firm grasp and yank, David sprang up, oblivious to the pain shooting through his left ankle, and ran alongside his mother.

Paired together, mother and son and father and son, they ran with all their strength, clumsily slipping with the lack of traction. Both pairs approached a jumbled collection of saplings circling another large oak, which forced each group to take a different route to get around.

Beyond the cluster of young and mature trees on the right, the terrain's slope increased sharply. Slowing his advance, Micah glanced back to see if the figure was closing on them, seeing multiple shadows giving chase.

He whipped his head around and yanked on Will's hand. "Come on and watch your step!" Planting his left foot in the soft soil of the hill, pulling his son behind him, followed by his right side stepping downward. In seconds, the two made it to the bottom and back to level ground, where again, Micah looked behind them and saw nothing. He forced his eyesight away from the top of the decline to search for Lynn and David but found no one. His twitchy eyes searched left, right, and toward the top of the hill. *Where are they? What happened to them? How? How did we lose them?*

Past the grouping of clustered trees on the left, the hill's decline sharpened southward, sending Lynn and David away from the others who were traveling southwest. The grade was steeper on this side, and Lynn over-corrected for it, falling forward, breaking the maternal chain of hands she had with her oldest son. She tumbled twice before gripping the side of a rotting stump jutting through the debris, sending a wake of needles and leaves down the hill. A long stream of crimson rolled down her left forearm as she gained control and focus after the fall.

David locked his knees midstride, leaned back, and fell on his ass, sliding to a stop near his mom. Without time to check for injuries, they both sprang up—ignoring the dirt soiling their clothes—continuing downward. Lynn, sure-footed now, glanced back, expecting to see the monster chasing them, but found nothing. With adrenaline fueling them, they continued southward down the slope, not knowing they had lost Micah and Will.

After a few dozen cautious yet swift strides, then wiping her bloody forearm on her jeans, Lynn looked to her right and left, expecting to see Micah close by. Throughout the run, she hadn't been able to think, only carry out primeval actions of survival. But glancing back again and finding no threat, her cognition slowly returned.

Panting, she stopped and placed her hands on her knees, allowing David to also catch his breath. Buckled over, she scoured her surroundings, searching for any sign of her husband. Panic sank in, and she regained the ability to scream but suppressed it, knowing they weren't safe yet. Micah had seen something, and it had scared the hell out of him. They had to keep moving, but the suddenness of the halt caused her ribs to scream with pain. She reached for them, cradling her side with her right arm. She also noticed a concerning limp in her son's leg as he attempted to shift from foot to foot, balancing on the steep decline.

Knowing something was wrong, a grimace struck her face. Hopefully, just a contusion, nothing broken. Her thoughts spun in her head, wondering, *How the hell are we going to continue and finally get to safety? And where are Micah and Will?*

There was nothing but silence all around them, creating even more stress and anxiety as she held her side, trying to hide the anguish she felt from the fall from her son's shaken eyes. She couldn't see anything or anyone, but there was a twisted feeling scratching its way up her spine. Like they were being watched.

25

WILL BUCKLED OVER, PANTING and trying to catch his breath. While he sucked in the rich mountain air, he watched his father's behavior escalate. Micah was spinning in circles, eyes shifting in all directions, trying to comprehend what had happened, how they had gotten separated.

They were just here with us! Where did they go? Where are they? Think, Micah! Think, you idiot!

He continued his inconsistent pacing and turns, still cautious that someone was closing on them. His heart demanded he scream Lynn's name, find them, and reunite, but the threat held his tongue. With fingers locked behind his neck, he slowed his pace, steadied his breathing, and attempted to calm himself. His stoic appearance and controlled breaths didn't have the same calming effect on his younger son. It made things worse.

"Where's Mommy?" The nine-year-old's voice was shaky and elevated. "Wh ... where's Dave, Daddy?"

Micah's eyes found his son, worry striking him like a wrecking ball, knowing they needed to be mute, like prey hiding in the brush. He grabbed his son by the forearm and pulled him close to his body, back to chest, covering his mouth with a soiled hand. He then backed behind a stunted pine, shrouding their presence, dragging his son with him.

Will released a muffled bawl, the fear taking control of his thoughts and actions. He reached up with clawing fingers, trying to remove the hand from his mouth, but hesitated once he heard a whisper in his ear.

"*Shh*. Quiet, now!" Firmness accented with each syllable.

Will turned his head and looked up, seeing his father's glowering eyes. Angry eyes, bloodshot eyes. Micah held an index finger to his lips, making sure Will understood the urgency. After a series of dramatic nods, Micah slowly uncoiled his fingers from his son's mouth.

"*Shh*. He's ... they're out there somewhere, watching and waiting." Micah's eyes, darting and panic-stricken, left his son and returned to the elevated forest they had just descended. His brow arched as he scanned.

Will dug deep and mustered some courage to release a whisper. "Who? Who are we running from?"

There was no response. Micah continued his relentless pursuit to find the threat, gripping his son tighter with each passing second. Listening. Watching. Praying.

Will's eyes followed his father's into the dense forest, not understanding the situation or the lethal consequences that hid there.

Again, he probed his father, tension magnified by the lack of communication. "Dad, you're scaring me." He looked up and back again, trying to capture his father's gaze, but was unsuccessful. "Dad, who's out there? Who's following us?"

"Quiet, boy!" Micah hissed, never looking at his son. "It's the mechanic, son. And others. They're looking for us."

A tear fell from Will's right eye, streaking down his cheek, as he looked away from Micah and back at the never-ending forest beyond. His knees were the first to shake as he watched the trees, silent and still. Then the rest of his body caught up, a steady tremble pulsing through his core. He tried to pull away from his father's death grip but gave up within seconds, realizing it was no use. But the shaking never subsided. Neither did the fear currently strangling him like a taut noose.

"Why ..." Will paused, a whimper resonating in his throat. "Why is he looking for us? What did we do?"

Micah leaned forward, ensuring his mouth was adjacent to Will's lobe. With detest smothering every word, he whispered. "I don't know for sure, son. But he's been planning something since yesterday. Since we first met him." Micah dropped his glare, whipping his head around and scanning the rest of the forest. "We need to keep moving, Will, and find your mom and brother too. Come on."

With that, he turned, pulling Will with him, still watching in all directions, and inching away from the fir that momentarily concealed their disappearance.

Having Will walk ahead of him, he slowly started moving back down the descent, which had leveled out to a minor grade. With each paranoid step, he called out in a hushed voice, cautious of his audible level. "Lynn! Lynn, where are you?"

The two continued their trek, pace increasing, fearing they had lost the rest of their family and what fate was in store past the next tree.

"What's wrong with your leg, David?" Lynn hobbled over to her son, still favoring her ribs, while eyeing the discomfort of the boy's awkward stance. "From the fall?"

The pain commenced now that they were motionless with the lack of steady adrenaline flow. Agony painted across his face as he looked up at her, tears welling in his eyes.

"Let me look at it, baby." Her tone was full of concern and infused with comfort, as only a loving mother can do. As she knelt to inspect the injury, pain shot to her ribs with each inch of the bend. A grimace followed. She bit her lip to keep the shriek from escaping, knowing she had to be strong.

David knew something was wrong, something abhorrent. He momentarily ignored the constant pain shooting through his leg and buried the selfishness of his misery. "Mom! Mom, what's wrong? You're hurt, huh?" His voice grew wearier with each spoken word, watching her suffer in pain.

She raised her unscathed forearm toward his back, trying to conceal the pain in her side, not making eye contact. Her mind was in shambles, thinking about her husband, the shop, and Clyde.

Was he following them? Was he hunting them? Is that why Micah spontaneously panicked and darted into the woods, forcing his family to follow without an explanation? All unanswerable questions.

So many fears and worries meandered through her psyche. But at the moment, a few dominated the chaos swirling within. *Where was Micah? David? Where did they disappear after the sudden rush?*

"I'm fine," she paused, gritting her teeth and finally looking at her son. "It's just a bruise, baby, that's all." Her eyes moved to the forest above them, again searching for the threat they had run from. "We need to keep moving and find your dad and

Will. Try not to worry about me, son." She looked down at her contused forearm, blood dripping in streaked tendrils toward the earth.

David saw her rapid eye movement and observed the blood trail falling to the forest floor in a slow trickle down her wrist. "Mom, you're hurt. You're bleeding everywhere."

This is bad, unbelievably bad. How the hell am I going to get us out of here? Where are you, Micah?

She knew he was right, that she endured something significant during the tumble down the decline. And it wasn't just the laceration on her arm, which she knew needed to be stitched. Each laborious breath filled her side with torment. She required medical attention. But her instincts demanded that she stay strong and hide the truth, knowing it would only cause more panic and alarm in the boy.

Her eyes flowed to her son, attempting a weak smile as she gazed upon his innocence. "It's a lot of blood, son. But it's not as bad as it looks. I promise." The smile widened as she spoke, seeing how the dialogue had diminished the dread on his face. "I'll be okay, baby. I just need to get it wrapped and apply some pressure so the blood will clot."

For now, the response waived his worries. He still didn't understand what had happened and why they bolted off through the woods. Or what looming threat hovered beyond sight out there in the open. But listening to her calm plea and knowing her love for him helped ease some of those unanswered questions.

As he watched her doing all she could to conceal the truth and protect him, a feeling of guilt crawled into his gut, remembering all the times he had acted so shitty toward her. All the back talk and negativity directed right at her and nobody else. He couldn't explain how his behavior was a product of his father and their home life, or that the resentment delivered was for Micah. There was just a constant feeling of hate and shame pulsating through his veins with every heartbeat, and it had to be released somewhere, and at someone. Tears developed again, nearly flowing from his lashes, but these weren't the result of his injured ankle. They were from recalling the pain his actions and words created. The pain he had caused his mother.

Lynn saw the sudden collapse in his demeanor, watching the tense persona evaporate, replaced by self-loathing. Empathy enveloped her core, feeling the pain and sorrow unfold before her eyes. No mother should ever have to witness what her eyes were showing her, and her thoughts twisted with self-regret, thinking the worst.

"Honey, everything is going to be okay. I'll be okay, and we'll find your dad and Will and—" Her loving rant stopped immediately as the forest quieted around them. No calming breeze or chirps from finches and jays. Silence engulfed them, as if a predator were spotted lurking in the brush, ready to pounce.

She spun around, searching and scanning the woods, terror flowing again. She forced herself in front of her son, barricading the boy's sight. *Where are you? Where? What the hell is happening? Micah!* Her thoughts raced.

After what seemed like minutes of stress, out of the corner of her eye, a shadow shifted between two trees. There was nothing there, though. Nothing she could see. *Was her mind playing tricks on her? Or was there something out there waiting patiently for the opportunity to strike?*

Without thinking, she screamed in the movement's direction, summoning whatever it was to come out and show itself.

She waited, staring directly at the two trees where she thought the shadow shifted, expecting the worst and prepared to fight. Nothing obliged. They were alone, listening for the sounds of the forest to resume. The eeriness of the moment never subsided, but it was time to move, regardless. They had to reunite with the rest of the family and get the hell away.

Lynn scanned her surroundings once again before wrapping an arm around David's shoulder and shuffling him away, intent on supporting his ankle and her ribs with each step. Instead of moving farther south, however, she led him east, horizontally—against the gradient of the slope. Along the way, she called her husband's name in a hushed yell, pausing frequently, hoping for a response through the chatter of the forest and its inhabitants, both known and unknown.

26

Will hadn't said a word in minutes, merely mimicking his father's steps, cautious of the pine cones and splintered branches littering the forest floor. He trembled as he moved. He was confused and scared. Micah's vagueness about the situation only intensified his worries. He stood there, watching his father's odd yet familiar behavior, wondering why the man that had helped them on the side of the freeway was now searching for them. Hunting them.

Ahead of them, the thick canopy of trees cleared, forcing a cautious slowing of their advancement. Micah held an arm out to his side, halting Will from taking another step. "Hold on, kiddo, let's take a break. I need a minute to think." Stress and worry building, his eyes searched in every direction, still looking for his missing family members. And anyone else. Once stopped, he reached out and braced himself against an oak, staring up at the morning sky. Micah hunched over, palms on his knees, eyes closed, trying to think, to plan, as his mind recalled all that had transpired. As long as they continued to move, Clyde's threat decreased, but they had to reunite with Lynn and David in order to escape this horror of a vacation.

Where are they? How did we get separated? Think, Micah, think! When did we lose them? The memories of the run looped in his brain. Slowly, visions warped in and swirled inside his head, capturing him in an intoxicated trance. As his mind bent and twisted for answers, he felt unconsciousness approaching. He fell to his knees, and blackness took control.

An unknown number of breaths later, a dark, imposing figure—larger than humanly possible— sauntering through the woods materialized in his vision. Within moments, the facial features assembled, bringing clarity to the towering foe. It was Clyde, who was confused and capricious with every menacing movement.

Micah observed this avatar, watching the behemoth spin in circles, scanning the horizon, searching for something. After several turns, the monster paused, statuesque. It turned and stared at him. Its mouth opened, jaw unhinging like a serpent as a scream flew from its throat. The magnitude of the shriek echoed in Micah's mind, forcing a shudder as he fell to his knees again, eyes tightly shut.

Will cocked his head, watching the mannerisms of his father. He noticed Micah's breathing accelerate, wondering what was happening and why? "D ... Dad? What's wrong?" He took a step back.

There was no acknowledgment. Micah's mind whipped in loops, trying to remember the events that led to the separation. He knelt on the forest floor, head solemnly hung to his chest, inhaling and exhaling rapidly as he spiraled further into the mental distortion of reality.

The enormous replication of Clyde vanished in a hazy mist after relinquishing another ear-splitting scream. Then, in a bright flash, Micah was running. He, Lynn, and the boys were all sprinting down the slope of the mountain together in widespread panic. He could see the expressions of every member of his kin. Fear, anguish, uncertainty. Terror struck deeper with each stride as he ran with them, glancing back occasionally, trying to glimpse their pursuer. But the sprint ended. One boy fell, twisting his foot in a root hidden amongst the debris of the forest floor, falling face-first into the loose layer of leaves and needles. Micah skidded to a stop, ripping through arid leaves, as did the others, to help the fallen.

He reached a hand toward his son, attempting to support the boy and get him back to his feet, but something stopped the progression after the two linked. The boy wouldn't budge. Micah's eyes moved to the boy's foot, still lodged in the jutted root. As he reached down to pry the boy's appendage free, the root moved, coiling farther up the boy's leg, tightening with each turn, constricting the limb. The boy attempted to scream, as he watched the root slither farther up his body and around his torso, but no sound came.

Then, uncannily, all around the four, roots as thick as logs sprang from the forest floor, gripping onto arms and ankles. Needles and leaves sprayed in the air like the aftermath of a collision with each subterranean thrust. The roots slowly engulfed the family, enclosing them in a ligneous prison. The circular fortress inched closer and closer, forcing out all light and hope as it solidified.

Will watched as his father began hyperventilating on his knees, clawing at the air, trying to break out of the trance and the timber cage. Micah violently lurched back, eyes finally opening. But they were lifeless, rolled backward, only revealing his bloodshot sclera. He was stuck, and his mind wouldn't release him back to reality.

The flailing continued, accompanied by whimpers and shrieks of horror as Will observed what was happening. He reeled backward, away from what his eyes were showing him, not comprehending the mental instability his father was displaying. A look of dread and desperation crawled across his face, jaw dropped, unable to do anything to stop the maddening behavior.

Within Micah's psyche, he screamed as the final vines and roots completed their task, closing out any hint of light and strangling his family in the darkness. Physically, Micah flung forward again, chin returning to rest on his chest. His breathing slowed.

Then, in a moment of déjà vu, a bright flash occurred, suffocating all sight, and the vision was over. He and his family were free. Once again, they were running, approaching a cluster of metallic trees towering into the heavens. Shades of rustic orange, browns, and grays mingled to form the barricade before them. All four slowed their pace, still whipping looks backward, searching for the solitary predator chasing them.

Micah looked over at Lynn, noticing her out of breath, perspiration glistening on her brow in the morning sun. She returned the look, locking eyes with him and screaming for help without making a sound. David appeared next to her, tears streaking his cheeks as they all finally came to a stop in front of the trees. Micah glanced down and found his younger son clinging to his soiled brown sweatshirt. Fists clenched into the cotton fabric, face buried. They all stood there, observing the colossal obstacle blocking their path.

Suddenly, the ground shook with tremors as if a fault line were exploding deep within the earth. A meandering crack appeared at the base of the metallic trees, swiftly moving past the family to the top of the incline, growing longer with each passing second. Micah watched as the forest floor opened up and separated into two, dividing the land.

As the jostling subsided, Micah found Will still clinging to his side, gripping tighter and sobbing with fear. But they were alone. In front of them was a twenty-foot-wide canyon where the earth had opened. Micah looked over the edge, cautious of his footing, noticing the nothingness within. Even with the looming sun illuminating the land above, the newly created cavity was void of any features. Total blackness engulfed the chasm below their feet, forcing a gasp as he stepped backward, holding onto his son.

His eyes left the darkness below his feet, now scanning across the canyon. There, huddled together, were Lynn and David, shaking with angst, staring back at him. He called out in a thunderous yell, his voice echoing against the walls of the void, "LYNN! LYNN!"

She appeared to return the anxious scream across the canyon, cupping her hands around her mouth. But nothing could be heard. All audible sounds exiting her throat seemed muted. Her arms flailed above her head, trying to communicate, trying to be seen and heard. But she failed.

Slowly, she and David faded away, extinguishing into a mist, vanishing against the density of the surrounding forest. His jaw dropped, observing the unexplainable view before him, watching half his family dissipate into nothingness. A final scream exited his mouth as the last physical remnants of Lynn and David escaped his mind, enclosing him within a gloomy casket of mourning.

A bright flash struck the setting, blinding his vivid vision and ending the suffering flowing through his mind. Reality crept back in with its end, flooding his senses, releasing Micah to smell the richness of the surrounding pines, to hear the chirps of the jays, and to feel the gust of the breeze rustling in the trees high above. Slowly, cognition of his presence returned, and he opened his eyes, seeing his son sitting on the forest floor cross-legged. The boy cradled a pine cone—missing most of its scales—in his hands, squeezing it with all his might, tears running down his cheeks as he trembled before his father.

Micah's mind teetered between reality and the dreamlike state he had just left, wondering what was real and what was only within his mind. His fractured psyche weighed each option, trying to decipher the riddle. With great effort, he lifted himself off his knees and approached his son.

"Will?" He paused, seeing how the boy flinched back from his approach. "Son, what did you just see? What happened to me?"

The boy could barely make eye contact, brushing away tears with the back of his hand. The pine cone he once cradled discarded to his right. A slight tremble coursed through him as he sat there, trying to avoid his father's eyes and words.

"Will ... Will, I'm sorry you had to see that, but I don't really know what just happened. I was trying to remember." He knelt, getting eye level with Will, trying to comfort his son. "I'm sorry, Will." He looked past his son to the incline they had descended. "I think I know where we lost your mom and brother, though. Look." He pointed to the top of the grade where the thick cluster of trees grew. "We have to go back up. I'm pretty sure they're waiting for us near there, okay?"

Will glanced up the incline and then back at Micah. Dread still lingered on his face as he finally responded. "But ... but isn't the mechanic up there somewhere? Isn't he looking for us?"

Micah shook his head, moving forward with the solace, even though his mind still contemplated Clyde's whereabouts. "I don't think so, boy. I'm pretty sure we lost him." He reached out and gently cupped Will's chin, making sure the boy was looking into his eyes. "Listen to me, William. I'm here and he can't hurt you. I won't let him or anyone else hurt any member of this family. Understand?"

A feeble and very unconvincing nod came from the boy's head.

A similar response came from Micah, staring into his son's brown eyes. A brief chuckle followed, lightening the tenseness of the exchange. "Good. We need to go, okay? Let's find your mom and David."

27

A SMALL GAME TRAIL ran northwest along the slope, barely noticeable to the untrained eye. Decades of small mammals scurrying up and down the grade disturbed the fallen leaves and needles. David saw it first, glimpsing a flash of gray fur disappearing around a pine's trunk. He thought it might help ease the agonizing pain in his ankle by following the thin path of hard-packed earth instead of the blanket of dead organic material.

He and his mother worked their way up it, supporting one another with laborious and painful strides. Lynn threw her arm around David's waist, easing him upwards while grimacing and holding her side. He rested an arm along her shoulders, taking weight off the ankle as they moved forward.

A rock outcropping jutted through the forest floor near the top of the incline, reaching a dozen or more feet above. Once they reached it, Lynn stopped and leaned against the granite, taking long breaths. A natural shelf in the rock formation allowed David to sit next to her, resting his injury. There was no time to relax, though. Lynn's eyes frantically scanned, searching for whatever was out there.

David sat and rubbed his ankle, exhaling slowly with each stroke. A grimace struck his face with each touch, regardless of how gentle he tried to be. Internally, he knew something was severely wrong, dislocation or fracture, and the pain did not outweigh the fear swirling within his mind.

Once her breathing slowed, Lynn glanced up at the morning sun, wondering how long and how far they had traveled. Direction seemed foreign as she dropped her eyes, looking around, wondering where they were and if they were getting closer to Micah and Will. Nothing but thick vegetation in all directions: oaks, pines, saplings, and the unfortunate rotting trees from centuries past. *Damnit, Micah! Damnit! Where are you? How did you lose us?*

Frustration and worry grew within her gut, not knowing their next move. *How could they continue with an injured ankle and possibly broken ribs? Where were they going? How long would it take for someone to find them, confront them, harm them? Could she protect her son if Clyde came at her?*

She halted her brooding thoughts and questions and looked at David, feeling empathy and anger simultaneously. This was wrong. This vacation was supposed to be their chance for renewal, absolution for past sins. Forgiveness, even. How did it come to this?

The anger intensified as she watched her son, but she couldn't subdue the feeling. She had to be strong. She couldn't allow the stress and anxiety to control her behavior and actions. A facade was needed to conceal how badly she was hurt, scared, and panicked by each sound transmitted around her. Survival and sanity depended on it.

"David, can you keep going? I mean, can you make it a little farther, baby?"

David released his swollen ankle, eyes welled up from the pain, and addressed her. "Yeah ... I think so, Mommy. It just hurts!" The last word elongated with a whimper.

"I know, I know, baby. But ... but your dad and brother," her voice cracked as brother exited her mouth, "are up there somewhere. Where it's flatter." She paused her motherly coo, staring at the last stretch of the incline. "We can do this together. Let's finish this and find them, okay?"

David nodded, attempting to mirror his mother's sham of positivity. He knew she was doing this for him, just like he knew she was hiding the severity of her injuries.

"All right then, son. Let me help you up." As she shuffled over, still holding her arm tight against her body to protect her ribs, she noticed a streak of blood on the back of the boy's shirt.

More aggressively than intended, she turned the boy's torso, lifted the soiled *Star Wars* T-shirt, and examined him, searching for a wound. She found nothing. Not a scrape or scratch.

"What, Mom? What is it?"

"I thought you were bleeding. There's a streak of blood on the back of your shirt." She looked down at her forearm, noticing how her cut had already clotted and looked terrible. Irritated and red. It needed to be cleansed. *This isn't from my arm. What the f—?*

Her eyes darted to the stone crag his back had rested against, seeing a blotch of crimson dripping below to a small oval pool near where he had sat. She followed the streak upwards, where the granite ended above their heads. Something severely injured or deceased was on top of the rock.

David saw the dread on her face as he watched her eyes shift upwards. Alarm setting in, his eyes followed hers to the top of the rock. He jumped, nearly rolling back down the incline. "What is that, Mom? Is it on me?" His voice was shrill and infused with panic. He whirled, hopping on one foot, trying to see the back of his shirt.

She stood, getting a few paces away from the dark puddle. She reached for his arm, gripping tighter than she realized, stabilizing his unbalanced turns. Her gaze left the blotted stone seat and again traveled upward, not wanting to know what happened but needing answers. Her neck craned back, trying to peer over the crest of the rock, but it was too high. This mystery had to be solved.

She gestured toward David, urging him to join her. There were no words between them. Her glare remained fixated on the top of the granite, trying to glimpse whatever was there, dead or wounded. She slowly scaled the incline, circling the large stone step by step, while David limped behind her and gripped the back of her shirt. Once she reached eye level, she discovered the mystery. A look of shock coincided with a flinch at the sight.

David clung to her as they stood and looked at the brutality. His hot breath brushed against the side of her face. "What is that, Mom? A rabbit or something? Wolf?"

She glanced back, noticing a little intrigue mixed with a splash of horror stretching across his face at the sight before him. A smirk crossed her lips, watching the glow in his eyes. "I don't know, baby, but whatever it is, it's dead."

After a series of challenging steps, the two reached the top of the outcropping. The view from atop the rock was unobstructed and allowed a closer look. David remained hovering behind his mother, nervous as they both approached.

Within feet now, Lynn broke her gaze of the gore, looking around the scene, searching. To her left, she found a splintered pine limb, a cluster of immature cones gripping it with might. She reached down, picked it up, and extended it toward the bloody mess. A firm poke, followed by another. Caution heightened as they watched, expecting a reaction from whatever was there.

The stick probed the matted fur a third time, and then with some effort, Lynn shifted underneath the bloody mess, lifting a part of it off the rock a few inches. Strings of sticky, brown, congealed blood clung to the carcass as it lifted, stretching longer with each inch raised off the surface.

The sight affected David, resulting in a series of gags and coughs as he turned away, unable to watch. Lynn heard the commotion behind her and dropped the stick to help her son. As she did, her peripheral vision caught something unexpected. A figure loomed above them, standing at the base of the incline. Watching them.

28

Reuniting with the lost was imperative, and no alternative was acceptable. They had to reconnect. Survival depended on it. The climb back up the steep slope was laborious and challenging, but necessary. Hidden roots protruded through the arid, sunbaked earth, blanketed by fallen leaves and shards of timber, creating unseen threats contrived to snag their feet and trip them up.

The mind-twisting trip down memory lane delivered Micah what he needed to start the search. After reflecting on the mind-altering trance, clues pointed to the tight cluster of large trees straddling the base of the incline. *It funneled us one way, and they went the other. That's where we'll start.*

Nearing the top, and after several rests to catch their labored breath, Micah stopped. Will stalled a few paces behind, hands on his knees, and buckled over with exhaustion. He turned and looked back at his son, sweat matting his oily hair in the morning sun. "Will? Boy, did you hear that?"

Will diverted his eyes from the slope, focusing on his disheveled father, panting heavily. He shook his head, not understanding what he was being asked.

Micah cocked his head, unsettled by what his senses were revealing. "You sure? I thought I heard a car in the distance."

Will held out his right arm, gesturing for him to wait. He struggled to gather the words to respond, confused in his own right by the inquiries. "A car? No, Dad. We're in the middle of the forest."

Micah chewed his lip, wondering what he had heard in the distance. *It sounded like a car. Was it a car? What the hell are you thinking, Micah?*

Moments passed as he stood there, overanalyzing and second-guessing himself. A reversion to past strategies snuck through the blur, deep breaths following. He closed his eyes, thinking, planning. *Control it, Micah, control it. You are in control.*

Will called out again, with no response. He watched his father, praying he didn't succumb to the trance-induced behavior from before. "Dad?"

An animal scurrying up a nearby pine brought Micah back. The sound of its claws gripping the brittle bark echoed through his skull. He opened his eyes, focusing on his son once more. "Never mind, Will. It ... was nothing."

Will stiffened as he erected himself, puzzlement across his face. He had seen enough of Micah's erraticism in the past to question the truth. But what his father presented during the vision frightened him. So much fear swirled inside his mind from this entire experience. He needed to count on Micah for protection, guidance, and to find his mother and brother. But his trust was wavering.

"Come on, Will. It levels out just past the groupings of trees, there." An index finger pointed ahead, thirty paces uphill at the cluster they had maneuvered around during the sprint. "They're up there, son, waiting for us. I promise, Will." A smile crossed his lips as he spoke, trying to sound confident, but precariousness danced in his eyes. He did not know what to believe.

Will gave no reply. He simply dropped his eyes to the ground again and proceeded with cautious, long strides upward, checking his footing by bouncing with each step.

Micah remained in front, glancing back every few steps and offering supportive yet speculative advice. Reaching the top, he faced his son, offering a hand to pull him to the top, which was reluctantly accepted. With Will safe on flat, stable ground, Micah buckled over, taking deep breaths as he watched his son collapse to the forest floor, fatigue taking over.

With the hard part of the journey complete, and after collecting themselves, they sought evidence or traces of the others. Ignoring the west side, which they had rounded together, they opted to go the east side, recalling this was the direction Lynn and David took during the chaos of the sprint. Hoping for a response, their muffled chants of "Lynn" and "David" whistled through the woods as they searched the forest floor for tracks.

A series of saplings branching off the main cluster ushered them farther east around a bend. Micah led, weary with each step, eyes dancing to his left and right as the vegetation thickened. The gradient became steeper as they continued, and Micah could see how the level ground broke away and diverted north. As they neared the break, he stopped, wondering if he was even heading in the right direction. No clues revealed themselves.

Frustration festered, tormenting his twisted thoughts. A series of erratic turns ensued as he searched, finding nothing but thick, overgrown forest obstructing clear views in all directions.

What should I do? What should I do? Think, Micah, think!

As desperation settled in, he abandoned the prudence of stealth and silence. A series of screams exited his lungs, magnified by the surrounding woods. "Lynn! Lynn! Where are you?"

"Dad! Be quiet! What are you doing?" Will held a finger to his lips, trying to get his father's attention. "You said we had to be quiet because...."

Micah continued yelling, ignoring his son's pleas. The erraticism escalated with each passing moment as he swirled, forcing his eyes to find a clear path in any direction, but it wasn't possible. The forest seemed to encircle him, slowly closing in on all sides, squeezing him tighter and tighter. *What the hell is happening? What is this?*

He watched as the thick canopy enclosed, blocking out the morning sun, bringing a sense of claustrophobia to the surroundings. Panic struck immediately as Micah searched for an escape, holding his arms out to stop the incoming branches. The scent of pine and oak filled his nose as he dropped to his knees, eyes shut tightly, shielding himself from the perceived inevitable. He tried to turn away from the encroaching onslaught. Limbs and vines entwined around his waist, ankles, and wrists, holding him. Squeezing the life out of him.

"DAD! DADDY!"

Micah's eyes popped open. Will's deafening, distraught scream snapped him free of his vision, steering him away from the eccentric delusion. Struggling with reality and these waking nightmares, he remained on his knees, eyes locked on his sobbing son. His mind teetered momentarily, striving to deliver some sense of understanding before re-establishing. *What is wrong? What the hell is wrong with you, Micah? Am I ... crazy?*

Suddenly, he diverted his empathetic eyes, looking beyond his son into the never-ending forest. His eyes moved to his left and right as he whirled a 360. He gestured at Will with both hands to stay still.

"*Shh*, boy."

Will's shaking and sobs escalated, not knowing if this was real or another erratic meltdown. How could he tell the difference?

"Will!" His voice was firm, overbearing. "Control it. You have to, son." He stepped closer as he walked, always scanning. "I know you're scared. Hell, I am too, Will, but I need you to listen to me right now. I heard it again."

Micah reached out and pulled Will to him, gripping the boy in a tight embrace, back to chest so that their eyes roamed together. "I heard it again, boy." His whisper in Will's ear was vengeful and odd. "The car."

Will looked over his shoulder at his father's grizzled face, craning his slender neck and trembling with fear as he listened. His gaze fixated on his father's eyes, watching them twitch as he scoured the environment. The voice protruding from Micah's throat was different, almost foreign to his ears. The smooth, subtle delivery of each syllable packed with contempt. *Who was this man? Where did my Dad go?*

"You can hear it, right? The hatchback?" Micah pulled his face away from Will's ear, cocking his head, listening to the sounds of the forest, never loosening his grip across Will's torso.

Instantly, a chuckle exited Micah's mouth, followed by a devious grin. *The fuckin' car was fine all along!* His theory and thoughts came to full fruition as his eyes met what his ears revealed. There it was, between hundreds of feet of dense forest and vegetation, floating along the sporadic tree line flowing west. The car. Their car. The damn hatchback that was the root of all the shit they had endured the last day and a half, driving along the meandering mountain road. Running, not parked in a hillbilly's shitty garage.

29

Panic raced through Lynn's veins like ice water as her vision focused on the man looming above. She stiffened, standing a little taller and guarding her son, instinct taking over.

He leered down at them, eyes beady and dark. A pocket knife danced in his hand as he cleaned his grimy fingernails. He paused his grooming, staring at the nails with approval before nodding in their direction, face twisted with disdain.

Lynn didn't respond to his nod, taking a few strides backward toward her son instead. She didn't know this man. It wasn't Clyde.

"What's a pretty li'l thing like you doin' out here?" His voice was high, lecherous.

Lynn returned the leer, observing the short man and his blue-collar attire. His lack of height was evident, even with the worn, brown construction boots adding an inch or two.

Eyes locked with hers, he called out a second time, the syllables slithering off his tongue. "Don't be coy, woman. Whatcha doin' out here, all alone with that ... boy?" He narrowed his eyes, waiting and expecting acknowledgment.

Lynn glanced at David, who returned her skeptical look. This stranger's reference to her son was revolting.

The man's greasy, long hair hanging out the back of his trucker hat and soiled coveralls tucked into the boots didn't hide his frailness. He seemed sickly, malnourished. His bony features made him look like a human hanger in oversized clothes.

Her gut feeling was to flee, run and never stop, but fear shuffled its way back in, paralyzing her. She took another step backward, blocking David from view, never glancing away from the dark, menacing orbs fixated on her.

He slowly folded up the knife, dropping it in his front pocket. "See ya found my boy's handiwork there." The man gestured toward the rocky crag behind them.

Lynn glanced back, seeing the rotting carcass baking in the morning sun. Her attention steered back to the stranger, unsure if he was a threat.

"What's wrong, woman? Cat got ya tongue or somethin'?" He stepped forward down the slope, cocking his head, a twisted grin forming across his face.

"What do you want?" The sudden response blurted out with agitation and worry, alarm ascending with each passing moment she watched him.

As he took another step, his grin morphed into a yellow, tobacco-stained, gap-toothed smile. "Well, well, well, I reckon she can speak after all." He dropped his glare briefly and stared at the forest floor. "I believe I asked ya a question, miss. Not sure who taught ya manners, but my momma always told me to answer people when they ask ya somethin'." There was a level of contempt and disappointment in his tone.

No response came this time. A slight tremble flowed through her body, not understanding what was happening, fearing the worst. *Was this guy some goon working with Clyde, hunting her and her son? Or was he just some creepy hillbilly getting his rocks off? What were his intentions?*

"Well, to each his own, I suppose." He released a saturated breath, rolling his eyes. "Damn boy can't help himself, though. Touched by the devil, that one is. Been killing critters since he was four." He broke his gaze and raised an eyebrow, thinking. "Maybe even three."

"Wh ... what the hell are you talking about? What do you want from us?" she screamed.

Instantly, the grin vanished, replaced with loathing. A menacing sneer crossed his face as he eyed her, watching, stalking. His eyes narrowed and focused as though honing in on a target in his crosshairs. "Guess you don't know manners, after all. Well, there's always a way to learn. Know what I mean ... pretty li'l thing?" Every word authoritative, lustful.

Lynn took another step back, watching as he reached into his pocket. "Did he send you? Clyde?" The inquiry belted from her throat, words jumbled together in desperation.

He paused, frozen by the question. After a few tense moments, he removed the pocket knife again, unfolding the blade and staring through her. A slight chuckle sprang forth, followed by the familiar grin. "Yeah, that's right. Clyde sent me." He held the knife down at his side, the sun's rays glistening off the polished steel. "Fat son of a bitch told me ya been real bad, and he wants me to bring ya to him."

Tears welled in her eyes, listening to the news. "Why? What did we do? We didn't do anything!"

He shook his head from side to side, clicking his tongue. "That's what they all say, darlin'. Every one of 'em."

Their eyes remained locked on each other. A silent standoff. Then he sprang forward, descending the slope, not stopping, heading right for them, knife clutched in his hand.

30

THE LAUGHS FLOWED UNCONTROLLABLY now, watching the car vanish from sight behind the tree line. Micah nearly buckled over from the fit, realizing how naïve he had been, how he had played right into this twisted lunatic's trap.

Moments passed as he collected himself, staring out through the vast forest, mind teetering.

He planned this. He knew we would run. Knew we couldn't handle the terrain, the challenges the forest brings. Now he's hunting us in our car. I'm betting we aren't the first either.

His head wavered as he pondered the thought. Still attempting to rationalize the man's actions. *The man and woman from the shop. The wallet, the purse. I bet they were the first.*

Will watched, observing his father, hearing the hysterical laughter followed by the odd looks as paranoia grasped hold. "Daddy, what's happening? What's wrong?"

The fear in the boy's voice brought Micah around, dropping the mind-bending thoughts. "Everything's fine, Will. Daddy's okay, I promise. It's just ... the damn car, boy."

The lie lingered in the air as he spoke, attempting to soothe and calm his son. He knew things weren't fine, their situation wasn't improving, and he wasn't helping. He was losing control; he felt it dwindling away with the breeze. Recapturing it was imperative if he was going to beat Clyde at his own game, reclaim his sanity. Reclaim Lynn.

Will shook his head, kneeling, squeezing his eyes shut, trying to leave this place, this hell he had been ushered into. He could neither believe a word his father spoke, nor trust his actions. Utter hopelessness swallowed him, knowing there was nothing he could do but follow Micah, irrational or not.

Micah approached, seeing the trouble unfold. This was his fault. He knew it. Deep down, he understood the harm he had caused and knew this wasn't the place to reconcile. They had to keep moving, searching for the others, before Clyde found them first.

He knelt, eye level with his son. "Will, I know you're scared. I am too, but you have to trust me and follow my lead. We have to keep moving, son. We have to find your mom and David before—" The speech paused as he watched his son, eyes still tightly shut. He realized he wasn't getting through to him, not making the difference he needed. "Son, you need to listen to me and do as I say, okay?"

The sudden change of tone struck a nerve, forcing a response. Will opened his eyes, his father inches from his face, sternness flowing with each breath. The proximity caused a flinch, and he leaned backward, afraid of what he saw, afraid of his father. He barely recognized the man in front of him, and it terrified him how different he appeared.

With raised eyebrows, a dark scowl, and a voice full of tension, Micah asked, "Did you hear me, young man?" Every word stretched out for emphasis.

Will's stress and anxiety brewed to a boil as he peered at his father, not knowing if a nod would suffice. Slowly, he dropped his eyes to the forest floor, feeling a spiraling mixture of confusion, hate, and terror. Not understanding his overwhelming feelings and without realizing his actions, he delivered a feeble nod, never looking up.

"Good." The glower distorted into a slick grin. This look was different, contorted and full of sickness. "Now we have to go. My gut tells me that the damn car is aiming right for Lynn and David."

For the first time in minutes, Will mustered the courage to speak, lifting his view to his ever-changing father. "Why ... why do you keep talking about a car, Dad?"

The sudden inquiry took him by surprise. "The car, son, our hatchback. We just watched it pass on the road over there." He paused as he gestured down the slope, taking in the vast wilderness and dense forest where the car meandered along the road. "The road's there."

His circumstance devoid of clarity, Will's confusion intensified. "Our car, Dad?"

Micah's face mimicked his son's, puzzlement stretching from ear to ear. "Our hatchback, Will. The tan one. It was right there, and that mechanic was driving it, remember?"

Will shook his head, trembles rippling through his body, trying to comprehend, trying to understand what was happening. He didn't know what to believe. "Wh ... what are you talking about, Dad?"

The look on Will's face and his words fractured Micah's mind. His eyes again became erratic, darting as he paced in circles, searching for answers. *It was real, and that son of a bitch drove it. I'm not going crazy. I'm not going crazy! It was real!*

Suddenly, a shriek echoed through the dense forest, sending nesting birds fluttering high in the sky. The source wasn't near, but Micah knew the direction, whipping his head to the east. The voice was known too. It was Lynn's, and it sounded like she was screaming for her life.

In less than a heartbeat, Micah reached down, grasped Will's shaking wrist, and ran in the scream's direction, pulling his son along.

31

Shock set in, taking control as she watched the man stumble down the slope, aiming right for them. His steps were awkward, unbalanced. Something was wrong with his stride, inebriation or genetics, Lynn couldn't tell. She ignored his movement and saw the darkness swirling within his beady eyes. Eyes of a psychopath, a killer. Void of human qualities.

Instinct forced its way through the paralysis, releasing Lynn from its grasp. She staggered backward, colliding into her son, her eyes focused on the knife in the man's fist, how the steel glistened in the morning sun.

Through her pain, she continued shuffling backward, keeping a distance from the menace bearing down on them, never averting her view. Hands held out toward the monster, gesturing for it to halt, her shriek drifted through the canopy. "Stop! Stay away from me! Stay away from my son!"

But the pleas were ignored. Her fear fueled the man's motivation, driving him, steering his actions. His pace quickened, even with the lopsided steps, closing the distance between them.

Lynn dropped her glare, turning away from the man and his demented stare. She heaved David's arm around her shoulder, escorting him farther down the steep slope, negating all progress they'd made following the game trail.

Watching the two supporting each other, the man paused his treacherous romp, eyeing his wounded prey to note their injuries. Salivating and refocused, he pounced and resumed the chase.

The two worked together, stride for stride, making their way away from the threat, slowly gaining distance with each laborious step. Lynn's ribs throbbed with excruciating pain. Through gritted teeth, she forced herself on, carrying the bulk of David's weight.

Threats, curses, and slurs poured from the pursuing stranger's mouth as his trophies lengthened their lead. Anger fueled his screams, knowing he was losing this race.

Lynn glanced over her shoulder, seeing the threat in the distance, knowing he would never stop. She also knew her body couldn't continue much longer. Her heart hammered in her chest as adrenaline pumped aggressively through her blood, but it wouldn't last. Exhaustion and affliction would eventually win out, crippling her efforts.

As she whipped her head around, her left foot landed in a cavity beneath the littered forest floor. She stumbled, bringing David down with her. The weight of her son buckled her knees, and she fell face-first as David collapsed on his side, arms rushing toward his ankle.

Lynn pushed her torso off the ground, hands grasping the dried vegetation for leverage, her vision directed behind her, terror streaking her eyes. The man bearing the blade was on their heels and closing fast. A twisted sneer crossed his face.

She spun around, ass scraping the ground, as she watched him getting closer and closer. She pushed herself backward in a crab walk, barring access to her son, screaming, pleading for help. Finally, she lifted herself off the forest floor, grasped David, and yanked the boy up. With his arm back around her shoulders, the trek downward continued much slower.

The agony of each step dictated her speed. She cradled her side, supporting the ribs with her free hand while trying to shoulder most of her son's weight. With each step, the pain escalated, pulsating through her. She couldn't continue. This sprint turned into a marathon, and crossing the finish line first escaped certainty. With flight out the window, it was time to fight. Fight for her family. Fight for her life.

Her eyes flicked to their pursuer once more. The distance between the two parties was maybe ten paces. Her vision meandered, scanning the area, searching for anything: rocks, branches, sticks, anything. Lying to her left was the remnant of an oak burned in a previous wildfire. The trunk, charred black, thick as a wine barrel, and several paces long, was positioned perpendicular to the grade.

Lynn turned and hobbled toward it, still supporting her son's weight. Once she reached the burnt tree, she rounded the stump, kneeling behind it. David dropped to the ground, his back leaning against the blackened bark. She looked at him, gazing at her firstborn, seeing the tears, quivering lips, and terror plastered across his face.

The curses, vulgar threats, and carnal wish list flowed heavier from the man's throat, knowing he was closing in, seconds away from fulfilling his sinful desires. He followed their lead, awkwardly, toward the fallen tree. The downward trek had ill effect on the permanent affliction of his left leg; the unbalance to his steps was more apparent with each stride.

Her frantic eyes scanned the ground, searching for a miracle. Behind her, the man's voice amplified. He was within five strides now.

David covered his ears with his hands, squeezing his eyes shut and cowering against the trunk.

She stood to face him, this monster. She clawed and ripped at the tree's trunk, pulling off pieces of charred bark, heaving bits in his direction. Pieces sailed left, right, and short as she screamed at him. Screamed for him to stop this madness.

The flying fragments forced him to freeze. He held up his hands, fingernails thick with blackened grime, blocking his face from any collision. In the frenzy, a thick chunk struck him square in the chest, but the scorched wood crumbled on contact, lacking significant punch. The bark wasn't a threat. Licking his lips, he pounced, reaching the tree.

She took one step backward, left heel digging into the slope, eyes locked on the man wielding the knife. The tree barred him from advancing, distancing her from demise. Her eyes flicked to her son, cradled against the trunk, before returning to the threat.

The obstacle barricaded him against his will. He lunged forward, stomach scraping against the burnt bark, swiping at her with the knife. Spittle flew from his mouth with each failed attempt. Curses flew from his yellow teeth.

Lynn flinched back with each fruitless thrust. Her eyes wandering, her mind fracturing. She wanted to run, force herself farther down the slope away from the danger, but ... her son. David. Maternal instinct broke through, driving the need to protect, the need to sustain. She forced herself forward, avoiding a sloppy swipe by the man, gripping his wrist with both hands.

He yanked and struggled to free himself, twisting his wrist, trying to maneuver the blade, cursing, slobbering.

Lynn struggled to hold on, watching his maniacal eyes. His frail frame hid the strength his drive provided. Her vision fled to the blade, slowly watching it creep toward her wrist, ready to slice in and tear the flesh. Her grip was loosening, failing her.

In the exchange's madness, the man's eyes left her and glanced to the right. The sick, twisted grimace dissolved instantly as his eyes bulged, pupils magnified. His view was David and the thick log the boy brought down on his temple.

32

THE BLOOD-STAINED LOG FELL to their right, settled amongst the brittle leaves and needles. David dropped it to the ground after striking the man and watching his limp body collapse. Hysteria ensued, realizing what he had done.

Lynn embraced her son as they crumpled to the forest floor. He wept in her arms, wringing the back of her shirt with clenched fists, letting all emotions exit his body. The occasional scuffle with Will occurred, chalk it up to sibling rivalry, but violence wasn't in his blood. He had never struck someone with ill intent before. Yet, in the moment of crisis, seeing his mother in peril, he acted.

After the sobs slowed, she pulled back, cupping his face with her palms, staring at him with loving eyes. "You did good, baby. Everything's okay now, son."

He watched her but couldn't respond. The emotional outpouring crippled his ability to speak, allowing only a series of stuttered breaths.

Slowly, her attention moved to the burnt tree. She stiffened, sitting taller, attempting to peer beyond the tree to see where the man was. The tip of a work boot caught her attention. She dropped her grip on David and staggered to her feet, advancing toward the tree, leaning over.

There he was, on his side, facing them, eyes shut. Thick saturation poured from the wound on his head, blood dripping down his neck. There was a subtle flare of his nostrils. He was alive.

Lynn studied the man, the grimy gray attire, his bony shoulders, the greasy hair, emotions swirling in her core as she shifted over him. Her attention now on the nametag embroidered in red cursive letters on his coveralls. It read: Sid.

The knife he wielded minutes before was too close to his limp right hand. She had to retrieve it, eliminate any potential for a second round if he woke. She leaned away from the tree, addressing David. "Baby? Baby, I'll be right back, okay?"

The stuttered breaths slowed as he looked at her, blank-faced, unsure how to respond. So many emotions flooded his mind. He was lost.

She didn't wait for a response, moving around the tree and leering at the unconscious man, her steps slow as she approached, fists clenched and ready. Once within feet, she knelt, stretching her right hand toward the fallen blade, shifting her eyes between the knife and the senseless maniac. Her hand inched closer, brushing against the forest floor, nearly touching the handle. Then she grabbed it, pulling it toward her in a rapid motion, and backed away from the man.

She looked at the knife, turning it over in her hand, mind racing with a series of what-if scenarios. These dark questions weighed her down, her stress and emotions full to overflowing. Her sight moved to David. He was still staring blankly at her. A flood of sadness and guilt struck her as she peered at him, knowing he saved her life. His life too. Her broken ribs wouldn't allow her to fight, to protect. She knew she would succumb and not make it through another attack. She held back the tears and folded the knife closed, placing it safely in her back pocket.

She dropped her eyes to the forest floor, walking around the tree in David's direction. Her head lifted once she was in front of him. "We need to keep moving. I don't want to be around if he wakes. When he wakes, baby."

David nodded, trying to stand, leveraging his weight against the charred trunk. She swooped in, putting his arm around her neck and supporting her ribs. Her gaze flowed to the open forest, wondering if they should continue heading farther south, away from the shop and away from Sid. They couldn't climb again, neither had the strength, and their injuries prevented it. Their only chance was to hope the terrain was flat enough for stable walking if they continued east. She glanced up at the sky, seeing the sun positioned almost above them, and stepped toward it. She whipped around after a few strides, wondering if her ears were deceiving her. Amongst the clatter of birds, scurrying animals, and leaves rustling in the breeze, she thought she heard her name screamed in the distance. *Micah?*

A half hour passed with little progress shuffling on the uneven ground, but they shambled forward, distancing themselves. Lynn glanced behind them every few steps, scanning the forest and listening to the surrounding sounds.

As they cleared a thick stand of sycamores, the forest opened up, revealing flat land and something else. A structure. A building similar to the shop, same weathered yellow and blue paint. Once she eyed it, she ducked behind a copse of trees, pulling David with her. They sat there, backs supported by the trunks, silent, motionless, unsure of what to do next.

After collecting her thoughts, Lynn peered around the tree that concealed them, watching for movement, taking in the aging property. It was your standard four wall structure. Dirty and gritty with a few dust-caked windows, the rest broken. It seemed abandoned, void of human activity or use. Long forgotten for many years.

This might give us a chance to rest, regroup, and collect our strength. God, where are you, Micah? I need you. David needs you.

She inched her head out, scanning left and right. Everything was still. Nothing signaling that anyone was currently using the building, or had recently. *It could be a shelter, as long as it's vacant.*

She stood, helping her son get to his feet, then they exited the dense forest, entering the sunny open space and heading straight for the strange structure in the middle of the woods.

PART FOUR

THE BUNKER

33

Lynn and David slinked forward, cautious with each weary step. Their senses were heightened as they walked through the cleared land, looking in all directions as they came to the building's entrance. Someone boarded up the front door with plywood, preventing squatters or trespassers from entering. The rusty nails holding the piece in place were failing, and Lynn pried it off in two yanks. She looked behind them at the clearing before they went inside.

Upon entering, they had to allow their eyes to adjust to the dimness. Lynn searched the wall for a light switch, fingers nimbly stretching across the corroding drywall, finding one after a few moments. But there were no lights.

Lynn hugged the left side of the hall, avoiding crates obstructing a clear path, still pulling David behind her. Every few steps, she looked back through the opened door, praying Sid hadn't awoken and tailed them.

She didn't know where she was going, but she had to keep moving. "Keep up, David. Move!" she whispered, yanking her son by the hand without looking back, searching for any trace of her husband. Her pace slowed as she neared a doorway along the hall and a similar door across from it. The entire hall had matching doorways across from one another about every twenty paces. The doors were all closed.

David didn't know what was happening, only to follow her lead. Every few tugs, he pleaded for an explanation. "What is this place? Is that man chasing us, Mom?" His voice was shaky, confused.

She looked back at him, trying to hide her nervousness. "I don't know, baby," she answered, heart still racing from the altercation with Sid. "We need to get out of sight." She reached down and gripped the door's handle, finding it locked. "Shit!"

A loud shriek from the forest echoed through the long hall. Lynn whipped her head around, eyes moving to the once barricaded opening, expecting to see Sid, Clyde, or someone else. But she didn't. She saw the fear in her son's eyes as she locked onto him. "Everything's okay, David. Keep moving. Come on!"

They continued down the hall, stepping over piles of trash and squeezing past an old mattress leaning on its side. A broken dresser blocked most of the path in front of them. Lynn's attention shot to another door across the hall. It wasn't closed. Something in the doorway was holding it open.

Lynn maneuvered through the obstacles, never letting go of her son's hand, glancing back repeatedly. "This one's open. Hurry!" With minimal strength, she pushed on the door with her free hand and shoulder, forcing the door to open far enough for both to slip through.

She pushed David through the opening first, keeping her eyes fixated on the entrance. After he entered, she, too, slipped through the gap. Before closing the door, she caught a glimpse of motion near the structure's entrance.

She cupped her mouth to prevent the scream's escape, gently closing the door with the other hand, and locking it. She backed away from the door, one step at a time, making sure David was behind her. *Where are you, Micah? Where the hell are you?*

David reached out to her, gripping the back of her shirt in desperation, pleading for answers. He buried his face in her back. Sobs of hysteria began as they continued to back away from the door, finally reaching a wall.

She faced her son, saying, "David. David, I need you to stop right now, baby." She forced his face from her wrinkled T-shirt by grabbing the sides of his face, his eyes sewn tightly shut. "We need to be quiet now. Do you understand, David? Do you?"

David squeezed his eyes tighter, nodding while mumbling incoherently.

Instinctively, she hugged his face to her body, gently stroking his hair and cupping the back of his head. He wailed into her torso while she spoke soft, quiet words convincing him to stop crying. This was her firstborn, the spark that ignited a mother's love, and she would do anything for him, even die. But that wasn't her plan today. Her plan was to protect, to escape whatever danger stalked them, and to survive.

The sobs lessened with each passing second that she cooed to him, eventually allowing her the opportunity to scan the room. On the wall they were backed up against was a narrow window, midday rays penetrating through it. However, even if she could open it, she wouldn't fit through it. Nothing but scattered newspaper and broken glass on her left. She scoured the rest of the room. To her surprise, she found another door on her right. She had to try it.

"David? David, honey ... we need to move, okay?" She gave him a slight shake, gripping his shoulders. "We need to go. Now, son." The words brought his face up from her body. "We need to be brave, okay?"

His eyes were open now, fixated on hers, seeing the love and hope she displayed. He didn't answer her question. A mere nod delivered his response.

With understanding established, she reached down, grabbed his hand, and led him to their right. The door they approached was much smaller than the one for this room. *But what was on the other side? A bathroom, living quarters?* These were minor thoughts floating in her mind, compared to the threat outside and the whereabouts of her husband and son. She couldn't think about that right now. She had to act.

Standing in front of the door, she reached for and turned the handle, opening it with ease. As it cracked, she buckled over, coughing and gagging. Dropping David's hand, she covered her mouth and nose, choking and dry heaving from the exposure. She took three steps back from the doorway, trying to prevent her son having the same experience by forcing him back with one arm. The fetid scent of death nearly brought her to her knees. In the moment, all thoughts of stealth and silence were forgotten as she coughed and wheezed, willing her body not to retch.

Panic struck David again, not understanding what just happened to his mother. He clung to her, trying to force her upright, hollering and screaming in distress.

Then, they heard it again. The scream. It was muffled but close. *Maybe right outside the building?* Lynn did her best to control the nausea as she turned and faced the locked door, spittle dripping from her open mouth. David was already behind her, driving his face into her back and gripping her T-shirt.

She never broke her stare, expecting the door to be broken down any instant. With tears streaking her cheeks, she guarded her son, the only way a mother could, prepared for whatever was about to happen.

The yell came again from the hall, but it wasn't what she expected. It was familiar, non-threatening. She dropped her guard, cocking her head to the side, listening, really listening.

It sounded again, nervous and anxious. "Lynn, David? Where are you?"

34

Lynn's eyes widened at the voice, and she rushed to the door, escaping David's grip. Reaching down for the handle, she flipped the lock and turned the knob, pulling the door open as far as she could. There he was in the dim light, anguish dripping from every pore, thinking the worst. Micah was here. He found them when all seemed lost. He followed through with his commitment as a husband and father.

She squeezed through the door's opening, bolting forward and wrapping her arms around his neck in a tight embrace. She sobbed into his chest. Tears of joy replaced tears of despair, knowing they were back together and safe. For now.

David peeked out of the doorway and quickly hobbled to Micah, embracing both his parents.

Lynn and Micah stood there holding one another, releasing all their pent-up emotions. Before their vacation, so much animosity and torment had developed. So many ill feelings, memories, and thoughts. But they were a family, and they were going to escape this situation. Together.

After a few more moments, Lynn lifted her head from his chest, and her eyes searched to the left and right. "Where's ... where's Will?"

The question piqued David's interest, and he looked at his father, waiting expectantly for the answer.

Micah stiffened, pulling back some. *Why the hell is she looking at me like that? Didn't I just rescue you two?* He looked down the hall to his right, toward the opened entrance, and then back at his wife's worried eyes. "He's fine. Everything's fine, babe."

She cocked her head, dropping the warm embrace and taking a step back. "You didn't answer my question, Micah. Where the hell's Will?"

He could see the anxiety creeping into her with each passing second, not knowing where her baby boy was. "I'm ... I'm sorry, Lynn. I didn't mean to worry you." He paused, looking down the hall. "He's outside."

Her glare shifted to the entrance before returning to Micah. "You just," eyes narrowed, "left him outside? Why isn't he here with us, Micah?"

Why doesn't she appreciate anything I've done for her? She realizes what I went through to find her, right?

He released a long breath. "I didn't know what I was walking into, Lynn." He stepped forward, trying to explain. "I hoped you two came in here, but I didn't know if someone else followed you." He held her eyes, reaching out and caressing her arms with gentle strokes. "I had to protect him, keep him safe, in case...." He trailed off, knowing she could finish the sentence.

After staring into his blue eyes for a few seconds, she nodded slightly. It was the right decision. He did what was necessary when everything else seemed lost. She didn't like the idea of her baby boy being alone in the middle of the woods, but at least he was safe. "Let's get him and leave." Pausing, she looked toward the open door. "That maniac's out there somewhere, and I'm not about to let him near us again."

Instantly, a silhouette formed in the entrance doorway. The sunshine illuminating the form. It was short, petite. It was Will. He poked his head into the opening, waiting for his eyes to adjust to the dimness. Then he saw her. And David too. He sprang forward, weaving amongst the crates and sliding around the old mattress. No sound came from his lips until he was in front of them. His family. The separation only lasted a few trying hours, yet it felt like an eternity.

Barreling forward, he wrapped his arms around Lynn's waist, holding on with all his might. His face buried in her torso as he wept. Tears of joy or sadness, he didn't know. But he was back with her and his brother. They were together.

Lynn held her baby boy, squeezing him despite the pain in her ribs.

David left Micah's side and embraced his brother, hugging him from behind while gripping Lynn's shirt. Micah watched as the three shared this moment, this love. It brought a smile to his face, seeing the compassion they shared with each other. A family reunited.

But the blissful feelings slowly vanished the longer he watched. Deep within, a new feeling came crawling from the dark pit. A feeling of self-righteousness, of envy, of jealousy.

I'm the hero, right? Why am I not receiving love and respect? What the hell is this? He clenched his jaw as he glared at them.

35

"Micah. Micah! Are you even listening to me?" Lynn demanded, her tone emitting urgency.

There was no response. He just stood there under the rusty light fixture, lips parted and mumbling. The sun coming through the broken window highlighted the profile of his stubbled face as he stared in her direction, but not at her. He was somewhere else, thinking. Dark thoughts and memories mixing like a twisted, potent cocktail.

Why don't they love me, respect me? Why? I'm a changed man. It was me who reunited everybody and tried to get us help. Me! They can't see what I've gone through, lived through? They didn't even care when my mother passed, when she suffered alone in that hospice bed. I was there, not them, all those long, somber nights. Now they're turning against me, together.

"Micah, I'm talking to you."

His mind refocused, and he looked at his wife, the woman who once loved him. The woman that now loathed him.

Why can't she see the real me?

"I'm sorry, babe. I was just thinking about how glad I am that we are back together." His face morphed, a weak smile attached to his lips.

Her brow furrowed as she cocked her head, staring back at him. "I'm happy too. I was so scared out there without you, without Will." Her vision drifted down to her son, still clinging to her side. "I thought I was going to lose him."

Micah stepped forward, inching closer to the three, concern flowing through his actions and words. "We were scared too, Lynn. What do you mean, lose him? Did something happen? Did that monster find you two? Clyde?"

She peered back at him, seeing the trouble manifesting. "No, no, it wasn't Clyde. But ... but some asshole tried to hurt us, Micah. Some skinny pervert with a knife. David here—"

Micah cut her off mid-sentence. "A knife? What the hell happened?" He stepped forward, looked her over, then reached down and cupped David's chin, lifting his face and searching for wounds or injuries. "Are you hurt? Did he hurt you, cut you somewhere?"

Lynn reached out and gently caressed Micah's arm with one hand while turning his face toward her with the other. "We're okay, Micah. Everything's okay. A little banged up from the forest."

Micah studied her attentively, listening concentratedly to each syllable of speech.

"David twisted his ankle, and I fell while running. I may have broken a rib or two, but we're okay. As long as we're together, we're okay." She released her massaging grip from Micah's forearm and cradled her side. A look of grimace followed as she gritted her teeth.

"Oh, no! How did you ... how did you get all the way here? In your condition? I mean ... the two of you?"

"Hey, hey, hey! It's okay, Micah. We worked together, that's all. And ... as I was saying, David here," she paused, staring at her son with pride and love, "he saved my life. He saved both our lives."

Micah's attention turned to his oldest son. "What! How? What happened?"

"Micah, don't worry, we're both fine. But it could have been bad if ..." her voice trailed off, tears welling in her eyes, "if David hadn't helped me out there against that maniac with the knife."

Micah urged her to continue with a series of rapid nods.

She raised her shaky hand, wiping away a tear. "That monster had his knife, and he was about to cut me with it when—"

"I hit him, Dad."

Both their heads swiveled, looking at David, astonished by the brashness of their son.

"What? You did what, David?" Micah's voice was shocked.

"He was going to hurt us, hurt Mom, so I hit him with a log. Knocked his ass out too." David crossed his arms across his chest, smirking.

Micah ignored the confident curse, staring at his son, marveling at the young man. "You saved your mother, son." He paused, smiling back. "You saved us all, boy."

Lynn stood behind David, placing a hand on each shoulder, staring down at her son with pride. "Yeah, you did, buddy. If you hadn't acted, I don't know what would have happened if...." Her look flowed to Micah as she spoke, the pride vanishing. "No, no, no, that's wrong. I know what would have happened."

Micah met her eyes, watching the uncertainty unfold, searching for hints, wondering why she couldn't move beyond the past. *This wasn't my fault! I don't know how we got separated. I would have helped, Lynn, but I had to drag Will with me the whole way.*

"What's important is that we're here together." Lynn glanced around the dingy hall, releasing her gentle grip from David. "But I hate this place. Pretty sure something dead is in the next room."

Micah stiffened, thinking about outside, being back in the woods, back in the unknown. He looked around as well, cringing. "Well, this place has definitely seen better days, but it is a shelter. Maybe we should stay, watch, and listen for them." His vision returned to his family, all bunched together, staring at him. "Outside, we're just stupid, grazing sheep waiting for the wolf to pounce and feast."

"What if they come here, Dad? The crazy mechanic or the knife guy David creamed?" Will asked.

David stepped forward, nodding, as various scenarios played out in his head.

"We just have to pray that doesn't happen, boys." Micah met his younger son's eyes, attempting to assure him this was a haven. "At least in here, we can hide, maybe defend ourselves if it comes to it."

Lynn shifted, anxiety bubbling again. "What are you saying, Micah? Stay in here and wait it out. Wait for those monsters to attack again? Micah, you weren't there. You didn't live through it like me and David."

"Lynn ... just listen to me, please!" Micah looked around the hall again, noticing the floor littered with debris and old, ripped trash bags. "Maybe there's something here we can use to protect ourselves. Maybe if we search this shithole, we'll find something useful."

Lynn placed a hand on each son's shoulder, staring at her husband, searching his blue eyes. Silent.

Micah returned the stare, holding it and not backing down. He believed in this plan. He still needed to protect his family despite his ill feelings. Safety required knowing your surroundings and being able to detect threats from any direction. That wasn't possible out in the open forest. Now that he understood Clyde wasn't giving up the hunt and additional threats were present, the forest was a deadly idea.

"Help me find something so we can end this. You can trust me, Lynn. We can do this together."

Lynn held her glare, listening to Micah's promising words, thinking. Thoughts of the present and past swirled in her mind, flooding her with emotions. She also considered keeping the knife in her back pocket a secret from him. Moments passed before she finally accepted his pleas and nodded in his direction. She wouldn't be much help with her broken ribs, but she would do her part, play her role. Her boys depended on it.

Micah smiled at her, acknowledging this was the only logical choice; they might stand a chance if they overnighted in this fetid nightmare of a structure. Then again, maybe they wouldn't need a chance.

36

THE FOUR SHUFFLED THROUGH the drab, dark hallway, dumping the contents of long-forgotten trash bags and rifling through cardboard boxes. Searching for anything useful. Will trudged along with Micah in the exit's direction while David rejoined his mother, looking through debris near the entrance, finding nothing.

Who left all this shit here? Micah thought, squatting, sifting through a pile of paper. *What was this place? It wasn't a mechanic's shop.* He stood and strolled to his right, eyeing something black, metallic.

"Dad, Dad? This orange box has old clothes in it." Will knelt, peeking inside. With his forefinger and thumb, he lifted a shirt from the box, studying it in the dim light.

"Okay, son. Keep looking, boy?" Micah stated, not turning to face Will. He was busy shuffling through a metal filing cabinet, tossing old photographs to the ground one at a time. *Old clothes, magazines, bills, and useless photos. Shit, there has to be something somewhere.* "Hey, Dad, there's a picture on it, like the picture on the shop."

Micah froze, slowly dropping the remaining photographs from his hand. His attention shifted, turning and staring at Will, seeing the boy holding a gray shirt with both hands examining it. "What, Will? A picture? Like ... the logo?"

Will held the shirt in front of him, holding it high so Micah could see.

Micah's eyes squinted, attempting to focus on the graphic design. There it was, all right. Clyde's shop, G. C. Motors Inc. stitched on the left breast, and the name Frank on the right in red cursive. *Was this another shop? What have they been up here doing?*

"See, Dad, right there." Will draped the shirt across his torso, pointing to the design. "It's like the one on the building."

"Yeah, Will, I see it, buddy. Good job." Micah cupped his chin in his hand, scratching the stubble.

From down the hall, a voice sprang out, collecting everyone's attention. It was Lynn, and it sounded like she made a discovery.

"Micah! Micah, come here, quick!"

Both he and Will sprang forward, moving down the hall in haste, avoiding the obstacles in their path. They were hovering over Lynn in mere seconds. Numerous U-Haul moving boxes were stacked waist-high against the hall's wall. One was open; all four huddled together to look inside.

"What is it, Mom?" Will's hands gripped the lip, peering over on his tiptoes.

"It's filled with purses, son. You know, the bags ladies carry on their shoulders?" She looked down at her son, giving him a nod. "Three of them, and they're old and used." She turned and faced Micah, her brow furrowed.

Micah leaned in as well, eyeing the leather and cloth bags with suspicion. After a few moments of silence, he reached in, grasping the strap of a light-colored one. Pulling it out and cradling it with both hands, he studied it, thinking. Instantly his eyes swelled, and he remembered. *The shop. The boxes in the shop. Shit, I didn't tell her.*

Studying his eyes and mannerism, Lynn witnessed the shift in his demeanor. "What ... what is it, Micah? What are these things? Why are they here?"

A subtle shake of Micah's head, trying to connect the dots. "I ... I don't know, babe. Goodwill items? Hand-me-downs forgotten in this dump?"

Lynn continued her stare, searching his blue eyes, knowing her husband, knowing when he was being dishonest.

Micah's attention returned to the box, looking over the handbags. *Shit, shit, shit! More purses equals more missing people. Dead people, probably. I bet all these boxes are full of the sick bastard's victims' belongings. I can't let her know I know the truth, though. She'll hate me even more, knowing I didn't tell her. God, what do I do?*

"What's in the others, Dad?" David asked.

"I'm sure it's more useless, old crap, son. Maybe the rest of some grandma's wardrobe or her dead husband's stuff?"

"Micah!" Lynn whipped her head in his direction.

"What?"

"Really? Dead grandmas? Is that what we need to fill their heads with, Micah?"

"Lynn, I don't know what this shit is or why it's here. It won't help us, though. We need to keep searching or come up with plan B."

"What alternative, Micah? There are two psychos running through the woods looking for us. One nearly ..." Lynn stopped her rant, swallowing hard. "One nearly ... killed me, Micah, and he would have killed David too." Her posture stiffened as she spoke, staring straight through her husband. "Is there something that can protect us? A knife, a gun? They're going to find us, Micah, and come in here and...."

Micah felt the intense pain and fear flowing through her core, and it hurt. Guilt crept in, digging its way inside his mind, grinding against his skull, followed by misery. He had nearly lost his wife and his son, and now he was questioning his sanity. And he couldn't control any of it.

Instead of responding, he reached out, gently pulling Lynn close to his body, embracing her. He cupped the back of her head, holding her tight against his chest, letting her release the hate, the anguish. Words would not fix their situation. Action was needed. And she was right; this abandoned dump had nothing of use, and the longer they stayed here, the closer they stayed to Clyde and Sid.

Tears ran down her cheeks as she gripped his sweatshirt, wringing it in her fists.

"*Shh, Shh*. I'm here, Lynn." His hands strayed to her face, holding each side with his palms, forcing her eyes upon his. "I wasn't there before, when you and David were attacked, but I'm here now, babe. I'm here."

She laid her head on his chest once more, looking at her two boys. A soft whisper came from her lips as her head slightly rose and fell with each of his breaths. "I know, Micah. I know, my love."

His brow furrowed at the loving response, glancing at the side of her face, wondering.

She lifted her head and looked at the box filled with old purses, releasing her grip from his shirt. "Let's keep looking. There are at least ten other boxes here. One has to have something in it we can use, right?"

Moments later, they set each box on the damp floor, flipping open the closed flaps. The four stood there viewing the contents of the boxes. More purses, billfolds, belts, shoes, and one had at least a dozen old license plates from California and nearby states.

"What the hell is this?" Lynn asked, eyes flipping to her husband.

"Just old crap that no one wanted, I guess, babe."

But his subconscious was working overtime, slowly fitting all the pieces together. *These are his trophies. No, no, that's not right. Their trophies, the two sick bastards. This is what's left of their victims after luring them in like sheep. He did the same with us, but ...*

He turned, looking out the formerly boarded-up door of the building, then returned to the boxes' contents. *But we got away. Are we the first?*

"Is there anything inside the wallets, Mom? Is there money in them?" David asked.

Lynn glanced at her son. "Only one way to find out, right?" She knelt, sliding a box toward her, causing the boys to flinch as it scraped against the concrete foundation. Reaching inside, she lifted a black leather tri-fold billfold to her face, studying it. It was warped, shaped from years in someone's back pocket. She opened it slowly and peered inside.

Empty. No cash, no pictures, no driver's license. Nothing.

Lynn faced her son. "I guess it's just old stuff left here to rot, Dave. There's nothing here for us. Let's look on the other side, near the exit, okay, guys?" Her attention flowed to Micah and Will, waiting for a response.

Her boys had already nodded and turned to stroll down the hall, but Micah stood there, eyes twitching.

"Babe? Micah?" She pointed down the hall, where David and Will were already stepping over piles of debris. "Are you ready to look down there?"

We got away, but why? How? This is another game, isn't it? That son of a bitch is still mocking me, screwing with my head. He knew we would come in here, start snooping around, and find his trinkets. It's all part of his twisted, sadistic plan. And I fell for it. I bet he knows I saw him in the car too.

"Micah? Are you coming?"

He snapped back from his thoughts after the question, staring at his wife. "Umm, yeah, yeah. Right behind you, babe."

He took two steps forward, then stiffened, cocking his head. *Was that a scream I just heard?* He shifted, peering out the entrance, listening to the unknown beyond the safety of the building. *Was that real?*

"Boys, slow down, okay? It's not a race, and I want you two as close as possible." Lynn's voice echoed through the long hall, bringing his focus back.

He tried to ignore his thoughts and followed her, glancing backward every few strides. *They're coming for us, and they know we're here. I can feel it.*

37

THE SOILED MATTRESS PARTIALLY hid their movements while they continued searching. Finding only more of the same: dusty trash bags, boxes, and rusty aluminum filing cabinets filled with junk. The four rummaged through most of it, finding nothing.

Micah's focus flipped between the litter and the entrance, watching, listening, knowing time was running out. This old building provided shelter—sanctuary from the openness of the woods—but lacked any form of comfort with its claustrophobic conditions, dimness, and fetid, musty smells. There was nothing of value here.

Lynn dropped a box of papers to the floor, unapologetic. She turned, facing her sons, "This is pointless, boys. It's just a bunch of old crap."

David and Will had rolled up pieces of thin cardboard in the middle of the search, engaged in an epic galactic duel.

"Come to the dark side, Will!" David attempted a Darth Vader impersonation, holding out his right hand and metaphorically strangling his little brother in a death grip. Will grasped at his neck, playing along with the charade, gargles emitting from his throat.

"Boys, quit the horseplay and help us find something." The annoyance in Lynn's voice resounded, and both dropped their makeshift lightsabers before returning to the hunt.

Micah turned, focusing on his sons, watching the two scurry off. "Boys! Look over there." Pointing in that direction, he eyed something dark near the corner of the hall.

Both boys flinched at their father's voice but didn't hesitate to obey, moving in the direction they were told.

Lynn walked up to Micah, the crunching of broken glass under her feet. She reached out for him, patting his forearm. "Well, this was a disaster, right?"

"Yeah, I don't know what I was thinking, digging through all this shit." He glanced over at the entrance, peering past the mattress. "But we need to leave. If we find the road, maybe we can flag someone down."

"Nobody uses that road, Micah. The only car we've seen or heard on it the past two days was that asshole's shitty truck."

Oh no. I didn't tell her about the car either. Will and I just saw Clyde driving it an hour ago, swerving around each curve.

"Micah, are you listening? You seem lost again." She gripped his arm, looking at his glassy eyes.

He shook his head, gathering his focus again. "Yeah, yeah, I'm fine, Lynn. I know the road's a long shot, but what else is there?"

"At least we're inside, where those bastards can't surprise us."

"That's what I'm worried about, Lynn, surprises. They're working together, and there are two doors to the hall. They could come in both doors, carrying guns or knives, and we'd be trapped."

Lynn didn't counter. Her attention fled to the entrance and boarded-up exit, whipping her head back and forth.

Micah could feel the stress boiling in her, so he stepped forward, pulling her close. "I don't want to scare you more, babe. I know you've been through a lot." He paused, scanning the entrance before returning his focus. "I wouldn't be able to live knowing they hurt you in this place."

She forced a weak smile as she locked onto those blue eyes, watching them twinkle in the dim light. "Then let's go. Get to the road and find help."

"Dad, Dad!"

A ruckus near the exit grabbed their attention. The boys were yelling about something near where Micah instructed them to look. Both whipped their heads in the direction and scampered over, avoiding a splintered crate set on its side.

"Come look at this, Dad!"

They found David and Will standing in the center of the hall, just inside the exit's threshold. Their backs were to their parents, and they were staring downward, motionless.

"Boys? What the hell is it? What did you find?"

David glanced over his shoulder, eyes dilated and large. "It's another door. But on the floor. With—"

"Yeah, it's like a trapdoor, Dad," Will interrupted. "We pulled up this nasty rug and found it. There's a big ring attached to it, like a handle." The nine-year-old's voice was accelerated, excited at the discovery.

"The hell are you two talking about?" Micah stepped forward, forcing his sons to part and make room. Lynn arrived seconds later, reaching down and gripping Will's hand, staring at the floor.

And there it was. A wooden door, square, about a yard in width and length, and badly damaged by moisture. It indeed had a dark metallic ring hinged on its center and similar metal casings riveted around its frame.

"What.... Why...." Lynn couldn't find the words.

Micah looked over at his wife. "Must be some sort of storm cellar. You know, like the one Dorothy's family went into in the movie."

"We don't have tornadoes here. It's California." She responded, never averting her eyes from the mystery.

"Hmmm," Micah rubbed the side of his face, eyeing the anomaly. "What else could it be used for?"

The four stood there in a row, staring, wondering, until Micah broke the silence.

He turned to his left, looking at Lynn and Will, cocking an eyebrow. Then he mirrored his actions at David standing on his right, gathering everything he needed from their faces.

"Let's find the answer to the riddle, guys." With that said, he stepped forward, leaving the three a pace behind. He knelt in front of the door, scanning it before slowly reaching out and grasping the ring. "Here goes nothing." He wrenched his arm upward, applying some torque, expecting the door to fling open, but it wouldn't budge. Surprised, he grabbed the ring with both hands, lifting, bracing with his back and legs. Nothing.

What the hell is wrong with this thing? Is it locked from the inside?

Micah released his grip, turned, and faced his family; his brow furrowed in puzzlement. He held out his palms face up and shrugged. "The damn thing won't budge."

"Is it locked, Dad?"

Micah ignored David's question, standing, refocusing on the mystery before him. *What is on the other side?*

Lynn cleared her throat. "We'll do it together, Micah. I can lift with my left side." She stepped forward, cradling her ribs, stood beside her husband, and nodded in assurance.

"Worth a shot, I guess."

Seconds later, three hands gripped the ring. Micah remained standing, buckled over the wooden door, bracing himself with sturdy legs. Lynn knelt, reaching across the door, protecting her side with her free hand.

Micah counted down from three, and they yanked. Micah leaned back, veins rippling in his neck and forehead. Lynn screamed from the pain in her side.

The wood shuddered, splintering and creaking, and the door sprang forth, forcing both parents to fall hard. A metal rod protruded from a hasp on the underside; it was broken, bent at a 90-degree angle.

Micah broke his fall with his hands, reaching backward to lessen the impact. He sat on his ass, winded and staring down at the open door. *Damn thing was locked from the inside. Shit, we broke the drawbolt too. Guess we're not relocking it. Hell, I'd be surprised if we could even get it closed again.*

He looked across the door, seeing his wife laying on her side, grimacing. "Lynn, are you hurt? Did you mess up your ribs even more?" In an instant, he was by her side, trying to support her, comfort her.

She gingerly lifted her torso from the cold, damp floor, bracing her weight with one arm. With gritted teeth, she nodded, assuring him she was okay, but it was a fib. She couldn't tell him the truth.

"Here, let me help you to your feet." He wrapped an arm around her slim waist, supporting her weight as they worked together to stand. She grimaced with each breath, clenching her jaw, sucking in air.

The boys approached, too, eyes full of concern and worry. They stepped in and helped her stabilize, one getting her arm around his shoulders and the other cradling her sides, cautious of her left. She fought through the pain, delivering both a wan smile.

Micah took a step back, watching them together again. Watching the love, the respect, the support they had for one another. His mind teetered, filled with envy, guilt, and shame. Memories flooded his consciousness, remembering when they used to embrace him the same way years ago. Holidays, trips, vacations, when he was the hero, the father they loved. But that was the past. There was no winning them back now. It didn't matter how hard he tried. The damage was done, and their feelings and opinions couldn't be changed.

His loathing stare left his family and landed on the splintered door hanging open. Shadows covered the opening, allowing minimal visibility, but he had an internal need to solve the mystery, to dig deeper. Ignoring the others, he got down on his knees, holding his breath due to the smell, and peered into the darkness.

38

MICAH COULD SEE THE vague silhouette of descending stairs. Faint illumination bloomed deeper within, making him believe there was a light source below. These concrete steps had to lead somewhere.

Lynn and the boys joined him, peering into the cavity, fear and intrigue mixing in their veins.

"What's down there?" David asked.

"I don't know, but from the smell," Lynn wrinkled her nose, acknowledging her son, "I'm staying up here."

Micah didn't answer his son's question or respond to Lynn. His perusal continued, eyes penetrating the black, wondering, imagining what waited at the bottom. Fixation grasped his mind, twisting and tightening with each turn of the vice.

"Micah? Are you considering going down there?"

Hearing his name snapped him out of his thoughts, bringing him back to reality. "What? Uh ... I don't know. I mean–yeah, maybe."

"Are you serious? It's pitch black, and who knows what, or who, is waiting down there, ready to pounce?"

Micah leaned in closer, listening. The sound of running water was distant in the background. "There's some light down there, babe, and I think I hear water too." He pointed to the bottom, where he glimpsed the last stair, mind meandering at the mystery. "Besides, we're alone. No soul has set foot down here in years."

"Are you sure about that? It looks like a perfect place for murderers to wait for idiotic trespassers like us."

Micah cocked a brow as he looked at her. "We're alone, Lynn. The answers we're looking for might be in that direction. Give me five minutes in there; if there's nothing, then there's nothing. At least we'll know."

A minute later, after more deliberation, Micah led the caravan down the steep stairs, pulling his sweatshirt up and covering his mouth. The three mirrored his actions, trying to dilute the putrid smell seeping from within. Concrete walls lined the steps, rough and cold to the touch as they descended. The faint light at the bottom grew with each step, finally revealing a room near the bottom, possibly more than one.

Micah skipped the last stair—stepping over it to avoid something black and saturated—with Will, David, and Lynn on his heels. His pupils slowly dilated with the sparse light, and he scanned the room. Like the hall, it was damp, cold, and cramped, but not as long. It felt like it was underground, though, with its concrete walls, floor, and ceiling. It was a bunker. His sight shifted to the back of the room, noticing two paths veering off from the room he and his family now stood in.

Will bumped into Micah, hovering close and peering around his father. "Dad, where are we?"

Micah glanced back, "We're beneath the hall, son, but more importantly, why was this room built?" He stepped forward, advancing into the unknown.

Lynn's foot finally touched the cold floor, supporting David and his ankle with each step down. "I don't like this, Micah." She surveyed the room and landed on the paths ahead. "Each way probably leads to one of those creeps."

Micah ignored the probable warning, taking short strides, stepping over scattered empty beer bottles. He eyed the walls as he advanced, reading the sporadic graffiti: Gorman, CA; AJMC; death to pigz.

"Dad, what do you think is down there?" David asked, peering over his little brother's shoulder and pointing at the paths.

His eyes fluttered, trying to control the hostility, the frustration brewing. "I don't know, but we need to find out, okay?"

"Micah, you said five minutes. I know it hasn't been that long, but I need to go. I can't handle being down here." Lynn looked at her two sons. "And I don't want them down here any longer. Let's get to the road, please!"

Micah locked onto her, leering at his wife. "Lynn, listen to me. I need this. I need to find out what is down here and why this shithole was built. There's something here, okay, and I need to find out what it is."

Lynn returned the stare, annoyance and doubt surfacing in her stance. "I'm not going in there, Micah. The boys and I are leaving."

"Why is everything always about you, Lynn? Are you so dense that you can't see what is right in front of you? This is our chance, our way out! When are you going to learn to listen?"

A look of disgust formed on her face as she stepped forward, getting between Micah and the boys. He hadn't spoken to her that way in months. Not since his days of heavy drinking and deceit after his mother passed. She shook her head, curling her upper lip without a verbal response. She wouldn't fuel the rage, the fire burning in his dark, fractured mind. No. That would only lead in one direction.

Micah held the glare, mind slowly regaining control of his actions and words. The hate inched away, suppressed with heavy breathing, leaving his thoughts to rationalize and clear.

Seconds of utter silence passed, absorbing the family's emotions and thoughts, sick memories of heated arguments. Tears and agony rushed through, swallowing the moment, filling their heads with the past. This was not the way.

Finally, Micah shrugged, turning away from his family and facing the paths in the near distance. Without addressing them, he stepped forward, leaving them behind. *Screw them. I'm going to help us, save us. It's going to be me, damnit, with or without your help, Lynn.*

"Dad, Dad, don't leave us!" The boys chanted in unison.

"Micah?" Lynn uttered incredulously.

The boys' mantric pleas forced his hand, and he paused, slowly turning his neck and looking past his shoulder. A meek smirk grew on his lips, realizing they actually needed him and couldn't make it without him. *Maybe I'm not the monster? Or are they just—*

"Dad, let me go with you. I don't want you to be alone, just ... you know, in case."

Micah's sight flew to David, peeking out from behind his mother's rigid, distressed stance.

The older brother looked at his mother, stepping out from her looming shadow. "Someone needs to be with him, and I can help, even with my ankle." He didn't wait for Lynn's rejection, advancing past her and Will, hobbling forward.

Micah's smile grew, filling with cockiness and arrogance, watching the boy approach, choosing his father. He delivered a slight nod, and the two stepped forward, David using the brittle concrete wall as a crutch.

As they reached the fork where the paths diverted from the main floor, the illumination diminished. Both new halls were dark. Micah leaned into the right path, squinting his eyes and listening. "Can you hear that, boy? Running water?"

David mirrored his father's actions, bracing against the wall and leaning forward into the shadows. "No, I don't hear anything, Dad."

"You sure? Like a stream or creek flowing?"

David shook his head, confusion gripping his mind.

How can he not hear that? "Hmm. Well, how the hell are we supposed to find out? I can't see anything past a few feet."

David began rummaging through his pockets with his free hand, pulling out a miracle. A small, cheap flashlight with Mickey Mouse stickers wrapped around it. A rubber on-off button on its end.

Micah looked down at the piece, then at his son. *A flashlight, really? Are you kidding me? We've been walking around in the dark and this little shit has a flashlight in his pocket?*

His brow furrowed, eyes narrowed, and there was a fury burning within. "You have a flashlight?"

David looked up at his father but didn't have the courage to answer. The rage swirling in Micah's eyes induced a tremble through David's core. The boy's eyes bloomed, knowing that look, expecting the wrath to unleash, to boom from his father's lips. He stepped backward, holding himself up with the wall, and bracing for the verbal bashing, but....

It never came.

Micah shook his head, eyes peering up at the crude ceiling, thinking. *Control it, Micah. Control it.* His mind drifted, thinking about his family, and that he stood in front of an absent-minded twelve-year-old. He also thought about their recent vacation, which soothed his nerves and calmed his breathing. Then, the memory of the flashlight came crashing in, like a wrecking ball destroying his consciousness. A black shawl gripped the light.

It was their second day in the park, and they had just exited an older ride with a pirate theme. They had held off riding it for the first day and a half, regardless of Will's enthusiasm to do so. David had clarified that he wanted nothing to do with pirates after listening to Stevenson's classic novel read in school. A certain captain with a peg leg caused a few sleepless nights, and the idea of facing such characters in a fun way wasn't appealing. Even if the theme of the ride was adventure and excitement.

After countless moments of pleading and begging from both Will and his father, David mustered up some courage and was ready to face his fears. As long as he could get something from the gift shop when the ride was over, of course. Lynn's idea, regardless of their tight money situation.

As they entered the shop, Will ran to the figurines, scooping up one in each hand, shouting with excitement as he reenacted a scene from the ride.

David, however, reluctantly strolled through, not seeing anything that wouldn't remind him of the captain from the book. Micah came up behind him and forced a hat on his head, adorned with the jolly roger, but he squirmed out of it, hating that it had touched him. He wanted nothing from this place, nothing at all.

Because of his indecisiveness, his parents had given up on buying him a gift, until they approached the cashier's desk. David's eyes dropped to the ground, and he moped, agitation festering as he listened to the excitement in his brother's voice. He was lost, swimming in an ocean of disappointment, until he finally looked up. There it was, alongside dozens more just like it. A miniature flashlight with Mickey's face on the side. A gift that he wanted, a gift that he might actually use sometime. His excitement as he turned it on for the first time didn't match his brother's, but he was happy, tucking it into his pocket for safekeeping. He was happy with anything after the past year and a half.

"Dad, I'm sorry. I don't know how I forgot about it."

The memory of the vacation slipped away as the boy spoke, bracing himself and leaning away from his father, apologizing for the slight. Micah's vision returned, eyeing his son. Looking at the boy, remorse and guilt filled his soul, knowing he was responsible for the fear bestowed.

"Hey, hey, don't worry about it, boy." He forced a wan smile, reaching over and mussing his son's hair. David flinched at the action, tense and nervous with the touch. "It's okay, David. You're not in trouble. I'm just glad you remembered it. We're going to need it."

His vision left his son and aimed into the darkness of the path. He held out his hand, palm up, never taking his eyes off the blackness of the unknown. "We won't be long," he stated, voice cold and elevated, never looking back at his wife or Will.

David glanced at the hand and then in the same direction as his father, into the darkness, the void. Without questioning, he placed the flashlight in Micah's palm.

"Micah? You're just going to leave us here!"

He ignored Lynn's question, never even looking back. "Let's find out what's in there, David. Ready?"

39

Lynn pulled Will in close, his back against her waist. Her arms looped under his armpits, fingers locked in a tight embrace across his chest as they watched Micah and David stroll into the dark pathway. She had forgotten about the flashlight, too, and seeing Micah power it on delivered a modicum of stress relief. She was still alone, though, in this dingy, damp bunker that smelled like death. Micah had left her. Just like before. Just like in the woods.

Micah and David's silhouettes eventually dissolved into the abyss, bringing about feelings suppressed for months. Feelings of betrayal, sorrow, shame, hate. She was fuming inside. Her anger toward Micah masked every other thought and emotion.

How dare that son of a bitch talk to me like that? In front of the kids? And then he leaves me here, with our poor little boy, scared and shivering in the darkness. He hasn't changed at all! Selfish asshole. Never has. Cared more about his mom than any of us. I'm ... through, done. When we get out of this—

"Mommy?" Will's quiet, disappointed voice interrupted her thoughts. "Why didn't you buy me one of those flashlights? It's not fair that Dave got one, but I didn't."

The petty complaint broke the silence and garnered her attention, breaking her free from her dark, corrosive thoughts. She looked down at her son, admiring the boy and smirking at the comment. "You didn't get one because you wanted Billy Bones and Long John Silver, remember? His light was two dollars, and your little pirates were two dollars, son. That's why."

Will looked up at her, disappointment flowing through his eyes. "Still don't think it's fair. My pirates are in the car, and Dad made us leave them."

Lynn sighed, thinking about the car, the bunker, and what might lie ahead. "I know, baby, I know. Dad and David will be back soon, and you can hold the flashlight, okay?" Her jaw clenched, thinking about them returning, about facing Micah.

Will turned around, silence gripping his voice. He fixated on the dark path, wondering where his father and brother were, wondering if she was right. *Would they be back soon?*

Micah and David slinked forward, welcoming the soft light emitting from the flashlight. Micah gripped it, holding it in front of the two, waving it in every direction with his son clinging to his sweatshirt with clenched fists. Their eyes followed the bouncing beam as it subtly illuminated sections of floor and wall for a split second before moving on. An eerie, utter stillness surrounded them with each step farther into the unknown.

"How far do you think it goes, boy?"

"I don't like this, Dad. I want to go back! We shouldn't be in here."

Micah paused and turned around, using the light to see his son, observing the nervousness. "I know, I know, son. I don't like it either, but we have to find out where this leads. Understand?"

David squeezed his eyes shut and shook his head no, never verbally answering his father.

Micah looked on, watching the boy tremble before him. "David! Quit your sniveling. It was your choice to come with me, and we are finishing this." He swiveled in place, waving the beam once more in the dark hallway. "Now, get yourself together, boy." He stepped forward, pulling David along unwillingly.

"No, no, no, Dad! Let's go back! Let's go back to Mom!"

"*Shh,* David. Quiet!" Micah took another step, cocking his head, listening. He shone the light down the hall, focusing on the center. "You can hear that, right? Water running?"

"Wh ... what? What are you talking about, Dad? I don't hear anything. Why do you keep asking me about water?"

Micah took another step, David right on his heels. He held the light steady, squinting his eyes and watching, searching for answers. "The water, son. There's a creek or stream flowing down there. You can't hear it?" He turned back to David, seeing the boy shake his head.

Hmmm, that's weird. I can hear it clear as day, and I know we're getting closer.

"Come on, boy. We're close now. I can feel it. Just a little farther."

Micah inched forward, forcing David to keep up or be left behind. He waved the faint light around, scanning the walls, the floor, and the ceiling, knowing the mystery was near. As the beam hit the right wall a few paces ahead of where they stood, it illuminated something for a split second. He bounced it back to the area where the image appeared, but it was gone. Startled, he jumped back a step, bumping into David. "Did you see that?" He asked, hand shaking as he tried to steady the light.

Confusion struck David right away as he peered around his father. "Huh? What'd you see, Dad? What was it?" The grip on his father's sweatshirt tightened.

"There was a person right there!" The beam of light bounced around the area. "Right there, Dave!"

"A person? What are you talking about?" The news caused his hands to tremble as he watched the light shine down the path on the right. "Who was it? That scary man with the truck?"

Micah stepped backward, his son shambling along. "No, no, I don't think so." He turned around, shining the light back in the direction they had come before returning it down the two paths. "It looked like a kid, but I don't know for sure."

David buried his face in Micah's back. "I want to go back, Dad. Back with Mom. Please, please, can we go!"

What the hell is a kid doing down here, and where'd he go? What is happening?

Micah turned sideways and grabbed his son, pulling him to his chest. "Hey, hey, it's okay. I'm here." His eyes motioned back to the hall, wondering if he had really seen anything. "Yeah, let's get back to Mom and Will. Stay in front of me, okay?"

David didn't respond. He leaned into his father while Micah gripped him by the shoulder, leading him away from the mystery that lies within it. Their pace quickened with each stride, neither wanting to be in darkness another second.

What was that? And where's the creek, the stream, whatever it is? What is this place?

Micah looked back one last time, shining the light down the hall, wondering if he saw something or if the darkness was playing tricks on him.

40

WILL STEPPED FORWARD, WIDE-EYED, pulling away from his mother's protective grip. "Mom, Mom! Look, look!" He pointed down the long, dark path, his heart racing. Something was there, faint but luminescent, similar to a candle flickering in the wind. And it was getting closer.

Lynn lifted her head from his shoulder. Her attention turned to the path, confused by Will's sudden outburst. Adrenaline pumped through her veins as she peered in the direction her son was pointing, failing to grasp the situation. Then she saw it. A flickering light in the distance, faint and moving in all directions.

"What is that, Mommy?"

"I'm not sure, baby." She squinted her eyes, staring into the darkness.

"Is that Dad and Dave?" Will's voice choked on the words.

She pulled him back to her, cradling him firmly. "Yeah, yeah, I hope so." Breaths passed before she nodded, looking at the light wobble. "I think they're finally back."

As they stared into the darkness, fixated on the light, something strange happened. That pale light bouncing around sporadically dissipated into nothingness, like a breeze smothering a candle wick. It vanished in a heartbeat.

Lynn's mouth dropped open as she peered into the pitch blackness, speechless and paralyzed. Will turned and buried his face in Lynn's torso, gripping her shirt. Neither spoke nor moved.

Then they heard it.

A single scream resonated within the darkness. It echoed throughout the bunker, bouncing off the concrete walls and floor toward them. Lynn and Will locked eyes, fear and uncertainty swallowing any attempt to act, to flee, to communicate.

Strained heartbeats passed in utter silence until a new sound emerged: hushed, hurried voices in the distance. Like the scream, these also grew with each passing second, getting louder and louder, more comprehensible. Lynn leaned forward, listening, trying to identify the source or sources. Suddenly, two objects burst out of the darkness, nearly colliding with her and Will. She shrieked, falling back, pulling Will with her, and striking the crumbling concrete wall. In the blur of chaos and confusion, her eyes adjusted, focused on the intruders.

Micah and David had returned, heavily panting and winded from a run. Each buckled over, palms on their knees, catching their breath. Tears streaked David's cheeks as he looked up and saw his mother, relief filling his eyes. Micah's eyes fell back into the void, into the darkness, searching for something. Without a threat discovered during his gaze, he looked over at his wife, who was saucer-eyed and pale as a ghost.

With her heart racing and adrenaline flowing, the anger stirred by Micah's words and nonchalant exit was non-existent. She was concerned, confused, and troubled by their expressions. She stammered, trying to speak, trying to gain understanding, but failed to release the words.

Micah stood, removing his hands from his knees, and with paranoid eyes, gave a sidelong glance at the dark path. His breathing slowed, and his attention returned to Lynn, shaking his head in denial and disbelief.

Lynn released her death grip on Will and forced herself off the wall, staggering toward Micah. "Wh ... What the hell happened, Micah? What'd you two see?"

Micah released a long breath, placing his hands behind his neck and periodically checking the path for threats. "I don't know for sure. I think we saw a kid in there, a young boy."

"Dead? Like a dead body?" Her mouth agape, not able to wait for a response.

He delivered a subtle shake of his head. "No, no, not dead. Whoever that kid was, he was alive. He looked straight at me and then vanished into the darkness."

"There's some random kid lurking around in the dark down here? Are you serious?"

"I don't know for sure. It was weird. I saw a face as I passed the light on the wall. When I swept back to the area, it was gone, disappeared in a split second." He threw up his hands and shrugged his shoulders, unsure if it was real.

Lynn's sight moved to David, seeing him still shaken by the experience. "David? Honey, are you okay? Did the boy scare you too?"

David wiped his eyes with his sleeve, still out of breath. Overwhelmed by trepid emotions, he forced himself to answer. "It was dark, and I couldn't see anything. I don't know what happened. I had my eyes closed. Dad saw him, and then we turned around to find you guys."

Lynn looked on with speculation, eyes switching between her son and husband. "Well, what did he look like? The kid?"

Micah released another long breath, eyes twitching throughout the bunker. "I don't know. Young boy, blonde hair, younger than Will, I think."

Will stepped forward, listening to his father. "Daddy, that sounds like the kid Dave and I were talking to before—"

Lynn cut him off before he could finish. "Are you telling me that creepy little kid's in here with us, Micah? He has a damn bow and arrow and gets his jollies by killing things. Are we next on his list?"

"Damnit, Lynn! I don't know for sure. I saw something, okay? He was there one second and gone the next!"

"What happened to the flashlight, Micah? Where is it?"

"I lost the damn thing, okay, Lynn?" His breathing elevated, eyes twitching with contempt. "Are you happy now? I dropped it on the ground, and David was crying, whining like a girl, and we had to get out! I couldn't stop and drop to the floor to find it, okay?" His eyes burrowed holes through her.

She ignored the hostility in his voice, trying to regain composure and control. This wasn't the time to force his hand or push him over the edge. She dropped her glare, thinking, trying to rationalize the facts. Moments passed before she looked up, but her attention wasn't directed toward Micah. Her eyes moved to her sons, David and Will, and focused on them. "Your five minutes are up, Micah. We're leaving. I'm taking the boys to the road, with or without you."

The confidence and authority flowing through her voice forced both boys to approach. They stood next to her, staring at Micah, staring at their father, expecting him to join them, but he didn't.

He stood there, eyeing his family, watching every flinch, every breath, every moment pass.

Why? Why am I the bad guy? I've made mistakes, sure, but I'm trying. Trying to find answers so others don't have to deal with this shit. Why can't they see what I'm doing, what I'm trying to accomplish here? Why is she so judgmental, hateful, and cruel?

He shook his head in disbelief, understanding the ultimatum he had just been given.

She finally did it. She's turned them against me, my own sons, my blood, my life. I knew this day would come, eventually. She's been plotting this shit for years, whispering in their ears, falsifying my intentions and motives. Painting this slanderous picture of the man that is supposed to be their hero, their protector. The deadbeat dad who can't be trusted or respected. She finally accomplished her goal. They don't love me.

Lynn shifted her view to Micah, seeing the rapid eye movement and mannerisms she knew all too well when his mind wavered. But she was through. Through with it all. The lies, the volatility, the terrible choices and decisions. Through.

"Come on, boys, I'll get *us* out of here."

With that said, she strolled away, headed for the stairs. Will and David looked at their father, expecting something to happen. But he just stood there, emotionless and lifeless, eyes bloodshot, glassy, and strained.

"Daddy?"

David grabbed his brother's hand and pulled him away toward the stairs with Lynn. "Come on, man. We have to go. He can't help us." They both turned away, shambling toward their mother.

Lynn never looked back, shaking her head in disappointment as she walked toward the narrow stairway. As her foot hit the bottom step, something sounded behind her and the boys, a loud clunk. She whipped around, seeing Micah's limp body sprawled face-down on the bunker's floor. He was unconscious, eyes shut, and a fresh laceration ran from his forehead to ear. Above him, standing in the middle of the bunker, was Sid. Dried blood caked the side of his twisted, gnarled face. He held a thick log in his right hand, crimson and dripping.

"Let's finish what we started, love!"

41

Staring into Sid's deranged eyes and seeing her husband's lifeless body on the concrete floor, a thunderous scream leapt from Lynn's throat. David and Will flinched, whipping around to see the threat lurching forward. Both scampered in haste, making their way up the stairway, zipping past their mother. Lynn beat the shock back and followed, taking two stairs with each stride, forgetting about the intense burning in her side.

The boys barreled through the door in the structure's floor. David turned and reached down into the opening, grasping his mother's hand and yanking her upward, out of the gloom. Animalistic screams echoed below them as Sid mounted the stairs, advancing with awkward strides, swinging the log, and hammering the walls.

Lynn gained her footing and turned around, staring into the cavity, seeing the monster's eyes gleaming as he ascended. The dark, maniacal eyes of a predator who's just tasted fresh blood. She knelt, reached for the door, and threw it closed. *Shit, the drawbolt! It's broken!*

They ran down the hall, abandoning the splintered door, passing the obstacles and mattress blocking most of the hall. Lynn's vision meandered, unsure where to run and what to do. Straight ahead was the entrance, and adjacent rooms veered off on either side. They had to reach the interstate and find help.

She bolted forward, pushing the boys in front, yelling directions. The bunker door whipped open and slammed against the concrete floor behind them. She ignored the crash and pushed on, approaching the entrance, seeing the brilliance of late afternoon. But the boys slowed their progression, skidding to a stop, forcing her to halt as well. A shadow approached from outside, a large, looming shadow.

"Shit!" Her stare darted to the left, seeing a door cracked open. Blackness engulfed the interior, blanketing the faint light from the hall. "In there, quick!"

Without hesitation, the boys darted in, squeezing through the opening. Their eyes hit the sliver between the door and the hall, watching for Lynn to join them. But she hesitated when she heard Sid lumbering out of the trapdoor, slapping the floor with his log, screaming obscenities.

Hidden by the mattress and not seeing who was casting the vast shadow outside, she bolted through the tight opening. Once inside, she whirled, grabbing the door's handle and pushing it closed without a sound. There was no lock. She stepped backward, fixated on the door. Eyes locked on the thin barrier between life and death. Slowly, she lifted a finger to her lips, turning her head and glancing at her sons.

From the hall, the lecherous, chaotic screams increased, encroaching. The thumping continued as the log whacked the walls.

Lynn paced away from the door and held her stance. David and Will found her in the darkness, gripping her waist and side. She mirrored their desperation, wrapping her arms around their quivering shoulders. They were laser-focused, watching the door. Praying. Hoping.

Suddenly, the hysterical screams and thumps stopped. The room they stood in, the dim hall, and the forest beyond all fell mute. Unnaturally silent.

The three huddled together in the pitch-black room, paralyzed. Listening, wondering where Sid was and why the madness stopped.

Whack! Whack!

It continued, following a pattern of two strikes and then a suffocating pause. Each thump hammering the wall forced a flinch. And it was getting louder, closer.

Whack! Whack!

Lynn squeezed her sons tighter, unaware of her suffocating grip and oblivious to her excruciating pain. Her eyes followed the sound, listening to it pound the exterior wall, moving from right to left, inching closer to the door. Closer to her and her sons.

She braced herself, stepping backward with both boys, expecting the door to fling open in a violent eruption. Her head shook, and tremors passed on to the rest of her body. David and Will buried their faces in her sides, hiding from the threat, the inevitable. Her stare held, body shivering, as they reached the back wall, leaning against it.

Heartbeats passed, but the door didn't come crashing down in a fury of chaos. The apprehension causing fear and stress to multiply. The silence was deafening, maddening.

Until ...

A muffled voice rang from the hall, forcing a gasp from Lynn. She dropped her death grip from her sons' shoulders and covered her mouth, looking at both with panic-stricken eyes. *He's there! Right there! Right outside!*

Another voice, faint and distant, followed, barely comprehensible. "Where are they, dipshit?" Lynn couldn't pinpoint the location but knew it must be Clyde. These two were working together, hunting their prey from opposite sides of the structure.

"You didn't see 'em? Where the hell they'd go?" A heated debate ensued between the two, followed by heavy footsteps passing the door as she and the boys listened. Only fragments of the conversation were clear: car, woods, gun. The sound of the footsteps ended down the hall near the entrance.

The silence continued, leaving Lynn and the boys to succumb to the shock slowly creeping up their spines. No one could speak or move. Their bodies refused. The three hovered together, unsure and unable to act. Petrified.

Minutes passed without an incident or sound. Complete, terrorizing silence. Lynn stared at her sons, lips parted, not knowing the next move. She finally forced herself to take a step toward the door, listening intently. Without an episode, she continued her advance, slow steps forward, alarm percolating.

"Mom, Mom, Mom! What are you doing? No, stop, wait!"

"*Shh!*" She held her finger to her lips, the whisper elongated.

Once she reached the door, she leaned in, placing her ear on the grain of the wood. Her breathing accelerated, and her heart rate increased. She held the position, attempting to solve the mystery behind the door. *Were they alone and safe? If so, why?*

No sound emitted from the hall. No whispers, no conversations, not the scuffing of boots on the concrete floor, or the crunching of broken glass under one's weight. The hall was empty, deserted.

Lynn retreated to her sons, hope and relief restored, despite the ongoing silence. David and Will held one another, soft sobs trickling as she approached. "I ... I think they're gone, boys. I can't hear anything out there."

Looking up at her in the dimness, shaking, neither said a word.

"The bad men left, guys. I heard them leave the building. We're alone. We're safe now. They don't know we're in here."

David forced a whispered response, ignoring her unconvincing words and grasping his mother by her arm. "What did the man do to Daddy? Is he alive and safe?"

The mention of Micah forced her back, reliving the violent scene in the bunker. "I don't know, baby. I don't."

"We have to go get him. Make sure he's okay! The man's going to backtrack, find him, hurt him!"

Lynn pulled the hysterical boy to her, massaging his back and cradling his head in her palm. "*Shh, Shh,* now! We need to be quiet in case someone's close by, David."

Will joined them, embracing the warmth and bleak comfort of the dire situation.

Lynn pulled back, making sure she had both boys' attention. "Now listen, both of you. I know you're scared and worried about yourselves and your father. This is bad. I'm not going to lie to you, but we need to keep our wits and stay sharp, okay? We have to get to the interstate! If Daddy is okay," she paused, swallowing firmly, "he'll find us there."

Neither replied. Just blank, somber looks.

"Boys!" A stiff shake was delivered to their shoulders, awakening them from their shock. "We need to save ourselves and find someone on the interstate to help us. Then we'll come back and find Daddy," a heavy sigh released, "if he doesn't meet us, okay?" She stared at her sons, nodding, expecting the gesture returned.

David fought through the torrent of emotions, staring up at her with a sullen face. "No."

Lynn's face shifted, taken aback by the boldness and tone of her son's response. "Wh ... what do you mean, no?"

"We're not leaving him, Mom. He's in there, hurting, and he needs us."

"David? That lunatic emerged from one of those dark paths. He's probably back there already, waiting, licking his chops, knowing we'll return. That sick kid is probably waiting down the other path, arrows at the ready, notched, and aimed!"

David shook his head in defiance, not rationalizing his mother's theory. "We can't just leave him, Mom. It's Dad! I know you two have been through a shit-storm, and you hate him, but he's still my father." He paused, looking over at Will, quivering. "Our father, Mom, and your husband. We have to make sure he's alive and bring him with us."

Lynn dropped her eyes to the floor, thinking about Micah, her husband, the man she said she would spend the rest of her life with. So much history, so much joy, beloved memories etched in cognitive stone. She shut her eyes, envisioning the man she fell in love with, the man with kind blue eyes, always wearing a smile. Those early years were glorious, filled with tranquility and promise, and she wasn't ready to abandon them. If they could survive this, they could bury the past, start fresh, and thrive once more. She had to try. She owed it to herself and the boys.

"Okay, you're right. Follow me."

42

Lynn held her ear to the wooden door, prudence taking over as she listened. The hall beyond returned the eerie silence, forcing a mild shudder through her core.

Only one way to find out.

She released a long breath through gritted teeth before reaching down and gripping the knob. She paused, slowly turning her head and observing David and Will behind her. Both bore the weariness of their plan, knowing the risk here was potentially fatal.

"Stay sharp and close, boys. If either of you see or hear anything, run, and don't stop. Don't wait for me or your father. Get to the interstate, and don't look back." She didn't wait for a response. Instead, she faced the door and turned the knob.

With the door unlatched, she pulled it open a few inches, keeping her free hand on its flat surface, prepared to slam it shut. She peered through the small opening, scanning the hall, finding it motionless and mute.

She forced herself through the nerves, senses boiling with each subtle movement. She inched forward, craning her neck through the opening and looking left and right before retreating. "It's empty. There's no one here," she said, hoping to assuage the boys' fear and instill a sense of calmness.

Her heart rate elevated as she opened the door wide enough to pass through, hesitant to advance, then stepped forward, sliding out of the dim room's safety. Her eyes scoped her surroundings, catching the soiled mattress, the debris littered throughout, and the broken shards of glass. She found no threat.

She gestured for the boys to follow, watching them sidestep out the jarred door. David exited first, pulling his younger brother by the hand. They mimicked their mother, searching the hall, wary of the unknown hiding amongst the rubble.

With the facade of safety established, Lynn started toward the hall's exit, hovering close to the wall. Both boys followed, mirroring her actions, maintaining proximity. Every few steps, she whirled, looking back toward the room and the entrance. The motionlessness and silence from within the hall remained, and the three trekked to the trapdoor.

The door in the concrete floor was still thrown open, splintered, and hanging awkwardly from its torn hinges. The bent drawbolt on the underside of the fabricated wood reminded Lynn of the chaos and cannibalistic rage of that monster, Sid. She leaned forward, looking down the dark stairway. As before, there was a faint illumination at the bottom. Her eyes followed the dim light, seeing the bottom stair and imagining what was beyond it. *Was Micah alive?*

A heavy exhale exited her mouth. "I want you two to stay here, watch and—" She paused, averting her stare from David and Will. "W ... watch and listen for anything, okay? And remember, if something happens while I'm down there, you run! William, you'll have to help your brother."

Standing shoulder-to-shoulder, the boys nodded, acknowledging understanding.

"Good, good." Her stare shifted to the stairway again, followed by another deep exhale. "All right, here I go. I'll be right back with your dad."

The stairway seemed tighter now, more cramped and confined, as she descended with slow, methodical steps, listening to the sole of her shoes hit each hard concrete surface. Her vision remained on the last stair, focused on the black goo, seeing the warm light's reflection.

Almost there. Four more steps.

Sulfur's rancidity hit her, filling her nostrils. She suppressed the nausea, staring upwards. With her breath held, she paused, craning her neck to get a view of her sons. Both huddled together, watching her advance through the trapdoor's opening. Their eyes were wide, worried, full of doubt and despair.

Keep going, keep going. He's down there, and he needs you. Do it for your love, your life, your boys. Together is the only way!

Her heart hammered in her chest, thumping in a rhythmic beat. The sound echoed in her ears, and she could feel the endorphins released, refocusing her motive.

Three left.

The ceiling seemed to drop the farther she advanced, causing her to dip her head. Her hands naturally crept upwards, palms sliding against the roughness, but her stare remained.

Here we go. Last one. I'm here, Micah. We're getting the hell out!

As her feet hit the floor of the bunker, a labored sigh poured out, chased by a silent gasp. She could see the two paths at the end. But....

Micah wasn't in the room.

It was empty.

Lynn's vision leapt from the floor to the dark corridors and back, but she was alone. The only evidence suggesting her husband had been there was the crimson puddle that poured from his head after the attack. The memory rushed in, taking over, filling her with dread. Her mind swirled, thinking about the incident, watching his limp body crumple to the floor. And then seeing those eyes of the madman, the orbs of evil, hate, and fury.

She refocused, staring at the puddle of blood congealing on the rigid floor, and then she saw it: a trail of blood leading away. It vanished into the darkness of the path.

"He's alive," she said, stepping backward and racing back to her sons. *"Where is he, though?"*

PART FIVE

END OF THE ROAD

43

"WHAT DO YOU MEAN, he's gone? Where did he go?" David searched his mother's face for answers.

"David, honey, it means he's okay. He's alive and on his way to the interstate right now." She stared into her son's eyes with care and comfort. "We need to meet him there, find help, and get home."

"But, he's hurt. The crazy man hit him with that log. There was blood ... so much ..." He trailed off, eyes drifting to the wall, not completing the sentence.

Lynn stepped forward, addressing both sons. "I know, I know, baby, but he's okay, I promise. We can't think about what we saw." She reached out, cupping David's chin, forcing him to look at her. "Rid your mind of the image because he's okay."

She had to say it despite not knowing if the statement was true, given her maternal needs to soothe and coddle. Truth is, her anxiety was at an all-time high after not finding her husband unconscious and battered, bleeding out on the grim bunker floor. Seeing the pool of congealing blood and the droplets leading away from the scene attacked her thoughts, filling her with panic. She worried he wasn't okay and that she would never see him again.

The boys' uneasiness and reluctance were evident as she eyed them, but this wasn't the time to ponder and sulk about what-ifs. The threats were lingering somewhere, ready to slash, and cut, and feed their sick desires. It was time to act, to go.

"We're going to find him, boys, but it won't be easy." She paused, clutching her side and gritting her teeth. "We can do this as long as we stay tight and swift. The two-lane road is north of us, back up the slope, but I can't make it. Neither can David with his ankle." Her eyes dropped to her oldest son and his swollen leg, empathy and guilt rising in her gut. "Our only chance, guys, is to head west and pray we hear cars. It will lead us to safety, to help, and to your father."

Will and David looked at each other and nodded, gestures laden with disinclination and tension.

"Good, good. Okay, stay close and right behind me." Her stance shifted as she spoke, staring at the forest through the doorway.

With the plan established, Lynn crept away from the bunker's opening, hugging the structure's wall. She side-stepped her way down the hall, passing the mattress and crates, avoiding scattered piles of broken glass. David and Will followed, replicating her actions with twitchy, nervous eyes, never getting more than a pace behind their mother.

The sun's vibrant rays filled the entrance with warmth as the three inched forward, watchful and alert. Lynn halted as they reached the end of the hall, staring down at her sneakers. The sunlight streaking the floor lit up her white toe caps, while the rest of her shoes and body remained hidden amongst the shadows of darkness. She stood there for a few moments, focused on her rapid, labored breathing.

Deep breath in through the nose, exhale slowly through the mouth. Repeat, Lynn, repeat. You can do this. The technique repeated for nearly a minute before she marched forward, peering out the doorway. The splintered, sun-bleached plywood she ripped away from the entrance to her right, nestled against the structure's wall. Her sight gently moved to the left, seeing crisp leaves scatter in the windy gusts as dusk approached. But all seemed quiet, lifeless. Until ...

Motion caught her eye. A flash of color appeared from behind the corner, the thin man with the log. Sid. He narrowed his beady eyes and locked onto her face. He held the log horizontally in one hand, gently patting it with his free palm.

Staring into his lustful eyes, shock consumed her, and she bolted back inside the doorway. "GO, GO, GO!"

Her screams startled the boys, and both flinched at the rapid change in her movements and demands. They whipped around and bolted away from the doorway, hugging the wall. Will flew down the hall, jumping over obstacles. David had to hover close to the wall, using the crumbling plaster as a crutch. With a fresh injection of adrenaline, Lynn ran, keeping David moving toward the back of the structure.

Behind them came the familiar growls and curses. He was already in the hall, coming for them, coming for blood.

Will darted back into the dark room, turning and facing the doorway. Within seconds, David and Lynn squeezed through the opening. Lynn whirled around and shoved the door closed, barring it with her shoulder. She held there, applying every ounce of strength she had left. There was no hiding this time.

Violent threats screamed from the hallway, getting louder, closer. Lynn glanced away from the door, catching her sons huddled together, backs against the wall. They had slid downwards, crouched under the window, hiding their faces, trembling.

Memories flooded her mind, thinking about the two of them running around the house as toddlers. Dancing and laughing. Spilling their SpaghettiOs and milk on the cream-colored carpet of their home. The first time David rode his bike without training wheels, his little brother cheered him on. Fond memories, loving memories. Memories before the lying and the betrayals. Memories of a good life stolen. She couldn't let this happen. This wasn't their end.

She faced the door and pushed, holding the doorknob in a death grip. She pushed with a new exuberance, digging deeper than physically possible. And then she returned the screams; bellowing growled curses. Fear no longer flooded her veins. She was mad, and her instinct to protect and survive exploded.

The door shuddered from the first blow, splinters showering above Lynn's head. The force of the impact knocked her back, but she barreled forward, holding it within its frame. David and Will screamed behind her, holding each other, tears flowing down their cheeks.

Another thunderous strike followed, sending shards of wood flying. Lynn held, gritting her teeth, calves burning, and still screaming at the top of her lungs. Beads of perspiration ran down her face, dripping to the floor.

A final blow collapsed a portion of the door, and Sid's arm flung through the opening. His grease-stained fingers searched and found Lynn, gripping a handful of her hair. He wrenched upwards, yanking her head. Her face slammed into the door, splinters scratching her cheek and neck.

Both boys ran to their flailing mother, gripping her around the waist and pulling backward. David reached for Sid's filthy hand, attempting to break the grip of slick hair and knuckles. He pried at the thumb and index finger, twisting and pulling to no avail, screams exiting his burning lungs.

David leaned in and planted his gaping mouth on the top of Sid's hand, teeth clenched and bearing down with maximum force. The bite broke the skin, and an agonizing scream sounded through the hall. Sid released the grip and yanked his arm from the hole, cursing.

Lynn nearly collapsed to the ground, but her sons supported her, dragging her away from the door. The three braced against the wall, eyes locked on the door, knowing it would fall. And all three prepared to fight, roaring in their adversary's direction.

Through the dim light and chaos, an eye appeared through the opening, dried blood encrusted around it. It searched the room, finding its prey, its feast. Sid pulled away from the opening and brought the log down again, shattering the door's top half. It crashed against the wall's plaster, scarcely holding on by the top hinge.

Lynn and the boys stilled, holding their breath, bracing for the inevitable. Sid stood in the hall, panting like a savage beast after the chase. Flicking his tongue across his lips, bloodshot eyes honed in, he locked on Lynn. And then he stepped forward.

His skinny arm reached through the opening and found the doorknob. With a twist of his wrist, the latch disengaged, and the door sprang open, exposing the room and all its splendors. With deviant intent, he reached up with both arms and gripped the frame, leering inside with his trademark vile grin. Blood pooled on the frame from his lacerated hand, droplets sliding to the floor.

Lynn held the monster's eyes, fists clenched and ready to strike. "Come on, you piece of shit! Come on!" She growled with gritted teeth. She was ready to end this nightmare.

Sid's smile widened, exposing his yellow teeth. He started forward, ready to feast, when two deafening blasts rang out from down the hall. His shoulder and neck erupted in a crimson fountain. He slammed against the doorframe, body flailing while he collapsed to the ground. He wasn't moving.

Lynn's shriek filled the room. Seeing the man's lifeless legs sprawled outside the doorway diminished all previous feelings. She held her boys tighter than she realized, shielding them from the violent scene. And then, through the chaos, her ears picked up a sound. Shoes crunching broken glass. Whoever the shooter was, they were approaching the room.

44

THE NEXT FEW MOMENTS distorted Lynn's mind like a branch after a snowstorm. The weight muffled understanding, bending it to the brink of snapping. Reality was gone, leaving in its wake insoluble thoughts and visions. *What the hell just happened? What was about to happen?* Deep down, she knew the answer to the latter.

She couldn't move, body tense, muscles locked and braced against the wall, holding her children, her life. She also couldn't look away, eyes glued to the hall where Sid sprawled lifeless. The doorframe itself seemed alive. Deep, laborious breathing. Inhaling, exhaling. A steady thumping pulse flowed around the jambs. This couldn't be real. Was she questioning her own sanity?

The slow, meticulous footsteps were growing louder, inching closer with each heartbeat. She shuddered at the sounds, flinching, knowing this was an unknown threat, a new monster prepared to sink its jagged teeth into her flesh. And she was helpless to stop it. Her body was too bruised and battered to continue the fight. This was the end. You can't outrun bullets.

Suddenly, the steps halted, leaving silence, which was worse. The door's pulse intensified, expanding and contracting in a terrorizing cycle. Tears welled in her eyes, expecting the utter silence to dissolve as soon as the beast revealed itself. She gripped her boys tighter, embracing them, loving them, while saying goodbye without a sound.

But the inevitable fury never came. A sound replaced it that also brought tears to her eyes, but tears of relief, of comfort. She thought she'd never hear it again. A wheezing, exasperated voice. Micah's voice.

"Lynn!"

She released a gasp and her grip around her sons. That sound, that voice, flooded her with what she needed to push on: hope. Lifting herself from the floor, she tried to respond, but the words refused to flow. With newly blossomed will, she trudged forward, barely noticing the persistent pain stifling her stride.

She paused at the doorway, emotions trumping her need to lean forward and peer into the hall. To see her husband, the man who returned from the dead to save her, to save their boys from that sick madman. The man who ended the terror, the threats. Her eyes closed as she hovered there, thinking about her life, their challenging life, before releasing a long breath. Then she opened her eyes and peered around the jamb.

He stood ten feet from the doorway, his right forearm braced against the exterior wall. Dried blood on his temple, streaking back behind his left ear. He slowly lifted his gaze from the floor, catching Lynn's profile through the doorway. Through hollow, weary eyes, he stared at his wife, unable to find the words.

Lynn limped forward, approaching her battered husband, ambiguity swimming in his eyes. Her breathing paused when she inspected the blackened blood wrapping his head. And then her sight lowered to the violent tool anchored in his right fist.

She swayed back an inch, eyes glued on the gun. Turning away from Micah, she viewed the warm corpse lying to her right. A shudder pulsed through her body and mind, reliving the scene. Reliving the snarls, the growls, the log, and—the knife. *The knife.* Slowly, she reached back and patted her pocket. *Still there.*

"Lynn?"

The sound blasted her ears, even at such a low mumble, and she whipped around. He hadn't shifted or moved, still braced against the wall, staring at her.

"Micah?" She broke through the shock and stepped into the hall, facing him. "What ... what did you do? Where did you get the—"

He cut her off. "Are you okay? The boys?" He stumbled forward, using the wall as support.

Her eyes flicked to the room, where Will and David stood in the center, shoulder-to-shoulder. "They're fine," she stated, knowing that wasn't true. Her view returned to the gun, then to Micah's eyes. "Where did you ..." she swallowed, trying to force the words out, "get that?"

His eyes hinted at some life when the words exited her throat, and he lifted the gun, staring at the intricate handle. Silence blanketed the hall for what seemed like minutes before he lowered it back to his side, and his attention returned to Lynn.

"I don't know. I don't remember," his voice trembled with uncertainty.

"Micah," she paused, disbelief surfacing in her mild actions and voice. "You have a gun in your hand and just killed someone. Where did you get it?"

No response. His eyes fixated on her, then the haziness and lifelessness returned.

She stiffened, watching the gun sway loosely against the wall and at his side. "Micah? You're scaring me!"

The worry in her voice brought him back, refocusing his senses. He shook off the haze and cleared his mind, redirecting his sight to Sid's body beyond Lynn. He looked at it in awe while his mind searched for the answers. W*as he really responsible for this graphic scene, this butchery? Why couldn't he remember?*

From the doorway, a slight motion caught his eye, and he followed the source. David stood there, just inside the room, leaning forward and peering at his father. No, that's not right. He was staring at the gun in his father's hand and sensing everything wasn't okay.

"Dave, are you okay, son?" His eyes widened, locked onto his firstborn. "Where's your brother?"

David flinched as his eyes hovered over Sid's body, then retreated into the dark room.

"David? Come back here, boy." He stepped forward, advancing toward the doorway. "Now!"

Lynn slid in front of the door, blocking the opening. "Micah, I'm going to ask you again. Where the hell did you get that thing?"

He could sense the shift in her tone, the caution and worry. Such a dramatic change, filled with indignation and trust issues. *Where was the love, support, and admiration for rescuing them? Why was she doing this again? Why was she treating him like a dog that just pissed on the family room rug?* His cognition was so hazy, yet so vivid. Was this real?

He felt the steel of the gun's handle against his fingers while he searched for some clarity, some answers. He dug deep within his consciousness, trying to make sense of what was happening, or what had happened, but no logical answers surfaced. Confusion withered his mind, and he was lost. He didn't even know where he was.

"Micah?" she tried again. "I don't like this. I need you. The boys need you. Talk to me."

The walls seemed to collapse, boxing him in like a caged beast. His eyes darted around the hall, looking for answers, looking for an escape from the madness, but he remained silent. He slowly lifted his free hand, cupping the top of his forehead and sliding it backward through his bloodied, greasy hair. The damp touch garnered his attention, and he looked at his palm, at the rich reds and browns staining his skin. He stared at it with the same hollow, dead eyes from moments before.

And then those blank, emotionless eyes shifted and focused on Lynn. But something new had evolved in them. Anger.

Lynn watched the transition and slowly retreated, stepping back a few paces into the room with her sons. The moment she heard Micah's raspy voice after the shooting, her heart flooded with hope. But something wasn't right. She had never seen him spiral this deep, so dark and irrational. She was afraid of this man. This wasn't her husband.

45

Like the darkness that engulfed the hall, swallowing the faint light, Micah was powerless to stop it from taking control of his mind. His thoughts swirled with ill memories. Feelings of shame, betrayal, wrath, and hate surfaced, plummeting him farther down the rabbit's hole. Gravity seemed to vanish, and he found himself free-falling through the abyss of black. Alone again.

Agony struck him head-on, and he buckled over, heart racing. Flashes of light strobed in his cortex, each one delivering a jolt of pain followed by recollection. But the pain was comforting. It made him feel alive, conscious of reality. Memories slowly materialized, and upon opening his eyes, he found himself back in Clyde's shop.

He found his footing in front of the office doorway, staring at a desk cluttered with invoices. The bookcase stood guard to his left, watching over the room like a sentinel on patrol. The box containing the old couple's purse and wallet still sat on the shelf, undisturbed, covered in a thick layer of aging dust.

He held something gripped tightly in his hand. As he lifted his hand to his eyes, his palm opened, revealing a single key on a key ring. He looked at it with intrigue, turning it over in his hand. *Chevy Malibu?*

The clatter of glass shattering rang out behind him, and he whirled, panic sinking in. A glass jar filled with old washers and nuts had fallen to the concrete floor. The contents and shards danced on the ground, finally ending their macabre capering.

His heart hammered in his chest. But there was no culprit, no one responsible for the sudden shock. He was alone in this strange place. Once his breath slowed, he looked at his hand once more, but the key ring was *gone*. He turned his hand over, wriggling his fingers, staring in awe as the tendons flexed and relaxed. *What the hell is going on?*

Another flash struck, staggering his steps. He braced himself against the office wall, eyes closing until the intensity passed.

Then the brightness and pain subsided, allowing him to see again. But he wasn't near Clyde's office any longer. His surroundings had morphed, changed within the blink of an eye. He was still in the shop, though.

A black metal filing cabinet with the bottom drawer pulled out flanked his sight. He advanced toward it, floating on a cloud of mist. Inside was a case that matched the black color of the steel surrounding it. He fixated on the case, watching the hasps unhinge without human touch. The lid sprang open, exposing the contents; it was empty.

Moments passed while he peered into the emptiness, wondering what his twisted mind was showing him. Wondering why he was here.

He reached for the case but paused, realizing his hand held another object. His fingers wrapped around the black steel grip, cold to the touch. He brought the gun up to eye level, examining it with darting eyes, admiring the precision, the craftsmanship. *How did I ... Have I had this the whole time?*

The flash returned, and he buckled over once again. The brightness intensified, forcing him to stagger to a knee. Then it stopped.

Silence surrounded him, and the darkness returned, engulfing the remaining wisps of illumination. After a few breaths, he opened his eyes, revealing the hallway littered with long-forgotten belongings. Reality crept in, and he felt alone, abandoned, and discarded like the trash piled around his shoes. *How did I get here?*

He stood, stabilizing himself with the support of the mattress standing, until it toppled over to the waste-ridden floor. Hearing the shuffling of bodies, his attention darted to the room ahead on his right. Muffled whispers and light footsteps collected in his ears, further disorienting his mind. *Lynn? Boys?*

He stepped forward, the crunching of glass screaming against the rubber of his soles. With haste strapped to every action, he took another step and called out, "Lynn!"

46

He watched Lynn disappear into the room, taking slow backward strides away from the doorframe. Her teary eyes, frightened, shifted between the smug look strapped to his face and the gun locked in his fist. As the darkness engulfed the last sliver of her face, the hate boiled. *She's doing it again. Leaving me when I need her most. I can't let this continue!*

He advanced toward the doorway, unaware of his next steps, unaware of his true intentions. But he knew something had to change. He couldn't allow the suffering to continue, or the desertion. They needed him, and he needed them to care and follow the lead of their loving patriarch. They would listen, follow, or....

As he rounded the doorway, staring into the blackness of the room, a shout echoed from behind him. A sound he wasn't expecting or prepared to hear. "Hey, asshole!"

The suddenness triggered a flinch, and he swiveled. His beady eyes steered toward the structure's entrance, pupils reacting to the sunlight. Instinctively, he raised the gun, pointing it at the agitated beast looming in the distance, just beyond the opening. Clyde stood there, shotgun pumped and pointed at the clear view of his prey.

The tension bloomed, and the two locked eyes, neither willing to back down or lower their firearm. Micah knew there was no resolution to the standoff sans bloodshed.

The hulking man glaring at Micah shouted again, breaking the silence and strain. "Better drop that, you thievin' son of a bitch! Don't make me kill you!"

Micah listened intently—picking up each syllable as it left the man's lips—but remained silent. His view narrowed, watching Clyde's shallow breathing and the sway in his stance. Every sense heightened by the intensity of the moment. Heartbeats passed before he responded.

"Stay away from my family, you psychopath! We didn't do anything to you! Leave us alone! We're not going to be another one of your," a snarl slid between his lips, "trophies."

"Trophies? Are you fuckin' crazy?"

"I saw the purses and wallets! How long have you been doing this, man? Abducting people and killing them?"

Clyde shook his head, confusion warping his stare. "What the ... Purses and wallets?"

"You know what I'm talking about. The ones on the bookcase. The ones from the two people you killed. Probably a poor couple needing help. You lured them here, slaughtered them after toying with them. Just like you are doing with us!"

"You're crazy. Going through all my personal shit. Those were my grandparents' belongings. Better shut your ass up before I blow a hole in your head, ya lyin' asshole!" His eyes tightened, aiming the shotgun for a kill shot.

Micah stiffened. "Back away, man. It's not happening."

"Hmm, a thief and a liar, eh?" Clyde snickered, the shotgun's barrel wavering at Micah's chest. "What'd you do to Sid? Is he dead?"

Micah ignored the inquiries, not thinking about his handiwork sprawled behind him. He held the big man's stare, fury and agitation burning in his blue eyes.

"Drop the gun, asshole, before it's too late!" Clyde sucked in a breath through clenched teeth. "Don't make me do this. I just want some answers."

"What the hell are you talking about? Answers?" Micah growled, feeling his finger flex and recoil around the trigger. *God, this guy's sicker than I thought. Still toying with me after everything. He's a maniac.*

Confusion exploded, and the darkness returned, warping his thoughts.

Clyde cleared his throat, disgust and hate lingering in his eyes. "Was this your plan all along, buddy? Why? I was trying to help—"

"Stop it! Stop the games, you piece of shit!" For the first time, Micah dropped his glare from the hulking monster, watching the darkness creep in amongst the walls and ceiling. "Stop the lies, NOW!"

"You're the liar, asshole! Breaking into my shop, stealing my gun. Who knows what else you rummaged through and took? Probably ransacked the whole place while I was out searching the nearby yards for a fuel pump. Shitty ass import."

"STOP IT! STOP IT!"

"Where's my Malibu key, motherfucker? Planning on taking it? A little joyride?"

"What—"

"Then you cut my damn phone cord and stole the handset." Clyde clicked his tongue. "Why? What the hell is your motive, man? Just get off on toying with people, taking advantage of their goodwill?"

"Stop it! Stop It! Stop lying!"

Micah suppressed the fury burning within his soul, knowing this was another sick game of cat and mouse.

"What the hell are you babbling about, psycho?" he growled, moving the gun's sights to the center of Clyde's head. "You cut the phone cord, so we couldn't call for help! You did this, and you're still tormenting me. Why?"

"You really are a piece of work, man. Lying at every turn. Are you even listening to yourself? Why the hell would I cut my own phone cord? It's my only means of communication out here, dipshit." Clyde clenched his jaw, shaking his head.

A slight shake pulsed through Micah's head, trying to control it. "I saw you. I saw you driving the hatchback. Driving through the forest a few hours ago! Why are you doing this?"

"The hell is wrong with you, buddy? That shitty ass car is still on blocks in the yard. You are fuckin' crazy!"

"STOP IT! STOP IT! STOP THE LIES!"

Clyde's eyes narrowed, watching the fury explode from Micah. He cocked his head and spat. "I can't believe you're actually married. How in the hell did you con her into saying 'I do'?"

Lynn's mention was too much. The thought of this monster thinking about his wife, visualizing her, undressing her with his eyes. All the twisted fantasies and thoughts. The cord snapped as the darkness blanketed him. And he pulled the trigger.

47

Lynn watched in terror as her husband crept around the corner, slowly revealing his torso. There was a stagger to each step, full of emptiness and misery. Dim light highlighted his sunken shoulders and head, and shadows concealed his twisted, contemptuous face. But she knew an emotionless smile grew there. Sickness dripping from each corner.

Before he could lurch into the room, he whipped around, startled and agitated. He screamed and cursed just outside the doorway, wrath burning deep in his voice. Lynn couldn't see the extended gun locked in his fist, but she knew he held it. Knew he aimed it at the man, the monster chasing them, toying with them, hunting them. Knew what was about to happen.

The two exchanged words and threats. Heated accusations and lies. Clyde continued with the deception and games, twisting facts. She knew Micah wasn't responsible for any of this. Seconds later, a shot rang out, bouncing violently through the hall. The sound shattered her ears, and the deafening blast was not alone. It was mirrored. There were two shots.

Flashes of light strobed with the blasts, and time slowed. Micah shifted backward, his balance interrupted, and slammed against the doorjamb. His sweatshirt, tattered with holes, now rippled with waves.

Lynn cringed at the sight but couldn't drop her stare. She couldn't scream, couldn't move, couldn't breathe.

Micah remained there, pinned against the doorframe for several seconds, shock apparent in his panicked eyes. He still held the firearm in his right hand, now pointed toward the ground.

With his free hand, he cradled his midsection. The left side of his sweatshirt bloomed with color, the faded brown darkening to crimson, painting his skin and fingertips. He stared in disbelief at the blood, eyes studying his palm, seeing the stained whorls of his fingerprints. *Son of a bitch shot me.*

And then the shock wore off. Pain radiated from the wound, spiraling throughout his core. The agony intensified, and a muffled moan escaped his clenched teeth. The darkness closed in once more, stalking its prey, pouncing like a parasite.

It took control.

A bright flash flickered, vibrant and harsh, against his closed lids. It forced his eyes open, and he peered at his surroundings. The pain throbbing in his gut was gone as he looked around, bewildered by the sights and sounds. All around was warm and comforting. *I know this place. I'm home.*

He sat in his leather La-Z-Boy, feet kicked up in front of their old Zenith. The Bulldogs were marching down the field against Stanford, and it was a nail-biter. His sons, years younger, jumped and shouted as each play commenced, celebrating alongside him. The atmosphere was peaceful, light, and fun. A time before the wilt and decay.

The smell of freshly baked cookies hung in the air, wafting around twinkling Christmas lights. As his vision swept the house, he noted the fireplace, the dining room, and the stairway leading to their bedrooms. Suddenly, laughter rang out from his left, and his eyes drifted there, knowing the source. Lynn stood in the kitchen, a yellow apron tied around her waist. Flour smudged a crease near her waistline where she had wiped her hand. Her aura glowed as she giggled with delight.

Next to her, sharing the kitchen duties, was his mother, Grace. She laughed alongside his wife, sounds of joy and happiness flooding the room. Color highlighted her cheeks, and a hint of gray streaked her hair. She looked youthful, passionate, and alive. Happy.

The two jostled one another, splashing soapy water back and forth. They were more than a mother-and-daughter-in-law. They were family, and they loved each other's company. Loved each other.

The boys continued their rambunctious jumps and excitement on his right, shouts and cheers exiting their lips. Oblivious to what was actually happening, they mirrored their loving father's actions when Fresno State scored. They were following his lead, showering him with love the way only children can.

He loved this life, this memory. His boys, his wife, and his mother, all under his roof. He built this life, this beautiful world, and sacrificed his own desires and needs to achieve it. Worked his ass off at every turn. He deserved it. A smile walked up his cheeks as he absorbed the moment, relishing every sight and sound. This was home, and he would not leave this place again.

But he was not in control.

The twinkle of the Christmas lights dimmed and dulled. The old Zenith's bright screen faded away in a mist of vapor, twirling amongst the approaching tendrils of darkness. He tried to stand, to scream for it to stop, but the blackness surrounded him, blanketing his mind.

The distant sound of a siren awoke his senses, ushering in pain's return. Not the pain from the gunshot wound, but the pain from the truth. The pain from what he lost.

The sound neared, and he snapped his eyes open. *What the hell is this? No, no, not this!*

The scent of rain—ozone—lingered in the air, and stars smiled down from above. But there was nothing happy about the memory.

An agonizing scream bore through the apartment behind him. The shriek froze his mind, paralyzing his body. He knew that scream all too well.

His vision remained fixated on the street past the yellowed strip of grass. A strobing light, red and blue, came into view, lumbering toward him at a steady pace. It brought the wail of the siren with it, ending its descent next to the walkway where he stood.

He forced his body to react, to face this demon that strangled his thoughts and his heart. Ignoring the cluster of shouts and the two EMTs shuffling past him, he peered over his shoulder, knowing this nightmare was real.

She was already on the gurney, frail, gray fingers clutching her throat. The exasperated screams echoed in the night as they rolled her closer and closer. He locked eyes with her, seeing the terror, the suffering bursting through like a ruptured boil. Tears streaking her cheeks, her screams escalated as she reached for him, the tendons in her arms popping and snapping.

He felt his arm lift and stray toward her, hearing the pain swimming in the gurgled cries. He held on with gentleness and care. His fingertips caressing the top of her withered hand, savoring the moment, silently letting her know he was there and he would fix this. He would find a way.

The screams suddenly muted, movement ceased, and time seemed to halt. He held her stare, watching the pained demeanor shift. The strains and spasms stopped, and she sat there, content. She seemed at peace, comforted by her son's loving presence and touch.

A sly smile formed, corners of her wrinkled mouth turning up. And then she spoke. Soft whispers.

"Micah ... Micah, my sweet boy. You're here. I knew you wouldn't let me go through this alone. You love your mother too much to let that happen." Seconds passed, and the two shared the moment in silence, appreciating their lives as mother and son. Appreciating the bond that could never break.

But the darkness didn't bring him here for pleasantries.

Instantly, her peaceful, loving smile faded, and her eyes narrowed. He could no longer see the clouds of delight shimmering through her soul. No, this woman was bitter, enraged, and loathing. Her fine hair flattened against her skull, her skin a paler shade of gray, with blue veins protruding from the paper-thin membrane. The walls of bliss and safety crashed around him the instant her mouth spilled the truth.

"How could you?" Her hand clamped down on his like an iron vice, twisting and tightening with each turn, and he was trapped. "How could you choose her over me, Micah? I'm your MOTHER!"

He tried to break free from her hate and the shame spiral, but he was helpless.

"You killed me, Micah," she wailed, spittle flinging from her thin, dry lips. "It was you! Why weren't you here when I needed you? You chose—HER! You let this happen! You chose that *bitch* over me! Kill her, Micah! Do it for your mother."

He could feel the bones of his hand and fingers shattering. The skin splitting, exposing pink muscle and white tendons. He tried to scream, hoping that would end the agony and shame, but his attempts were strangled. There was no escape from the darkness—it steered this vessel now—and the blanket engulfed all his senses.

The strobing effect reintroduced itself after a few moments, bright light followed by the dark shawl. Flashes of blue iridescence pumped through his shut eyes, each series weaker and weaker until they died. He breathed in, flexing his free hand, mind pounding. Memories and reality collided, merging and fusing together like a poisonous concoction, ready to explode.

As he opened his eyes, the intense pain from the gunshot returned, but he ignored it, locking it away somewhere deep in the caverns of his splintered consciousness. There was no time to feel, to think. There was only time to end the misery.

Slowly, he craned his neck and peered into the room's darkness, knowing Lynn was in there, knowing what he had to do for his mother. And the sick smile flooded his face.

48

THE THREE CLUSTERED UNDER the window, hands gripping fabric and flesh. The boys buried their faces in their mother's sides, mumbling sobs. Neither could bear the scene, nor understand what was happening. They covered their heads and ears, squeezing their eyes shut.

Lynn wasn't so fortunate; she couldn't avert her eyes from the stalking beast. There was nowhere to hide, to escape. She was trapped, and her predator had his ears pinned and teeth bared, ready to pounce.

The faint rays penetrating the narrow window seemed to glow, highlighting the room and its precious contents. Micah pushed himself off the doorframe and shambled inside, bracing himself against the brittle wall. All his senses exploded, heightened to a degree that was unnatural, unworldly. He could smell their breath, feel their touch, taste their fear. But he was only there for her, for Lynn.

"Lynnnnnnn." The word left his tongue on a wave of contempt as he stepped away from the wall, plaster falling to the ground. He held the gun pointed diagonally toward the musty concrete floor.

"Come here, babe. Let's not keep *Daddy* waiting."

Lynn's throat boiled, needing to release a scream, but it wouldn't come. She sat against the wall, holding her two sons, unable to look away. Every muscle in her exhausted body contracted, squeezing without mercy, as she watched her husband get closer and closer. Even through the dimness, she could see the faint hue of his blue eyes. But they were wrong. They were empty, lifeless. Monstrous.

The sick call sprang from his lips again once he was within a few feet. "Lynn." Each word he spoke scratched at her psyche, shattering her soul. She watched as his free hand raised, lifting the gun, and aimed it at her face.

Finally, the scream fell from her mouth. "Micah! What are you doing? What ... Why ..." Incoherence triggered free-flowing tears and sobs.

A heinous smile widened across his lips as he witnessed her terrified pleas. "*Shh ... don't scream, babe.*" He held his index finger to his lips. "Everything's okay. Everything will soon be as it should be. You know this has to happen. This is the only way to make things right."

"Micah! It's me! Your wife." She released her grip on Will and held out a hand, trying to shield herself from the inevitable. "No, no, no! Stop ... stop. Please, Micah!"

"Goodbye, babe. Mother forgives you for your treachery, for your sins."

"What? What? Micah!"

The stagger of his stance dissolved as he watched her plead and beg, and his focus heightened, eyes narrowing in on the sight of the gun. Focusing on the quivering target fronting the end of the barrel, his finger curled around the trigger, primed to squeeze and end the misery.

But then he stopped. The slight sway of his stance returned as he stared at her—per his view—bobbing like a buoy in a calm bay. The twisted, sick smile faded, and his eyes fluttered, twitching under the chaos of his mind. He removed his finger from the cold steel trigger and lowered the gun. Then it all went black.

His eyes flickered in the darkness while his mind searched for answers, for understanding. All around was calm, silent, void of motion. A feeling of weight-lessness lingered, like he was floating through a cloud. But the tranquility and bliss ended, and the strobing flashes returned.

The light intensified with rapid bursts, burrowing through his closed lids. Faster and faster, they struck him, burning his skin and senses, then they ceased as quickly as they began, leaving him once more alone in utter darkness.

Moments passed before his cognition engaged. His eyes remained closed, but he found himself in a seated position, feeling life evolve around him. There was a crispness in the air, bustling with the morning chill, and he could hear the faint coos of mourning doves nearby.

He tapped the soft padding of the chair's arm with his fingertips while taking in everything his senses were revealing. *Where am I? What is this?* he wondered as he opened his eyes to the haze surrounding him.

Clouds loomed low, hovering as far as he could see, yet no scent of forthcoming rain presented itself. Sporadic, towering pines and willows peppered the yellow grass around his seat, and he found he wasn't alone. He was in the middle of a row, flanked by other matching chairs and blurred occupants. Soft whispers snuck out from all directions, billowing through his ears as he tried to bring clarity to the vision.

A woman sat on his left, clad in a long, black lace dress. Her face was hidden, covered by a sheer veil, yet he couldn't make out her features. She remained silent, only a faint sniffle showing life as she wiped her eye with a black handkerchief.

"Lynn?" he whispered.

He leaned forward, eyes drifting past the woman to the others in the row. Two young boys sat next to her, but he couldn't identify them. Something was wrong with their faces. They were hazy, blurred, partially erased. They wore matching black suits, slightly wrinkled. The two slouched in their chairs, solemnity oozing from their auras.

Dave? Will? What the hell is this? More figures flanked his right, all wearing the familiar funereal black and exchanging hushed whispers. Mourners surrounded him.

Slowly, the muddle of obscurity lifted, exposing the vision's truth. Before him was a dark mahogany casket supported by a steel bier. A mound of freshly dug earth encrusted the area, loaminess infusing the air.

As his eyes adjusted to the scene, he stepped toward the intricate coffin, eyes glued to the closed crown and watching his foggy breath linger in the air like a ghost in the mist. *This isn't right. This isn't what happened. Why is it closed?*

After three more cautious steps, he stopped, staring downward and taking in the rich, vibrant patterns of the wood. His sight hovered over the brass fittings, hinges, and handles, remembering the artificial, rehearsed sales pitch of the mortician. *Fuckin' gluttonous leech.*

He stood there for several seconds, taking in the memory, reliving the chilly morning he laid his mother to rest. Suddenly, the pain, the mourning, rushed back in, taking over and tormenting his mind with misery. Without realizing his actions, he wailed and screamed at the casket, trying to drive the agony away. Trying to bury it in the depths of his unconscious so he wouldn't feel it again. He spun in circles, fists clenched as the tears spilled. He dropped to his knees, screaming for the vision to end. But the memory would neither fade nor accommodate his wishes.

A powerful thud resonated from inside the casket, forcing Micah to stop his belligerence and bawling. He froze, watching the polished wood reverberate from the strike until it stilled. He glanced behind him, hoping the other attendees witnessed the event, but their blurred faces ignored him. They carried on, embracing each other and whispering loving words of support.

As he turned back to the casket, the thud ceased. Quickly, he sprang to his feet. His sight remained on the casket as he continued his retreat until his calf and ankle clipped his chair. A gasp escaped his throat from the contact, and he nearly tripped and fell over. After he steadied himself, his eyes fixed on the pulsing lid again.

The crown seemed alive, expanding and contracting like a beast's labored breaths. The ornate wood cracked and twisted with each pulse, exposing a convoluted web of meandering lines. Then, after another series of swelling shifts, it exploded in a violent burst of luminescence.

Micah shielded himself from the blast, whipping his torso sideways and holding out both hands to protect his face. Shards of dagger-like wood and splinters peppered his black suit, his exposed palms, and wrists, then fell harmlessly to the yellow grass below his feet. His hands instinctively went to his body, searching for wounds and cuts, finding nothing. He was unscathed.

He glanced to his left, observing the seated woman and boys flanking him. All three wore the onslaught of the blast, fragments of wood piercing their legs, chests, and blurred faces. Splinters dotted the younger boy's forehead where vibrant crimson wailed from the wounds, flowing down his hazy face. But they didn't notice the explosion, nor their pierced hemorrhaging physiques. All three carried on as though nothing happened.

What the hell was that? What is this? This didn't happen. Why am I seeing this?

An uncontrollable force seemed to grip his attention, forcing his eyes to shift back to the shattered casket. Wisps of smoke floated in the air above it, then slowly dissipated to clarity. And there she was. His mother. Grace.

She seemed at peace, her head propped up on a fluffed white pillow. She wore her favorite blue silk dress and a subtle pink blush on her healthy, full cheeks. Her face framed by thick auburn hair, lacking any hint of the silver after her decline. This was not a woman plagued by disease, stolen by rot and decay. She couldn't be dead. There was too much life thriving in her. She was merely in a deep slumber.

He took her in for several moments, admiring her beauty, remembering her laugh, her gleeful persona. The creases of his mouth curled, revealing a feeling he lacked for so long. Happiness. Memories of elation swept in, filling the void that created the monster he had become. This is how he remembered her before the curse took root. This was his mother.

Shock crept back in, planting its embryo, as he watched her eyes spring open. Slowly, she turned her head, locking onto his eyes. The peaceful, loving appearance shattered as she lifted her head from the pillow, sitting up with smugness.

"You!" Her head shook, contempt flaking off with each movement. "You don't love me anymore, boy. Why?" she growled through gritted teeth. "After everything I've done for you. Why haven't you done it? Why isn't she dead?"

Shrinking under the words, Micah watched his mother's facade peel away, revealing the veritable monster. The frailness and sagging skin morphed, depleting the youthful vibrance. Her thick lock of wavy hair deteriorated, leaving strings of silver and gray.

She raised her hand, pointing a gnarled, bony finger at him. "You are weak, boy. Pathetic. I'm your damn mother, Micah! What are you waiting for? She did this to us. DO IT!"

The words hit him like a truck, barreling over him, looping in his mind again and again. *Do it! You're weak! Pathetic! I'm your mother ... mother ... mother ... mother.... Do it!*

The words lingered, forcing him down the rabbit hole of despair and misery, boxing him in and taking control once more. Then, the dark shawl returned, leaving only gloom and blackness, and the vision ended.

49

A DEEP GASP LEAPT from Micah's mouth when reality resurfaced, and the pain from the gunshot rushed back in. He clenched his teeth, and he realized a new pain near his sternum accompanied the wound in his gut.

Lynn was in front of him when he opened his eyes, but she stood, no longer cowering on the dingy floor. She faced him, tears streaking her cheeks, and she shook like a branch in a windstorm. Her right shoulder arched forward, and her arm extended toward his chest, making contact.

Micah's eyes left her grieving face, feeling the shame and guilt building back up, knowing what he had to do. *Do it! Do it for me, Micah. For your mother!*

His sight followed her shaking arm to the center of his torso. There, lodged in her fist, was an object, a metallic object. The blade of a knife thrust deep within him, piercing his chest. And blood wept from this new wound.

Once his mind comprehended what his eyes revealed, he rocked backward, breaking the bond of contact. The sudden movement forced a flinch from Lynn, and she released the knife, watching his face twist with confusion as he glared at her.

After another distancing step, his fingers loosened, and the gun fell to the floor. Both hands reached for the blade's handle, gripping it with newly slick, stained fingers, yet he didn't pull it free. His eyes swelled, filled with panic and remorse before he stumbled, nearly losing balance. He struck the room's wall, stabilizing for a few seconds before sliding down to a seated position.

Lynn crept back, rejoining the boys under the window as the action unfolded. Her heart racked with pain, regret, and shame. She couldn't believe what she had done. This was her husband, the father to her children. The man to whom she said, "I Do." No, that wasn't true. That man died with his mother. Whoever he was now, this facade, this shell, mimicked Micah, but he wasn't her husband.

Her eyes strayed away for a split second, watching Will and David huddled together, still hiding their faces, hands plastered over their ears. They hadn't seen what transpired. They didn't watch their mother plunge a knife into their father's chest. And that was a good thing. They didn't need to live with this guilt, as well.

Suddenly, another saturated gasp escaped from Micah, and her sight returned to her husband, watching him twitch and convulse.

Micah released the knife's handle, staring at his hands, watching the life drip from his fingertips as he looked past his hands, locking onto his family. So many feelings blended, swirling together in a rage of agony. *Lynn. Dave. Will. His life, his legacy. What the hell happened?*

Instantly, the pain intensified, and he released a yelp through a clenched jaw. After a heartbeat, his arms went limp, dropping to his sides, and his rapid breaths grew shallower. His eyes glazed over as he stared at the nothingness before him. Death was the only escape from the madness.

Lynn froze, watching his body shudder, then still. She broke through the terror, calling out to him. "Micah? Micah? Can you hear me?"

There was no response.

She crawled forward on her hands and knees, ignoring the debris littering the floor. As she approached, she could faintly see his chest rise and fall, but the breaths were weak and few.

What have I done?

She slowly reached out with a trembling hand, brushing his thigh. "Micah? Babe?"

He remained motionless, unresponsive to her touch or calls. His head hung low, chin set against his bleeding chest, and she could see the blood pooling underneath him.

"No, no, no, no, no...." she mumbled. Without care, she leaned in, taking a seated position against the wall. She wrapped her arm around his shoulder, pulling him toward her, cradling him in a warm embrace. She cupped the back of his head while the tears flowed.

The boys watched in silence, still holding each other, not understanding the implications of what had occurred, nor the truth Lynn held. He would die in the next few minutes because of her, but what choice did she have?

With his face nestled against her neck, she could feel his slowed heartbeat and the rattle of his faint breath against her cheek. *How did this happen? Why? Why, Micah? What the hell happened to you? How did this happen?*

After what seemed like an hour of reckless thoughts and self-loathing, she felt him shift, a slight movement. She pulled back, watching him lift his right palm from the floor and gently pat his pants pocket twice.

"Micah, I'm here, babe." She placed her hand on his, feeling his cooling skin, trying to comfort him, to help him in any way she could. "I'm right here." She leaned in again, a soft breath brushing his forehead. She waited for a response, any hint that he was still with her. Under her hand, she felt the slight movement again, the two pats on his pocket.

"Mi ... Micah? What is it? Are you in pain? Can you tell me, babe?" She leaned in closer, listening and praying for a response. "Micah? What do you need me to do?" But the movement didn't repeat.

Her view fixated on his chest, praying to watch it rise and fall. It never rose again. A final breath exited his mouth. A long exhale carrying all the demons plaguing his mind, tormenting his soul. After years of misery, he could be at peace. He was gone.

Her tears flowed as she cradled his limp, lifeless body, followed by screams of despair and agony. Will and David broke the stranglehold of fear and cuddled her, mirroring the mourning and grief. All three sat there, releasing everything they still held on to. Releasing their father.

Darkness swirled in from all around, blanketing the surrounding light and forcing it from existence. He could feel it pick him up and carry him away, guiding him from the memories, from the guilt and shame of life. Taking him away from Lynn and the boys. He felt weightless, like a cloud hovering in a gentle wind, sailing along an atmospheric stream. All around was peaceful, serene, and void of the bitter fruit lingering in his thoughts. Until the first flash strobed.

The flash was steady, illuminating the abyss then burning out before repeating. This series continued for several moments before he saw something else within the darkness. A faint light loomed in the distance. This wasn't like the strobes, though. This light was constant, revealing the beauty of warmth amongst the ashes of death. And it seemed to call to him. The flow carried him toward it, whisking him away with the current.

As he neared, he heard whispers, both soft and inviting. The faint words seemed to roll over him, entering his ears, his skin, his heart, becoming a part of his flesh, his blood, his being. He couldn't make out the words, but they comforted him and assured him he was safe on this journey.

Once he was close enough, he realized the light was a doorway, an opening to a setting he couldn't believe. There weren't just hues of blinding white inside, but a myriad of colors, all delivering peace and tranquility to his mind.

And someone was there, waiting inside with open arms. A figure dressed in a long, flowing white dress waved him forward, guiding him into blissfulness. Radiance surrounded her, covering her presence in an unnatural orange glow, an aura of love, compassion, and hope. Her eyes were warm, and her loving smile extinguished any last feelings of shame, guilt, and hate that burrowed and clung to his psyche. He followed her into the light, absorbing the brilliance and shedding his physical life. It was Grace, and he was finally at peace.

50

THE WAILS AND SOBS finally slowed after time, allowing Lynn to regain some perspective and clarity. To think. She dropped her sight from Micah and looked at her sons, locking onto their reddened, dejected eyes. She could feel their pain and misery, knowing her action was both the cause, and the only solution.

She also knew she wouldn't recover from this. How could she, or anyone? She knew the truth would haunt her, attach itself like a festering boil ready to rupture. But she still needed to protect her sons and get them off this damn rock. And she wasn't going to tell them the truth. When the truth tears you apart from the inside, ignorance is bliss.

Despite the pain in her heart, her side, and her mind, she regained control.

"Boys," she began. "I ... I need your help. We have to keep moving. Get to the freeway and find someone. Find help."

Neither boy said a word, nor could they remove their stares from their father. Silence wrapped their bodies and held them still, engulfing them in a blanket of disbelief.

Lynn's focus returned to Micah, gripping his limp hand, knowing this moment would be the last time she touched him. She brought the hand to her lips and gently kissed his skin, lips trembling. She held the moment for several heartbeats, praying to awaken from this nightmare, knowing she wouldn't be so fortunate. And she said goodbye without speaking.

As she was laying his hand back down upon his blood-soaked sweatshirt, it slipped away, falling lifelessly to the concrete floor. The motion seemed distorted, slowed in time, unnatural. His fingers, flesh, veins, and tendons jolted with the impact before coming to cessation amongst a collection of brittle, cracked leaves. She watched his hand for several seconds, feeling the bile and grief rise in the back of her throat. But she had to push through those feelings, bury them. Her eyes darted, searching for anything that would lessen the pain, forcing her thoughts away from what occurred. That's when her stare drifted to his front pants pocket.

She could see he had something hidden under the stained denim. It was small, circular, creating a small, slightly raised protrusion in the material. Her mind focused, trying to think and plan. *What is that? What's in there?* she wondered, biting her lip.

She reached down, patting the object before giving it a slight rub. *Is that a half-dollar? What the hell?*

Instinctively, she reached her nimble fingers into the opening, feeling for the enigma. It was a ring, warm to the touch, and made of metal. She looped her index finger around it and pulled it free from the darkness.

She held the trinket close to her eyes with one finger looped through the opening, studying it, acknowledging that it was a key ring. A single brass key dangled from the metallic circle along with a stylized piece of rubber. The latter had two sides of detailed print: a souped-up classic car from the '60s, wheels flaming on the topside, and the word Chevrolet in blue on the underside.

As it twirled under the faint light, turning this way and that, she remembered. The car. The primed one parked at the shop. *What the hell are you doing with this, Micah? You were going to steal it and get us home, huh?* She shook her head, lip curled as she thought.

Her mind worked, playing out scenarios and weighing the threats. She possibly held their exit, their escape, in her hand. *But what if the Malibu didn't start? What if they made their way back to the shop, and it wouldn't turn over? What if Micah's shot missed Clyde, and he was lurking in the woods, waiting for the opportunity to spring?* There were a thousand what-ifs raging through her brain and complicating her decision-making. But sitting here, mourning her loss, not making a rational choice, wouldn't deliver them to safety. No, something had to happen.

She cleared her throat and wiped the remaining tears from her eyes. Her defeated posture stiffened, and she spoke with conviction, with authority. "Boys, change of plans. We're going back to the shop, and I'm getting us home. I know there's at least one vehicle that runs waiting for us."

Both boys looked up, staring at the strength in her appearance, listening to the bravery accented in each word, but they remained silent.

"You guys see this? Daddy took this for us. To get us out of here," she paused, holding the key toward them. "This is our ticket back on the road and home, boys. But it won't be easy. Not that anything that has happened in the last two days has been easy."

Dave broke the silence, eyes weary as he spoke. "Why would we go back, Mom? We've been running from that guy. What about getting to the freeway?"

She halted a response, thinking about his words, questioning the plan for a moment before reassuring both of them. "I really don't know where it is, baby. South, east, west?" She shrugged, trying to ease the stress swimming in his eyes. "But there's at least one car that runs back at the shop. And there's no one left that can hurt us."

Will inched forward, listening to her words, and delivered a meek nod.

She turned to her youngest, comforting his ill thoughts with a smile before addressing both. "This will work, boys. But we have to do it together- every step and inch climbed. We'll need each other to make it back to the top. We can do this."

Will wrinkled his brow. "But what about—" he paused his words, looking down at his father, tears swelling again. "What about Dad?"

"Yeah, Mom. We're not going to just ... just leave him here, are we?" David asked.

She sat there for several moments, watching her sons squirm in a puddle of impatience, watching their nervous eyes fill with anticipation. She knew the answer to the inquiries, and she hated it. Hated every part, but only three had a chance at surviving this nightmare. Only three would find a way home.

"Your father," she started before pausing, wrinkling her brow while searching for the right words. "We have to leave him."

"But—"

She didn't allow David to finish. "Listen, baby. Just listen, please. Both of you." Her eyes flew back to her husband, feeling the disgust rise again. *What the hell happened, Micah? Why were you going to hurt me? Us?*

She locked onto her sons once more. "We don't have a choice, boys. *I* have to get you to safety. *I* have to get you home." A deep breath exited her lungs, followed by a swallow. "We can't stay with Daddy or take him with us. It's the only way."

"What? Wh ... why, Mom?"

Lynn reached out, gripping David by his shoulders and silencing him with a look only a mother could deliver. "There's no other way, David. With my broken ribs and your sprained ankle, it's going to take the little strength we have left to get to the car." Her eyes narrowed. "I know this is hard, but if we are getting out of here, we have to leave him." The ill feelings returned as she said the words, crawling up from her gut and poisoning her mind.

Both boys' eyes welled as they listened to her strong, maternal words. This was wrong. But what part of this catastrophe was right? Eventually, they succumbed to her truth, knowing her words were the only way home, even if it felt like a betrayal.

"Listen, boys, once we get out of here and find a phone, I'll pull over and call the police. They'll come and find out what happened. They'll," her voice cracked, breaking the strong speech, "find your father and bring him home to us. He deserves better than this."

"Really?" Will mumbled, looking up at her.

"I promise, baby, but we have to do this."

They both knew she was right, even if the idea sickened them. Neither said a word, but the communication was clear.

After some time, and forcing herself through the misery and pain, Lynn lifted herself up and braced against the wall. Will followed her lead, getting David's arm around his neck and helping his brother to his feet. None spoke as they prepared to leave the room, glancing at Micah a final time, but they all thought the same thing: the real challenge lay ahead.

51

Lynn approached the doorway, shifting her eyes from Sid. She couldn't look at the monster, knowing the sickening thoughts would resurface.

She leaned her head out past the threshold, vision fixed on the entrance, listening and watching. A mild breeze blew through the opening, ushering in crisp scents of the mountainside and a few brittle leaves, but all else was calm and still.

"You guys, ready?" she whispered without turning and facing the boys, eyes still locked on the daylight. She knew they weren't, and she questioned her readiness, too.

Their responses were forced and unconvincing. Both boys wore signs of shock and grief as they followed Lynn's lead, not wanting to say their last goodbyes to Micah.

"All right. Let's go."

Lynn inched through the doorframe, turned left, and hugged the wall. After a step, she reached backward with an open hand, gesturing with her fingers. Will reached out, linking hands and following wary steps into the hall. David formed the last link of the chain, holding Will's free hand and supporting himself against the wall.

They moved silently through the hall, past the fallen mattress and boxes. Every few steps, Lynn glanced back, assuring the boys were right behind her, delivering hopeful nods. She suppressed her reservations about this plan, stuffing them deep inside, knowing they would only cause more panic and alarm. They had all suffered enough of that, but she still didn't know if her husband's shot had met its mark. *Were they still in peril? Where was Clyde?*

The caravan continued forward, approaching the forest and the setting sun. Lynn stopped a few feet before the opening, darting eyes scanning in all directions, noticing the shotgun to her right in the dirt. As she continued her search, that's when she saw him. Clyde.

He was a distance from the structure, back propped against an oak's trunk. He wasn't moving. She could see that the bullet struck him square in the chest. Blood pooled around the tattered flannel shirt he wore and soaked into his overalls. She could also see where he dragged himself along the dirt before resting against the giant tree.

The sight sickened her, and she felt the bile return to her throat. No one should witness this violence, this butchery. *Why? What did we do to you?* She thought, staring at the man.

She was also overtaken by relief. He couldn't hurt them now, even if he still possessed a pulse. She prayed he was dead, but she needed proof. She needed to know Micah protected them and saved them. He deserved that.

Without thinking it through, she stepped out of the structure, releasing Will's hand. She turned and instructed both boys to stay inside, no matter what happened, before stepping out into the open area and walking toward the man.

She cleared the distance in a few strides, getting within ten feet of him. This was close enough. She scanned him, seeing the life ooze from the wound, seeing his head dipped, chin resting on his broad chest. She also saw a slight flare of his nostrils. Faintly breathing.

"Hey. Hey, you son of a bitch." She forced the words out, anger and fear creeping up her spine.

Nothing.

Inching forward, she called out again, this time with some authority. "Open your eyes, asshole. I know you can hear me!"

The booming demand caused a shudder in his body. His eyes fluttered before opening—hollow, blank eyes—finding her after a few tense moments of searching.

"Yeah, I knew you were still there." Lynn took a prideful step forward, eyes cast down on this menace, this monster that destroyed her family. Any residual fear peeled away as she locked onto him, watching him struggle to maintain consciousness. He was as good as dead already.

A cough flung from his lips, bringing blood with it. The crimson mucus mixed with his saliva, sticky strands hanging from his chin as he looked up at her.

She knelt, getting low enough to keep his focus. "Why?" she asked, fury and hate boiling in her mind. "Why did you target us, bring us into your sick game? Why ... did you kill my husband, destroy my FAMILY?"

His eyes flickered again, and a grimace painted his expression. He turned his head and spat before returning to face her. "Help."

A chuckle sprang forth upon hearing his audacious plea. The impudence made her cringe, wondering how this heartless beast had the balls to ask for anything. "Help?" She shook her head, marveling at the proclamation. "Are you kidding me? You stole the world from me! Rot in hell!" she screamed through gritted teeth.

Clyde made a subtle movement, lifting his right hand from the brittle leaves surrounding the tree trunk. The motion caused Lynn to flinch, and she stood, backing away, eyes narrowed. The man lifted his chin, words trapped in his saturated, bloody throat. Eventually, the words spewed from his lips, mumbled and low. "I ... was tryin' to help ..." he paused, swallowing blood before a violent cough erupted from his core again. "Fix your car, get you home."

She stared down at him, watching the twitches and paltry flails, wanting to end his life and get her vengeance. She hated this man, hated every ounce of his being. He was the root of her suffering, her pain, and misery. He caused this, yet he sat there, lies oozing from his wretched mouth like this was a joke. Death was knocking on the door, and this monster's tongue still quipped deception.

"Stop the lies and tell me why you did it. Look me in the eye, bastard, and tell me why you targeted us! Why were you going to kill me and my—?"

"Just ... tryin' ... to ... help ... you. Get you ... back ... home."

"Stop it. Stop the lies, NOW!" Her voice boomed as she rushed forward, cocking her right fist back, ready to strike.

As she hovered over him, ready to release her fury and hate, Clyde's eyes glazed over, losing the faint hint of life lingering within. He still stared at her, but the haze brought the inevitable. Mouth agape, his final breath escaped.

Lynn slowly dropped her arm, fist unclenched, and a slight shake traveled through her limbs. Her stare remained on the dead man leaning against the tree, feeling both relief and pain. She and the boys were free, yet the void was brewing once again in her heart. She was a widow, alone.

So much violence and terror rushed through each thought, infecting her like a parasite. Her mind twisted with what she had seen and Clyde's dying words. She pondered each carefully fabricated deceit, dwelling on the corruption. *How could this monster continue with the lies, knowing he was dying, bleeding out? How could he continue his sick game?* Several moments passed before she buried the pain and collected herself.

She released a labored sigh, breaking her gaze from the dead man, cogs and gears working and searching for answers. Tears welled once again as her mind shifted to a different theory. *What if it is true? What if he was telling the truth? No, no, no. That isn't possible. But....*

Above her, a gentle breeze swam through the oak's limbs, garnering her focus. She stared up, catching the dying light in the orange sky. The leaves shook and swayed, pulled heavily in the wind's direction before coming to a rest. Once they stilled, she turned around, taking slow strides back to her waiting children. She chewed her bottom lip, eyes glued to the forest floor with each pace.

52

Lynn said little about Clyde or Micah once she collected her sons. She barely spoke at all. Simple instructions and encouragement sprang from her lips. She knew a million questions looped in the boys' fragmented minds, but the severity of their task was pressing. She needed them focused, clearheaded. They had a ticket home. They just had to get to it.

Close to an hour passed before they reached the top of the incline. All three collapsed to the forest floor once the ground leveled out, feeling the pains and aches blanket their bruised bodies. Lynn lay there for several minutes, collecting her breath. She stared into the darkening sky, seeing the first star twinkle through the dim.

Once rested, she sat up, seeing both boys laying on their sides, facing one another. They whispered choked words back and forth a few feet away. Her mind teetered, weighed down by grief and shame from the sight. She didn't know what they were talking about or what they believed happened. She was content knowing they walked away with only a few injuries. There was no need to burden them, to molest their memories with the truth. At some point, questions would arise, and she told herself she would protect Micah's legacy. He died in that building, saving them, ending the terror of the lunatics hunting them. She would protect them and him.

An owl hoot drifted on the breeze to her left. She whirled at the sound, heart pounding. She scanned the towering oaks, eyes searching for the source, finding nothing before her sight landed on the building in the distance, the shop.

Saplings and brush hid most of the structure, yet there it was. In the dim light, the sun-bleached yellow looked off-white, contrasting with the dull blue trim, but the sight brought relief. Three hundred feet and they were home free.

She hurried the boys along, ignoring the splintering pains, both physical and emotional, as they closed in on the firebreak separating the shop from the wildness of the forest. She knelt near the boundary behind a copse of juvenile pines, peering through limp branches. David and Will mimicked her actions, brushing needles away from their line of sight. The Malibu was there, parked in the dirt lot, patiently waiting.

There it is. That car's going to start.

She scoured the area; all was still and silent. After a few deep breaths and feeling her heart hammer in her chest, she stood and linked hands with Will and David. Then they stepped out into the open.

The three made their way across the dirt lot in seconds, coming to rest next to the classic car. David and Will's eyes fluttered in all directions with each step, flinching at every sound the twilight brought. Lynn ignored the sounds. Her mission was clear.

She approached and lifted the door handle; it was unlocked. With a gentle pull, the door sprang open in a wide arc, and she slid inside, sitting on the worn leather bucket seat. The feeling was comforting after the hell she had been through. She left the door ajar, and her sons occupied the space, watching her every move.

David leaned forward, pleading with his eyes. "Is it going to start, Mom?"

She ignored the nervous question, trying to vanquish her tormenting thoughts and visions, and looked around the interior.

A set of military dog tags hung from the rearview mirror. Her eyes focused on the stamped writing, reading the former soldier's name: Clyde Benjamin Mooney. She didn't need this knowledge. In fact, she despised knowing the man's full name. His last words still tore a hole in her heart, and she didn't know what to believe. *Could anything he said be true?* After a few painful breaths, she pushed past the thoughts swarming through her mind and pulled out the key ring.

She glanced at her sons for a split second before her attention refocused. *It's going to start. It has to. He did this for us. Micah.*

The key slid inside the ignition with little effort, and after releasing a deep breath, she cranked it forward. The engine roared to life.

Both boys stepped back from the powerful rumble, eyes tense and wide. They stood there, listening to the power beneath the hood. Listening to the beautiful melody of the V8, feeling its vibration. In that moment, the sound instilled something in all of them, something that had been stripped from their grasp, something they had almost given up on. Hope.

Lynn stepped out of the car, grimacing from the pain in her side. With a clenched jaw, she waved her boys forward. Neither could hear her voice over the engine, but they understood her gesture.

Will climbed inside and over the center console and gear stick, calling shotgun. A sly smile crept across his lips as he looked over at his older brother. After Lynn slid the bucket seat forward, David sighed before clambering through the tight opening. Comfort wasn't his first pressing need, but the bench seat would allow him to stretch out and elevate his swollen ankle.

With the boys safely inside, Lynn took a single step forward. Reluctance gripped her, however, and she paused before climbing back in. She stood there for several moments, arms crossed and resting on the car's roof. Her puffy, bloodshot eyes moved along the tree line surrounding the property, not sure what she was looking for. She was lost. She didn't know what to think or feel. There was a void pulling at her heart. An emptiness filling her with misery, forcing her face-first down the spiraling black hole.

A gentle touch on her stomach broke the melancholic moment, bringing her back from the hell she had entered: a deep cavity siphoning her drive to protect and survive.

She leaned down, staring through the door's opening. Will's eyes—that same bright blue as his father's—matched the calming smile on his face. The sight triggered a mirroring smile and an accompanying nod meant to convey comfort. After glancing David's way and repeating the nod, she slid into the seat and closed the door. The agony wasn't gone, but the looks on their faces buried it with a thin layer.

"Seatbelts, boys!" The demand was barely audible over the car's engine as she adjusted the rearview mirror. Her hand moved lower, pulling a knob on the dash. The car's headlights came to life, illuminating the siding of the shop.

She glanced to her right and into the back seat, inspecting their restraints before reaching down and gripping the gearshift. Then she dropped the Malibu into reverse, flooring the gas pedal.

The tires spun against the dirt, spitting gravel and dust into the night. As Lynn glanced into the rearview mirror, she slammed on the brakes. Someone was behind the car.

53

Dust lingered in the air, tendrils of floating earth reaching out like a curtain in the breeze. Inside the car, Lynn held her glare through the rearview mirror, watching the man. She shook. The red of the taillights accentuated his pale face and emotionless expression. In the reflection, he returned her look. She remembered him from yesterday. *Tank?*

David and Will shuffled in their seats, glancing at their mother, then at the man. The relief they felt upon entering the car vanished in a heartbeat. Now realizing the horror wasn't over, fear replaced it.

Tank held his ground for several moments, and a slight sway wavered his stance. Suddenly, his stare drifted to the ground, and he shifted a small stone around with his foot. Then his head rose again, locking onto Lynn. He was smiling. Not a smirk or a grin. A toothy beam running ear to ear, but the worst thing about the sight was the man's eyes. *Sid* had the same maniacal eyes.

The look struck Lynn forcefully, and she shrank in her seat, breaking his gaze. Her fingers tightened around the steering wheel, strangling the red leather. Tense moments passed before she reached up with her trembling hand and adjusted the mirror. Tank was gone.

She shifted in her seat, whipping around to regain sight. She scanned the yard through the back window, searching and coming up empty. *What the ... Where the hell did you go? Where are you, asshole?*

In her peripheral vision, Will ducked in the bucket seat beside her. He hid his face, burying it in his palms. She whirled her sight toward the motion, staring out the dusty window. Tank's smile grew wider as he leaned forward and tapped the glass.

"Mom, Mom, Mom!" David screamed from the back seat.

Without warning, Lynn's foot left the brake and floored the gas. The Malibu sped in reverse, leaving the maniac standing there. The smile left his face as he turned his head, watching the distance grow between them. After several car lengths, she spun the steering wheel, and the vehicle turned accordingly. She stepped on the clutch, shifted the car into drive, and aimed it straight at the natural tunnel hiding this place.

Lynn glared in the rearview mirror as she steered the car, watching the man shrink. Tank didn't give chase. He stood there, glaring as the car distanced itself. From the surrounding darkness, other faces emerged, joining this new threat. Too many to count in the split second she saw them. A small army.

The Malibu raced down the mountain road, hugging each twist and turn, ignoring the twenty-five mile per hour signs peppered around each bend. Lynn never let off the gas until the glow of fluorescent lighting forced her to slow. The few shops blanketing the interstate's off-ramp were on her right. The sight filled her with relief, knowing she and the boys were finally safe. She pulled the car into the Beacon Station lot, parking next to a white Dodge van.

She could see an employee helping a small family inside. Part laughter, part solemnity spewed from her lips at the sight, and she cupped both hands over her mouth.

We made it. We made it, we...

After a few seconds, she glanced over at Will, who had perked up and was leaning forward. His eyes were glued to the subtle movements inside the store, watching the same employee and family. Something formed across his face that she wasn't sure she would ever see again. A grin.

We're free.

After craning her neck to check on David, she saw a similar look. His eyes glistened as he, too, leaned forward, giving in to the hope revealing itself. She knew the horror was over.

We're safe. It's over. It's finally over.

With the back of her hand, she wiped away the tears and caught an object in her periphery. A blue object lined with glass located to the left of the Station—a phone booth. It was time to fulfill the promise she made to David and Will. She had to call the cops. They would sort out all the chaos and carnage. They would return her husband after a thorough investigation and discovering the appalling truth. And all the other victims before them could finally rest. Closure.

After dialing zero and listening to three mind-numbing rings, a voice chimed in—brusque, deep, male. It was the California Highway Patrol responding from the Gorman satellite office, two miles up the interstate.

With minimal hysteria in her voice, Lynn recounted the events that transpired—Clyde, Sid, the bunker, Micah. Oh, Micah. She told the man everything he needed to know about Micah and withheld any doubt floating in her mind about Clyde. She had to protect her husband's legacy.

The officer responded with calm, comforting, empathetic words assuring her that the terror was over.

Lynn wept into the handset, thanking the man between emotional breakdowns, then recovering her composure. She listened to his explicit instructions, nodding her head at the end of each of his sentences. She and her sons were safe, and help was on the way.

Fifteen agonizing minutes later, a cruiser approached the old Beacon Station, blue and red lights flashing sans siren. The car crept into the lot, slowly halting at an angle next to the Malibu.

Lynn didn't wait for the officer to exit. She sprang from the safety of the car, nearly collapsing as she shambled toward his car. She shifted from foot to foot as she waited for the man staring through the window to exit. Reaching for the pad and pencil on the passenger seat before opening the car door. His height was notable, and the campaign hat he wore hid his facial features in a veil of darkness. As he stood there, two more squad cars came speeding down the interstate exit, turning toward Clyde's shop.

After introducing himself and reassuring safety with deliberate words, the boys joined their mother outside in the lot. They stared at the man with bewildered, wide eyes. They could feel the man's presence throw a metaphorical net around them, protecting them from the night and its horrors.

Moments later, the boys and Lynn huddled tightly around the trunk of the squad car. Lynn's voice dominated the conversation, only allowing the occasional

"Yeah," or "Mom, Mom, don't forget ..." from her sons' shaky voices. As her story spilled from fatigued lips, the officer frantically wrote on his pad, trying to piece together the puzzle of mayhem.

After collecting himself, the officer led the three to a bench outside the gas station's side window. Lynn sat in the middle, flanked by her sons. The quaint store was empty now, just the employee inside, wiping down counters and tidying up the merchandise. Periodically, he glanced toward the group—concern and intrigue evident—before returning to his duties.

With Lynn and the boys sitting on the wooden slats of the bench, the highway patrolman reviewed his notes, attempting to merge the words escaping him. The story he held in his grasp was grotesque, horrid, like nothing he had heard or discovered during his years working this interstate. There was the occasional car accident or eighteen-wheeler catching fire, but nothing close to what he read. Unconvinced, he questioned the validity of Lynn's claims. The facts would come to fruition. They always did.

Before he could recite his notes back to Lynn and begin some follow-up questions, the two-way radio clipped to his belt perked to life. Another patrolman spoke through the speaker, stating he was at the property. The next few statements forced Lynn into a shell of despair and panic.

"Hey, Peters, Gonzalez and I are here at the old mechanic's shop. Place is dark and quiet. Seems abandoned. Gonzalez is down the hill searching for this mystery building. There are some fresh tire marks, but no vehicles parked outside. No sign of an old truck or tan hatchback. You sure this is the place? Doesn't seem like anyone has been here in years. Over."

Officer Peters lifted the radio to his parched lips while his eyes drifted to Lynn. Her skin paled, and her eyes went blank. "Did I hear that right, Michelson? Repeat. You don't see a tan import with a hatchback or a truck without paint, only primer? You don't see any vehicles? Over."

Silence.

"Michelson, repeat. Over." Peters hovered closer, watching Lynn tremble and pull her sons closer. His brow furrowed.

No response.

"Officer Michelson, do you read me? Over."

Breaths later, the static of the radio returned with a chirp. "Apologies, Peters. Gonzalez called me down to the building. He found it. Without our flashlights, he would have never seen it. But ..."

The silence returned, leaving all in anticipation. Lynn tried to speak, but her words were strangled, muted. She couldn't breathe. She shook her head, murmuring low in her throat.

Officer Peters drew closer, trying to use some comforting words and slow gestures to calm her. Michelson's voice came through the radio once more. "There's nothing here, Peters. No signs of a struggle, no blood, no bodies. No one's been here for years. Neither Gonzalez nor I see anything incriminating here. Over."

The radio died with a chirp.

Peters continued watching Lynn, analyzing what he just heard and the story he had written. His eyes narrowed, skepticism evident. Eventually, he spoke. "Miss, I don't know what happened out there, but we will find out. At daybreak, we'll scour the grounds and sort this out. In the meantime, is there anything else you're not telling me? Anything you wish to add or... confess?"

She looked at this man, twitching with fear, and remained speechless.

A long exhale exited his mouth, followed by a subtle shake of his head as he turned away from them.

His gaze returned, his mind working and sorting through information and scenarios as he bit his lower lip. "Nothing's going to get solved tonight. You guys are hurt, though. I can see that." He paused, examining the blood stains and rips in their clothes. "I'm taking you to the hospital to be examined and treated, and then we can continue discussing this case. Sound good?"

Both boys looked at their mother, needing her guidance. Lynn couldn't return their attention. The trembling continued—shock taking its toll on her body—and her unblinking stare remained on Officer Peters.

With no resistance, the boys lifted their mother to stand with them. Each tucked their head under her arms and hefted, supporting her back with their free hands. In less than a few minutes, all three were in the back of the cruiser.

54

Lynn's head rolled forward and rested on her chest when the cruiser reversed, preparing to exit the parking lot. Her vision came and went, blackness contrasting with haze. She could hear her sons whispering, feel them tapping her arms, trying to wake her from the fog. Shock had sunk its teeth in deep. Nothing made sense, and her mind buckled, leaving her in a pit of madness.

As the car barreled off the curb, her body mirrored the motion, and her weight collapsed on Will, sitting to her right. The boy did his best to straighten her upright, tears filling his eyes as he continued his failed attempts to wake her from the trance. But the darkness had won.

The cruiser veered onto the mountain road. As it sped up, the engine's growl brought Lynn about, and she looked around the cab with glassy, fuddled eyes. Her sons jostled beside her, and she could see their lips parting, but their voices were muffled. Toward the front of the vehicle, she could see Officer Peter's shoulders and head. The metal safety barrier distorted his bulky frame.

Her eyes slowly drifted out the window, catching the wide entrance to the interstate. Fluorescent lighting illuminated the street and the large signs labeling the route. But the car didn't turn. It continued down the mountain road, bypassing the green sign for Exit 202.

Lynn leaned forward with slow blinks, the tips of her fingers poking through the barrier's beige diamonds. "Sir... where are you going? The on-ramp is back ..." Her neck craned, following the road to safety as the car continued forward.

Officer Peters shifted in his seat yet remained silent.

"Officer ... why didn't we get on the highway?" Her voice was hushed, confused, as reality slowly crept back in. "I thought you were taking us to the hospital? Is this another route or something?" Her attention returned to the man driving, watching the side of his jaw grind away on a piece of gum.

Only silence from the front seat.

Lynn's body stiffened, and her mind wandered. Fear and panic shuffled their way back in, adrenaline pumping through her blood, accelerating her heart rate. The instinct to survive took control, and she leaned forward, getting inches away from the barrier. "Officer Peters. Where are you taking us? The fuckin' hospital isn't this way!"

His focused stare left the road for a split second when he shot Lynn a side-glance. Never breaking his silence.

"Why ... why aren't you saying anything? Where are you taking us, Officer Peters? Where?" Her voice raised with each word, and she shook the barrier forcibly.

The commotion caught his full attention, and he turned his head to address her. "Hey, damnit! Quit that shit." His stare returned to the road, steering the car around a bend. "We'll be there soon, okay? Calm the fuck down, and shut up!"

Lynn released her grip on the metal and leaned back with weary, wide eyes. She watched his profile clamp down on the gum, grinding his jaw.

After a few moments of silence, his head turned, wild dark eyes glaring at the three in his back seat. "We're not going to the hospital."

Lynn froze, unable to speak, move, or breathe. The hammering in her chest exploded, and darkness poured in, distorting her vision.

"Oh, and my name's not really Peters. It's ... Mooney. I think you've already met my big brother."

The words forced her deeper into the bottomless cavity, blanketing her senses with hopelessness and resignation. Paralysis set in, steering her farther into the darkness. Through the warping haze, Lynn's ears picked up on a familiar sound, the rhythmic ticking of a turn signal. Seconds later, the car slowed and turned left, crossing the single yellow line dividing the old mountain road. Ancient trees suffocated the moonlight as it entered the canopy. The shop was straight ahead. Finally, the car stopped, and the void swallowed her whole.

Lynn sprang forward, the deafening wail of the cruiser's siren ringing in her ears. Reaching out and grasping the barrier with stiff fingers, she gasped for precious air. The blue and red lights spun in unison, highlighting the view while her eyes circled the area.

Through the haze, she could see a large building to her right, bright lights beyond the glass doors of an entrance. Inside, men and women wearing white uniforms and coats were bustling around.

Where are we? What happened? Where'd he bring us?

Slowly, her vision stabilized. The siren wailed again, and Lynn heard a car door open and shut. Two men rushed from the glass doors. One met Officer Peters near the cruiser's hood, and the other lingered near, holding his hand above his eyes. One man peered into the back seat, watching Lynn squirm with anticipation. His attention seesawed between the injured occupants of the car and the officer.

Lynn leaned into the window, glancing upward. Centered high above the entrance was a cross illuminated by a spotlight. Under the symbol were words in bright red neon. She whispered the words as she read them, "Memorial Hospital of Bakersfield."

We're home? What happened? What the ... How did we ...

"Hey, Mom, you're awake."

The sudden break in silence caused her to recoil, and she snapped her gaze toward the voice. Her sight landed on David. He yawned and was rubbing his eyes.

"You've been asleep for almost two hours, you know. I think we're home. The cop drove us all the way here. Said the clinics on the mountain were trash."

Clinics? He brought us to the hospital? What the ...

Stupefied, she glanced through the barrier, eyeing the clock on the dash. Its hands read 12:17 a.m. It was Wednesday morning.

Panic faded away, and her senses returned as she looked around. She could feel Will on her right, rolled up in a tight ball. He was silent, motionless. Sleeping. They were safe and home. They had escaped the nightmare.

The whole thing was a ... It was a dream, only a horrifying, cruel dream.

She dropped her sight into her lap, reflecting on the chaos, the woods, and the bunker. Her eyes fluttered while her mind worked, digging for reasoning.

"Micah!" The name leapt from her lips like a light switch flipped on. She looked around the vehicle, seeing Will still sound asleep, before glancing at David on her left, a mix of confusion and solemnity on his face.

A shockwave of memories swept through her mind like a spiraling vortex: moments of tranquility during the two-night stay at Disneyland, the clamor from the flat tire, the shop, running through the woods, Sid, Clyde, and Micah. Her husband stood before her, peering down at her with his baby blues. He wasn't happy, though. The look he wore was wrong—vile, contemptuous. This wasn't her husband. She could also see the knife in her hand and where she had plunged it to protect them.

"Mom? Are you okay? What's wrong?"

Lynn broke free from the dream, redirecting her attention to her son. She could hear the crack of his voice as he spoke, tears welling as he choked on the last few words. But she couldn't answer him. Reality set in, and she knew it all happened. It was real. Every memory and thought before she entered the cruiser a few hours ago. She knew it now, and the guilt crushed her soul.

Suddenly, the passenger side door opened. The two men and a nurse peered into the back seat. One by one, they ushered Lynn and the boys out, placing them in wheelchairs and rolling them toward the hospital entrance. Officer Peters kept pace.

David and Will entered first, rushed upon at the glass doors by one man and the nurse. The large panes parted when the chairs and their occupants came close and then abruptly closed with the boys inside.

The other man, pushing Lynn, stalled, stopping and speaking to the officer. Lynn ignored their conversation, staring at her reflection in the glass door several feet ahead. The bruises, the dried blood, the dark, puffy circles under her bloodshot eyes. Her shattered mind tormented her, realizing the truth.

Micah was gone, and they would never recover his body. Whoever this clan of murdering psychopaths was, they would cover their tracks to conceal their crimes. And it wouldn't end with her and the boys either. They had escaped, but more families would be lured into the hills, abducted, and hunted. She understood that now.

It's never going to stop, and no one will ever believe me. This was her final thought before she felt the push from behind, and the glass doors parted.

ACKNOWLEDGEMENTS

So many need to be thanked for supporting me in this journey.

Without the patience and love of my wife, this book would have never been completed. You are my life, babe.

I also need to thank my loving children, Emma, Aubrey, Aria, and Luke. Thank you for inspiring me with your contagious smiles, laughter, and unconditional support.

To my secondary family, the Lopez's, for always being supportive, listening to my ideas, reading unfinished, raw pieces, and always showering me with positive vibes.

To my amazing cover artist, Ross Nischler, thank you for bringing the world of Exit 202 to life. Can't wait to see what you design for me next.

Thank you Dani Yeager at Hack and Slash Editing, my incredible editor. You cleaned up my mess with expertise and an uncanny crispness. All I can say is 'wow.'

Finally, I need to thank a fellow author who I deeply respect and admire. Thank you A.G. Mock. You've always been willing to lend advice and steer me in a productive direction. You rock, brother.

ABOUT THE AUTHOR

FROM AN EARLY AGE, J.B. knew he could create mind-blowing, emotionally charged stories filled with enigmatic characters and story arcs. Fond, nostalgic memories still loop in his mind about the three or four-page thrillers he wrote in middle-school for his friends. Around the same time, he discovered Stephen King and Dean Koontz. Both prolific writers influenced his creativity and helped hone his love for the craft. But the love remained dormant for years.

In the early stages of the Covid pandemic, JB's genuine passion came to fruition. Now happily married and a father, his inspiration bloomed after hearing his second daughter's desire to write a novella. Day after day, the two sat at the kitchen table, exchanging ideas, creating treacherous villains, and building a majestic fantasy world through the use of a pen. He was hooked, and the passion to write came rushing back like an avalanche.

Since then, he has completed two manuscripts: The Streets of Floria and Exit 202. You can also find his numerous short stories published through online magazines and websites. His current work in progress (WIP) titled The Chronicles of Barbasos, is an anthology of shorts, due out early 2024.

JB lives in sunny California with his wife and four children; three daughters and a son. Oh, and there's his writing partner; his gray tabby, Max. When he isn't writing, he loves to read, play golf, and listen to 80s rock and 90s metal.

Visit **jbarnold-author.com** for updates and future projects.

Milton Keynes UK
Ingram Content Group UK Ltd.
UKHW051005171123
432592UK00021B/156/J